CHILDREN OF THE COMET

CHILDREN OF THE COMET

DONALD MOFFITT

OPEN ROAD

INTEGRATED MEDIA

NEW YORK

Cover design by Mauricio Díaz

978-1-4976-8294-8

Published in 2015 by Open Road Integrated Media, Inc.
345 Hudson Street
New York, NY 10014
www.openroadmedia.com

Again, for Ann
Till a' the seas gang dry, my dear,
And the rocks melt wi' the sun.

CHILDREN OF THE COMET

How high can a tree on a comet grow? The answer is surprising. On any celestial body whose diameter is of the order of ten miles or less, the force of gravity is so weak that a tree can grow infinitely high. Ordinary wood is strong enough to lift its own weight to an arbitrary distance from the center of gravity. This means that from a comet of ten-mile diameter, trees can grow out for hundreds of miles, collecting the energy of sunlight from an area thousands of times as large as the area of the comet itself. Countless millions of comets are out there, amply supplied with water, carbon, and nitrogen—the basic constituents of living cells. They lack only two essential requirements for human settlement, namely warmth and air. And now biological engineering will come to our rescue. We shall learn how to grow trees on comets.

—FREEMAN DYSON
"THE WORLD, THE FLESH, AND THE DEVIL"

[HAPTER 1

6,000,000,000 A.D.
The Oort Cloud

Torris, son of Parn the Facemaker, sat a little apart from the other initiates who were waiting for their turns with Claz the Priest. It was cold where he sat, farther from the fire than he liked, with his back resting against a massive stray Tree root that had penetrated the ice cave. But his distance served to separate him from the other boys and their horseplay. As the son of Parn, he would be Facemaker himself someday, and he always had to maintain a certain distance. His father had relentlessly drilled that into him.

Claz finished with the postulant he'd been instructing. The boy rejoined the group, moving in a series of slow-motion bounces in the comet's feeble gravity. He was proudly showing off the stencil Claz had pasted to his cheek, where his mark of manhood would be etched in frostbite during the Climb ceremony.

From his priestly alcove across the ice cave, Claz signaled impatiently for the next initiate.

The noisiest of them, a boy named Brank, stood up promptly before any of the others could respond, but not so quickly that his feet lost contact with the ground. Brank was long for his age, as long as a grown man, and had sprouted a scraggly beard that brushed against the transparent Face of his hand-sewn airsuit already. Torris didn't like him very much. Brank was a brash character with a bit of a mean streak who liked to pick on the smaller boys and was known to take things that were not his.

Torris watched as Brank crossed the cavern, somehow managing to strut despite his low-gravity shuffle. But when he reached the priest's niche, he adopted a subservient posture.

Claz wasn't fooled. He gestured impatiently for Brank to kneel and peel back the hood of his airsuit.

Brank's catechism seemed to go on longer than usual. Torris couldn't make out the words from where he sat, but Brank's tone of voice seemed to grow more and more stubborn, and Claz's grew more and more angry. At last, Claz dismissed his errant postulant with a dissatisfied gesture, and when Brank joined his friends and started acting up, the priest exploded.

"What are you boys hanging around for? Those of you who are finished here, make yourselves useful! Go outside and fetch firewood! And you, Brank, you can fetch a few buckets of air to refresh the fire!"

Brank started to mutter a complaint, and Torris could make out something about "children's chores."

Claz heard it too. "You are a child, and a useless one at that!" he snapped. "You may have the size and shape of a man, but you will not be a man until you make the Climb and bring back your Tree dream. Now go!"

Brank and a few confederates left with ill grace. The others sat, cowed for the moment. Claz's gaze lit on Torris, and he motioned him over.

Kneeling in front of Claz, his elongated legs folded under him, Torris recited the creed of the Tree. " . . . and we give thanks to the Tree, which clutches the world in its roots, which created man and preserves him from the dark," he finally finished, relieved that he hadn't seriously stumbled at any of the difficult parts.

Satisfied, the old man leaned back and said, "Now, Torris, my boy, do you understand why you are making the Climb and why you must receive the mark of manhood to prove it?"

"I . . . I think so. It is so that I may prove myself as a man, and so that I may receive the dream the Tree gives me."

Claz nodded his approval. "Some bring back great dreams, some little dreams or petty ones. Some, I suspect, bring back no dream at all but pretend to have received some nonsense they think will sound like a true dream. And there are always those who are afraid of the great dark and never complete the Climb, and who are known because they bring back no proof of having reached the crown, or who bring back a seed pod they've found trapped in the lower branches, or worse, stolen from another Climber—the most heinous of sins. I suspect that ne'er-do-well Brank will be one of those. But I've watched you grow up, and I expect great things from you—greater even than making Faces for the tribe like your father."

At that point, Brank returned with a bucket of frozen air in each hand, the transparent Face of his airsuit tilted upward and covered with patches of frost. He dropped the buckets carelessly, almost contemptuously, by the fire, where they immediately started to melt and steam, making the flames flare up and turn a brighter orange. As he turned to go, he glanced over toward the priest's niche, where Claz was spreading his hands palms outward to confer his blessing. Brank's lip curled at the sight, and he shot Torris a look of sheer hatred.

CHAPTER 2

Almost the entire tribe was gathered outside the tunnel entrance to see the Climbers off. Torris estimated at least ten hands of them, not counting the babies some of the mothers were holding in translucent air sacks.

"Hold still," his father said, checking the seams of Torris's airsuit yet again. Sounds didn't carry in the airlessness of the outside, but by necessity he was as adept as anybody else at reading lips and speaking in finger talk.

The stars were bright and fierce despite the ruddy light cast by the red star that moved. The sky was emptier of stars than it once had been, but Torris could not know that. The other two stars that moved, a white dot and an orange one that were bright enough to cast shadows, stayed aloof from the red star and rose in tandem a little afterward—or, as Claz put it, "shared the same epicycle"—adding their iota of light and heat to the bleak icescape. According to Claz, the white star and the orange one were sisters, while the big red star was a "stepsister."

What Claz meant, no one could fathom, but he was the tribe's numberer as well as its priest and he often spoke in riddles.

Torris craned his neck to try to see the top of the Tree. But that was impossible, of course. The top was far away and hidden behind miles and miles of twisting green branches. Claz

9

had once said that the Tree was twice as tall as the world was big around, but how anyone, even a numberer, could know such a thing was a mystery.

Still, the thought made him shiver. He was going to have to climb that unthinkable distance no matter how many turns of the world it took.

Torris tried not to show impatience as his father checked his equipment yet again. Parn carefully coiled the rope—more than ten man-lengths of it with a grappling hook at the end—and draped it across Torris's shoulder along with the stubby little bow and a quiver holding the ten bone-tipped arrows that were permitted by custom. Both the climbing rope and the bowstring were made of web beast silk rather than the animal sinews that most people used. As Facemaker, Parn would provide nothing but the best for his only son.

"Remember," he said behind his faceplate with the exaggerated lip movements of no-air talk, "there are two kinds of web beasts: those that use their silk to spin webs for catching, and those that hunt and spin silk ropes to anchor themselves when they swing at their prey. If you're careless enough to get caught in a web and a web spinner starts toward you, don't try to use your bow. You won't be fast enough. Use your spear. Thrust, don't throw. Aim for the center of the cluster of eyes. And don't let go of the spear. That way you'll be able to hold it off while it's dying."

"Yes, Father."

"On the other hand, if you're being stalked by one of the hunting variety and you see it start its swing toward you, you'll have all the time in the world to nock an arrow, aim, and send it through the creature. It's just a question of keeping your head.

You have to calculate the angle of the swing and the length and timing of the arc as it keeps lengthening. Your brain will do all that for you without your thinking about it, as long as you don't panic. Remember that the creature is helpless while it's dangling, and that the force of the arrow will spoil its own timing, so when it drops it won't land on top of you if you stay alert. Their poison is dangerous even when they're dead. Can you remember all that?"

He waited for a reply, his expression stern.

Torris tried to make his nod look earnest. He'd heard it all a thousand times while he was growing up.

"As for flutterers and tree snakes and other such creatures, there's no single formula for dealing with them. You've been on meatbeast hunts with me and the other men, and you know what to expect."

He held Torris at arm's length and looked him over with a nod of approval. The flawless new airsuit had been sewn together out of everted meatbeast gut by Firstmother. It would probably be the last one he'd need. She'd sighed when she'd fitted it to him. "You've stopped growing, Torris," she'd said. "Your last suit was getting much too tight, and perhaps I waited too long, but I wanted to be sure."

And now, seeing that Parn was through with him, she came diffidently forward and gave him a farewell hug. "Be careful, my precious Torris, and may the God-Tree protect you," she said in voicetalk, her faceplate touching his, sounding thin and faint through the resin mask but still understandable. She'd wanted her words to be private, not to be read by others.

She released him and stepped aside so Secondmother could say goodbye. Secondmother was hardly older than Torris himself, and she was big with child. She smiled, too shy to speak, and handed him the caddy of food she'd prepared for the breaking of his fast.

Parn stepped in again. "Don't gobble up your climbfeast as soon as you're out of sight of the ground, as some of those whelps will do," he said. "Remember that your fast still has a day to go. And try to save a little. After you've had your climbfeast you'll have to rely on what you can hunt or forage, and you might not get lucky right away."

Torris nodded, but he had stopped paying attention. He was lightheaded from two days of fasting, but he was too eager to get started to think about being hungry. He wished his father would stop talking so that he could join the straggling group of Climbers who were starting to assemble.

But his father wasn't finished with him. Torris tried to look as if he were listening. He understood that his father probably was trying to hang on to these last moments as long as possible.

"And remember," Parn droned silently on in finger talk, "no matter how hungry you get, your first priority is to capture a stovebeast. The heatholder in your suit is only good for a day at best. The Tree is full of the picked skeletons of those who valued their stomachs more than their warmth."

Over by the gnarled slope of the Tree's base, Claz was getting ready for the final benediction, and the Climbers were gathering in a ragged semicircle around him. But Parn's only concession was to hurry his words a little. " . . . and the three airskins that a Climber is allowed won't last forever either. Replenish them as you go along, and never allow yourself more than one empty. Two empties and you're in trouble. The best place to drill a vent is . . . " It was too much. Even Parn realized it, and he broke off abruptly.

Torris moved his lips in a hasty goodbye and bounded off in an alarming series of high-flying arcs.

Claz was being mercifully brief. The Climb ceremony was in its third day, and there was nothing left to say. He gave a final blessing, making the ritual gestures that had been passed down by priests through the ages, symbolizing the sweeping arc of the triple stars with a swoop of his right hand and sketching their intricate dance with a wiggle of fingers.

Torris dutifully gave the proper responses and wished fervently that he could scratch the frostbitten itch under the stencil.

The Climbers chose their routes and spread out along the base of the Tree. Each Climber had to make his journey alone. It was forbidden to receive or give help to another Climber, or even approach him if your paths happened to cross.

Torris had already picked his spot—a gnarled channel that rose straight up and disappeared into the lower branches and that was narrow enough to afford a purchase on either side. Some of the boys looked for knobby projections or other random handholds, but a long groove like the one he'd chosen was better, giving you an uninterrupted head start.

He looked around at his fellow Climbers. A few of them had already started up the trunk. Far down the line, almost where the curve of the enormous base of the Tree cut off his view, he saw Brank, who seemed to be checking out the Climbers on either side of him but making no effort to start his own Climb. If his gaze had lit on Torris, he was too far away to tell.

But abruptly he sprang for the Tree, slamming into it about three man-lengths up, where there was nothing to grab hold of. The slow rotation of the world was starting to make him float slowly toward the outer darkness, but while he was still within arm's length of the trunk, he made a grab for his knife and stabbed it violently into the bark. It held, leaving him hanging, legs streaming outward.

Torris was appalled at the stupidity of Brank's gamble. If the blade had hit a hard spot or hadn't penetrated deeply enough to hold, the recoil from the blow would have propelled Brank irrevocably into the black sky, and not one of the men watching from below would have lifted a finger to save him. Brank's contact with the Tree had given him a Climber's untouchability, and it was forbidden to help him. It was a wise taboo; it helped the tribe shed its inept members before they could weaken it with their seed.

Torris did not wait to see how Brank continued his Climb. He centered himself in the groove, made a quick calculation, and leaped upward, his legs dangling free and his long arms hanging at his sides. His leap had carried him up about five man-lengths, and before he could drift out of reach, he pressed his palms against the walls of the niche on either side. He weighed only a few ounces, and the slight pressure was enough to hold him in place. He started to climb, using just his hands and letting his legs hang free. He didn't need legs at this stage, and it was quicker to pull himself along by hand.

He found his first stovebeast before the Tree turned nightward. It was wedged in a crook between the trunk and one of the massive branches, where it could quietly lap up the insects and other small prey that were attracted by its heat. It was about the size of a grown person's head, a furry round ball with four vestigial limbs that were good for nothing but clinging.

He pried it loose and dropped it in his backpack, letting his other one go. He could feel it immediately trying to attach itself to the inner surface next to his back, its life-giving warmth starting to spread through his suit. It would be good for a few days without being fed, and he could turn it loose when he found another firebelly to replace it.

They were not good to eat, though there were those who had to learn that the hard way. If you cut a stovebeast open, there was no actual fire inside, only a flood of noxious fluids that combined somehow to produce that flameless heat.

Torris resumed his Climb. The tunnel entrances to the tribe's cave were far out of sight between the twisting branches. He had some distance to go before he allowed himself to find a nest for the night. He could see how the Tree's leaves had turned almost edge-on to catch the last vestiges of the red star's heat. Claz said that the Trees used the pressure of starlight, if there was such a thing, to hunt down fresh comets to snare in their roots whenever they sucked the old ones dry. But that was just legend.

Still, one often saw a distant Tree floating free in space without an iceball or clutching an iceball that was shrunken to almost nothing so that it showed a ball of bare roots that were beginning to turn green to catch starlight. One wondered what other tribes did on such worlds. Did they hollow out caves in the God-Tree itself? Live in the branches? Or did they migrate to another God-Tree that might have drifted close enough? If so, the whole tribe would have to make that dangerous leap, not just the intrepid young men who launched themselves into the dark on bride raids whenever the opportunity presented itself.

Torris was feeling hunger now, but he resolved to wait out his fast till morning. He concentrated on climbing and looking out for predators. He was high enough to be in wild territory now, beyond the tribe's traditional hunting grounds. The more dangerous beasts had not been hunted out here.

Another hour of climbing and he flushed a covey of tree-hoppers that darted off in all directions. They were four-legged, like most life found in the Tree, with long, prehensile bushy tails. The little creatures somehow never seemed to launch themselves inadvertently into open space; here in the thick of the branches, they almost always managed to fetch up against a twig or cluster of leaves. He didn't bother to chase after any of them with net and spear. Tomorrow would be soon enough.

He was high enough, and he was getting drowsy. He found a sheltered spot in the lee of a branch and laid out his climbing kit. With a bone awl, he tapped into the Tree's vascular system and at first found only the thin clear resin that his father used to cast faceplates. He drilled deeper into the cambium and obtained a trickle of the watery sweet fluid that was good to drink. He filled a couple of small skins with this. Finally his persistence was rewarded with a gush of air from a cavity where it had collected. He used it to replenish the depleted air sack, adding the airflow to the remaining slush, where, increment by increment, it became slush itself. It took a long time, and when the frozen air had lost the ability to add to itself, he channeled the airstream directly into his sleeping sack through a tube made of meatbeast gut.

That done, he crawled into his sleeping sack, sealed its neck around the improvised breathing tube, and raised his faceplate to inhale the Tree's gift of air. It had a pleasant resinous smell like carpentered wood. He yawned and dropped off to sleep, the comforting warmth of the stovebeast pressed against his back.

CHAPTER 3

A dim, ruddy glow was filtering through the translucent sack and jerked Torris awake. The red star was in the sky again, and it was time to get moving.

He was ravenous. He tore open the packet of food that Secondmother had prepared for him and felt around inside. The first thing his hand encountered was a folded slice of tree fungus filled with minced meatbeast steak, marinated in its own juices and other flavorings. He wolfed it down immediately, then ate another. He was reaching for a third when he remembered his father's injunction, and he resealed the sack to save some of the food till later. He regretted not having set snares for the fleeing treehoppers the night before; he was going to have to be self-sufficient from now on.

He extricated himself partially from his airsuit and sponged himself off as best he could, using as little as possible of the precious meltwater he had brought with him; the sweetwater he had extracted from the Tree would have left him sticky.

Gratefully, he relieved himself with the help of the suit's facilities. He would open the second valve outside to drain the small reservoir.

Once again, the stovebeast attached itself to the small of his back, where it would recharge the suit's heatholder in the bargain. He would be glad to get out of the sleeping sack. The furry little firebelly, finding itself in an enclosed space, had lessened its heat output to compensate, but it was still uncomfortably hot inside the sack.

His weapons and the coil of fine silk rope were lying where he had left them on the branch's upper surface, held in place by the iceball's miniscule gravity, though they had fetched up against a protruding twig because of the even slighter force imparted by the Tree's ponderous rotation. That force would become greater as one proceeded outward along a branch, but here, close to the trunk, it was inconsiderable.

He thought it over and decided he didn't really need a climbing rope at this early stage; a spear that could be used as a harpoon would be more useful. He untied the grappling hook and passed the rope end through the small loop at the butt of the spear. Then he recoiled the rope carefully and fastened the other end to his belt.

Next he folded the sleeping sack flat and tucked it under his belt. He shouldered his bow and quiver, took a cautionary look around for wildlife, and resumed his Climb.

He climbed without stopping for a couple of hours. He was making good progress and thinking about taking a break when he saw the flutterbeast. It was hunting in the upper branches, and it saw him too.

It was huge—larger than a meatbeast—a dull black in color, with huge wings for enfolding its prey. The wings also helped the flutterbeast move from branch to branch, slapping those blanketing members against anything they touched. If it drifted out of reach of the Tree, it would turn its narrow face spaceward and spit a gob of reaction mass. There were wicked claws like grappling hooks at the first joint of the membrane's leading edges, for grasping a branch or a victim.

Instinctively, Torris pressed himself back against the shelter of the trunk—a useless move, because the flutterbeast could still get to him. The creature was flapping its way downward from branch to branch, its pink mouth opening and closing to show its fangs.

Slowly and deliberately, Torris drew an arrow from the quiver, nocked it, and pulled back the bowstring. He tracked the flutterbeast as it made its way closer.

Then it sprang. Its spreading wings blotted out the stars, and its pink mouth gaped wide. Torris let the arrow loose. The creature's wings jerked at the impact and brushed against his faceplate before it was sailing outward, impelled by the force of the arrow.

Quickly, it twisted its neckless head and spat. But the momentum imparted by the arrow was too great for it to overcome. Torris watched as it grew smaller against the background of stars until it shrank from sight.

He gave himself a few moments to recover, and when his heart finally slowed down, he continued his Climb.

CHAPTER 4

Four turns of the world later, the climbing had become almost routine. It was one handhold after another in a mind-numbing, repetitive rhythm, an occasional wriggle of his lower body keeping his straying legs aligned. There was no detectable up or down here on the great wall of the trunk; you'd have to proceed laterally at least a mile or so along a branch before you'd begin to have any sensation of weight—and then your "down" was outward, not in the direction that your eye and positional memory told you it ought to be.

Despite the advantage that near-weightlessness gave him, Torris was exhausted at the end of each long day of climbing. At dark, he crawled stiffly into his sleeping sack with his muscles screaming and his hands turned to cramped claws. He estimated that he'd made about forty miles so far. Four times now, he'd stopped to make camp. He was on his third stovebeast.

He'd faced no serious threats since the flutterbeast. He'd avoided any number of web traps, clubbed a small tree snake with the butt of his spear and flung it—squirming and spitting—into space, and warded off a swarm of carrion moths that had been attracted by the small game he'd managed to bag. He still had seven arrows left.

The dressed carcass of the meatbeast he'd killed that morning floated behind him in an improvised harness made of a length of climbing rope. Having no weight, the carcass wasn't a burden, but he still had to strain against its mass, and he still had to stop every once in a while to untangle it from the branches. Climbing was nothing but hard, unrelenting work. There was no hint of the mystic experience that older Climbers said a Climb was supposed to be.

He paused to look around. A few man-lengths ahead through the foliage, the sheltered crotch of a branch looked inviting. The approach was relatively unobstructed, giving a good enough view of anything that might be lurking nearby. Even from here, he could see evidence of an expanse of young bark that signaled a burst of growth of provascular tissue from rapidly dividing cambium cells. It was a promising place to tap into the Tree's vascular system for water and air.

He decided to camp there for the night. A few more tugs brought him to the protective hollow where trunk and branch met. He reeled the meatbeast carcass in after him. With practiced movement, he soon had his sleeping sack set up and the few needed utensils within easy reach. He then proceeded to cut a few thin slices of meat from the carcass and minced them, to be eaten raw. Cooking was a luxury away from the fires of the cave he lived in, but a dip in the fermented sauce that Secondmother had packed would make the meal palatable. He chopped up some of the treeweed sprouts he'd gathered to be kneaded together with the minced meat after he'd thawed it out in the air sack.

He surveyed his supper preparations with satisfaction, then cached his equipment and the rest of his supplies in a convenient cavity nearby, reserving his bow, quiver, and spearhead.

Exhausted, he crawled into his bubble of air and sealed it

after him. He raised his faceplate and let enough stovebeast heat escape to raise the temperature to above freezing. It was becoming increasingly hard to keep his eyes open. He'd barely finished his still-cold supper before falling asleep.

Something woke him early. He was still sodden with sleep, and at first he didn't know where he was. Then a flicker of movement caught his eye, and he came instantly alert.

He groped for an arrow and drew it from the quiver. It would have to do for a handheld weapon. There was no time to string the bow. And the shaft for the spear, too long for the sleeping sack, had been left outside. No time to regret that. But the arrow was as long as his forearm—longer than his knife or the spearhead, even with its threaded shank for a handle.

He felt the edges of his faceplate to be sure it was tight in its gasket, then unzipped the sleeping sack in one swift motion. The air pressure in the sack popped him outside like a seed out of its pod.

He twisted convulsively in midflight, landing feet first and right-side up. The comet's miniscule gravity planted him, however tentatively, on the branch's upper surface. Gripping the arrow, he quickly scanned the immediate area.

There was nothing.

He widened his search and saw movement in the middle distance, where the branch joined the trunk. The figure he saw, already half-obscured, disappeared into the foliage before he had a chance to get a good look.

It wasn't any kind of animal. It definitely had been a human shape, someone in an airsuit. He hadn't seen enough to make out the suit's identifying beadwork. But it had to be another Climber—a rogue Climber who did not respect the rules.

A glance at the sheltered hollow where he'd left his food cache stopped him. His supplies and belongings, what was left of them, were scattered all over the area. Two of his three airskins seemed to be gone, and the third had been wantonly slashed apart. A heartbreaking peek over the branch's edge showed him the hacked-up remains of the meatbeast carcass, drifting two branches farther down, already out of reach. It hadn't picked up much speed yet, so he must have missed catching the intruder by only a few minutes.

He couldn't afford to brood. He rummaged through the debris to see what he could salvage. There was an awl from his sewing kit and a half spool of web beast silk with it. He used them to sew the airskin back together, caulking the jagged seams with a generous slather of the animal glue used for repairing suit leaks, glad his father had insisted he carry some in an outside pocket.

He scraped as much of the spilled air as he could from the surrounding bark and scooped it into the airbag. Then he did what he should have done the night before: he drilled for air, let it congeal, and filled the air sack.

Belatedly he set the snares he had neglected to attend to before retiring, and by nightfall he was rewarded with four small treehoppers that would last him until he could find larger game. He promptly skinned and gutted them and stowed them away for later. By this time the two Sisters and the Stepsister had set, and he finished his remaining chores by ordinary starlight. He'd found the spear's shaft among the discarded miscellany—without the spearhead, his stalker hadn't thought it worth taking. He screwed the spear together and tested it for tightness. This time he'd sleep with the sleeping sack on top of it, face down and the zipper aligned, the spear ready to hand the instant he emerged.

Already nodding, struggling to keep his eyes open, he prepared to squirm into the inflated sack without sacrificing too much air. He had a good flow going from the new tap.

He'd lost a whole day. He wasn't worried about a return visit from the intruder that night. By this time, whoever it was would be miles above him.

He climbed for another two days without incident. A couple of times he thought he'd caught a fleeting glimpse of another Climber a few miles away, someone who quickly disappeared when Torris nocked an arrow, but if it was indeed the thief trying to keep pace with him, he made no attempt to get closer. He knew now that Torris had been alerted.

Torris remained cautious. A man ruthless enough to steal another Climber's food and air might be ruthless enough to kill him if he survived. Dead men tell no tales. The penalty for the enormity of stealing from another Climber was to be Shunned; the penalty for murder was expulsion from the tribe. That was a death sentence in itself. To be cast from the Tree into the outer darkness without enough air to reach another God-Tree was a punishment that no one, to Torris's knowledge, had ever survived.

After another five fingers of days, he was beginning to catch an occasional glimpse of the crown through gaps in the branches, and he estimated that he was halfway to his goal.

There hadn't been a hint of his elusive follower in all that time, and he decided that he'd finally lost him. But he wasn't tempted to relax. It was just when things were going well that people tended to let down their guard. At least that was what his father had always drummed into his head. By now he'd replenished his air and drinking water and had a fresh firebelly, after a frightening interval when he hadn't been able to find a replacement. He'd managed to bag another meatbeast—this far from the tribe's territory the lumbering creatures had lost all fear of man—and his larder was well stocked. It was no time to get careless.

It was his caution that trapped him.

He'd just attained another branch. He hoisted himself over the edge and peered around. It was a good place for a web spinner to weave a snare—a place where a migrating animal might venture an exploring limb.

Sure enough, there was a web there. His eye picked out a dry radial through the sticky labyrinth of crosshairs and followed it to the beast's lair. He located a beady cluster of eyes some distance away, half-hidden by an overhanging branchlet. The beast wasn't likely to rush out until its prey was caught in the web, but Torris nocked an arrow anyway.

He levered himself gingerly to a standing position and took a step sideways just to give himself an extra margin of safety, his eyes still on the nightmare in the shadows.

He felt the noose draw tight around his ankle too late. He was jerked off his feet, his spear and bow sent spinning out of reach. He found himself dangling upside down, swinging back and forth in dreamlike slow motion, the cord kept barely taut by the comet's insignificant gravity but still keeping him out of reach of anything he could grab to jackknife himself free.

From above he could see the scattered leaves that had so cleverly concealed the trap, laid down painstakingly in a pattern meant to seem random. Twisting his neck, he could see the tip of the long twig to which the cord had been attached. It was at least five man-lengths above him, and the base of the twig at the other end was anchored some five man-lengths farther along on the branch. The trap would have been powerful enough to snare a meatbeast and fast enough to snare a flutterer. Someone had gone to a lot of trouble.

But that wasn't his immediate worry. The web beast had been jarred to attention by the springing of the trap. It had partly emerged from its hiding place and was eyeing him with obvious interest.

He stopped struggling immediately. The beast crawled all the way out of its hiding place. Frozen with fear, Torris could do nothing but watch it.

And then, suddenly, the stubby end of an arrow was sprouting out of the web beast's cluster of eyes. The creature thrashed about frantically, spattering gobs of thickening blood, finally landing upside down, glued to the sticky spokes of its web, its eight hairy legs twitching.

As Torris watched, a bulky figure in a padded airsuit stepped out from behind a branchlet and started toward him, skirting the edges of the web but not bothering to glance at the dying web beast. The airsuit was an unfamiliar design. He had never seen anything like it. Instead of decorative beadwork to identify its wearer, it was embroidered in intricate patterns of many colors that covered the torso and branched out along the arms and legs.

Someone from another Tree, then. A hunter or someone on an ill-advised bride raid. Ill-advised because the nearest Tree, the one that the bachelors of Torris's tribe had been eagerly discussing for half a lifetime, was still too far away for a crossing and would not be reachable for many, many more turns of the world.

But this one had survived the leap. Torris had never heard of such a thing. The fellow must be very determined indeed.

Torris knew what you were supposed to do when you encountered someone from another tribe. You were supposed to kill him or her. His father had been telling him that since he was a small boy and had been given his first knife.

The stranger must have been having some of the same thoughts. As he approached Torris, he was already drawing another arrow out of its quiver.

Torris struggled helplessly. He still had his own knife, but he was hanging upside down by one leg, without the leverage to use it or even to throw it effectively.

Besides, the stranger wasn't going to get close enough to let him try. He stopped a couple of body lengths away and fitted another arrow to his bow.

Torris had the knife in his hand, waiting for a chance that wasn't going to come. The stranger looked up at him almost regretfully.

At that moment, the faceplate tilted toward him, and he got his first good look at the face of the person who was going to kill him.

It was a woman.

CHAPTER 5

3,500,000,000 A.D.
Quasar 3C-273

Two and a half billion light-years away, and two and a half billion years in Torris's past, a man named Joorn Gant floated in space above a cloud-marbled planet and watched helplessly as his ship disappeared.

A friend tugged at his arm. "Come on, Joorn. There's nothing you can do about it."

"Vandals," Joorn muttered. "They don't know what they're doing."

Less than two miles away, in low orbit above the planet that the colonists had named Rebirth, a swarm of spacesuited workmen began to dismantle the immense colony ship *Time's Beginning*, cannibalizing it for parts that would not be needed anymore. The journeyers had spent two and a half billion years—less than two generations to them—chasing down a quasar and had found, as they expected, that the quasar had burnt itself out, leaving behind the usual billion-sun black hole and a freshly minted galaxy. It was a young galaxy and a good place to start over.

"We've reached our goal, haven't we?" his companion said

bitterly. "We found our Earthlike planet and our longer-lived K-type sun, and we're well along in the job of making babies. We don't need *Time's Beginning* anymore, do we? The young folk are impatient, and you can't blame them. They don't want to waste any more time looking for something better. Leave it to future generations to fill this galaxy. It'll only take a paltry thirty million years of logarithmic expansion, according to the First Civilization theory that sent us here in the first place."

He turned his head for a rueful look at the gigantic shape of the starship silhouetted against the planet below. They were close enough to see swarms of mite-sized specks that were spacesuited workmen crawling over its blackened and pitted surface. Jets briefly flared, and one of the enormous habitat modules came free and started drifting slowly away from the core of the ship, a score of the silvery specks clinging to it. As the two of them watched, a nearby tug closed in and took possession of it.

"That doesn't sound like the Delbert Karn I know," Joorn replied. He stared accusingly at Karn. "It seems to me that it was only a couple of months ago that you stormed into a Council meeting with a crowd of your followers and made an impassioned speech demanding that they leave what's left of the ship intact and turn it over to you and your followers."

"I'm through with words," Karn said heatedly. "Our only hope is direct action."

"What are you talking about?"

"Talk is useless. Our faction numbers over three thousand now. And not just the old fogies like you and me. They're bright young people who aren't ready to settle for a latecomer like 3C-273. They're fired by our old dream of chasing down a quasar at the boundary of the observable Universe, a quasar that was present at the creation."

"An impossible dream, Delbert. The quasars that gave birth to the original galaxies are fifteen billion light-years away. The more the Universe expands, the faster they race away. You can never catch up, no matter how closely you crowd the speed of light. You'd be chasing a chimera."

"The human mind is a chimera, my old friend. Life is a chimera. Maybe the Universe itself is a chimera. My young people think that those of their contemporaries who are content to plant themselves here are hopeless dullards. And they think that your faction, the would-be returnees, are irrational sentimentalists."

"Irrational?" Joorn flared. "You're calling *us* irrational?"

"The home you people want to return to will have ceased to exist by the time you got there. The sun will be a red giant, on its way to becoming a white dwarf. It will have swallowed Earth. The net drift of Alpha Centauri toward Sol means that by the time you got there, the solar system will be part of a multiple star system with four stars—a red giant on the way down the Main Sequence to becoming a white dwarf, a white dwarf that had enough original mass to beat it there, and a K-type star that was small enough and long-lived enough to survive as a viable sun, only somewhat dimmer than Sol was in its prime. With Proxima Centauri circling the whole shebang at a distance. The Oort clouds of the three other stars will have merged to become a forest of comets. Not to mention that just about now"—Karn pretended to look at an imaginary wristwatch—"the Andromeda galaxy will have collided with the Milky Way."

"The Milky Way is still our home," Joorn protested, with anguish in his voice. "The cradle of the human race, even though we didn't know the First Ones already owned it. There'll still be plenty of real estate there. Maybe one or two of the planets of the Centaurian system will have survived. Maybe Earth will have solidified enough to form a crust that life can be planted on. We planted it here, didn't we? Maybe enough of Jupiter's atmosphere will have boiled away to leave a rocky core we can terraform. The Others must have gone extinct in the two and a half billion years that have already passed. We own our home galaxy again."

When Karn spoke again, he didn't bother to disguise his pity. "Fairy tales, my friend. You're telling yourself fairy tales."

"I'm only an unemployed ship's captain, not an astrophysics genius like you. But I've done all the math too—the life span of G3 and K5 stars, the rate of Alpha Centauri's drift toward Sol, the consequences of the collision with Andromeda—I've run and rerun the old computer models that show the gravitational distortion of both galaxies and two spiral galaxies becoming one big elliptical galaxy. And I'll tell you this. There's one thing you've left out of all your calculations."

"Which is?"

"The power of the homing instinct. The yearning. It trumps everything else."

"Give it up, Joorn. Between the two of us, we could bring the Council around. Otherwise . . . "

"Otherwise what?"

Karn became evasive. "I'm going to bring my case before the Council one last time. Then we'll see."

With a faint sense of alarm, Joorn said, "Don't do anything rash, Delbert."

"Rash? Don't trouble yourself about it, Joorn. Just go on dreaming your dreams, and I'll dream mine."

Without another word, they both triggered their altitude jets and spun on their vertical axes, turning together to watch as the habitat module maneuvered into position for atmospheric entry, carrying yet another twenty thousand inhabitants to the growing settlement on the ground.

CHAPTER 6

Only a few hundred people were left in a habitat module that had been home to thousands for most of their lifetimes. Joorn could almost feel its emptiness as a tangible presence as he propelled himself through the vast echoing corridors with a small handheld fan—the most practical way to travel now that there was no more up and down.

He passed only a half dozen people on the way to his quarters, swimming like him through the stagnant air with the help of their little propellers. Most of them didn't bother to stop. They gave him a negligent wave—or in the case of the older ones, an actual salute—and perhaps a "Hello, Captain," or "How goes it?" One old shipmate, pulling his wife along with a hand at her elbow, pointed his fan in the opposite direction long enough to say, "It's going to feel strange to leave the old thing, but the rep from the Council says they'll have housing for us any day now."

He'd replied, "You'll get used to it, Stefan. We all will."

The man's wife, her eyes moist, started to say something, but the air currents drew them out of earshot.

Another half mile of travel took him to what had been the captain's suite. It was lonely enough now, with his wife gone these many years and his son, Alten, working on Rebirth's still-untamed surface, lending his engineer's talents to the job of getting a civilization going.

He looked around at the main salon. It was spartan enough. He'd spent the years since his wife's death simplifying. But there were still the mementos from an Earth that no longer existed. An Oriental rug hanging on one wall—a relic of the centuries when they still made such things by hand. An actual piano of carved rosewood; his wife had played old music on it, and he hadn't had the heart to get rid of it. A glass dome enclosing an arrangement of dried leaves from a rain forest that had been long gone even then. A velvet sofa. Framed prints of paintings by vanished painters. A sculpted model of *Time's Beginning*, with its long shaft surrounded by the oblate spheres of the habitat modules and the forward umbrella to ward off the deadly radiation that came from slamming into interstellar hydrogen at more than ninety-nine percent of the speed of light. There was no resemblance to the earlier starships with their spinning wheels to simulate gravity; *Time's Beginning* had been designed to accelerate, then decelerate, at one G for the entire two and a half billion years.

He took a shower to get rid of the grime and sweat of the spacesuit, then thought about supper. He wasn't hungry, but he still presided over a captain's table of sorts, and he owed it to the others to put in an appearance.

There was still time to make a call to his son on the planet's surface. Alten, as far as he knew, was working at a construction site a few miles from the growing city of Rebirth's capital-to-be, New Brussels.

He tried to dial him up and was informed by the *Time's Beginning* communication center that the relay satellite—the first and so far only one—was currently behind the planet but that his call could be placed in two hours.

When he got back from dinner, he was a little depressed. He'd had to preside over an argument between one of the Endgamist majority and an obnoxious member of Karn's firebrand party. The dispute got complicated when a colonist with a third point of view became vehement. "We've only planted settlements in four star systems in 3C-273, including this one!" he'd said, thumping the table for emphasis. "That's not what I call seeding the galaxy. We've still got four habitat modules left, each with its own shuttle and everything needed to get started. I say let's finish the job!"

Joorn didn't want to take sides, but he managed to get them to calm down. "It ate up an extra twelve years of lifetime to do those other three stars, building up our gamma from scratch each time," he'd said diplomatically. "I can understand why most people are travel-weary. But look at the bright side. We'll inherit the four unused habitats and their starter kits, won't we? We'll have five times the resources and five times the people. That's quite a head start over the other three focal points we planted. That'll make this colony the crown jewel of the galaxy."

"And it'll *still* take twenty million years for the colonization front to fill the galaxy," the Karn partisan grumbled. "That is, if the human species hasn't evolved itself out of existence by then."

The Endgamist got in one last barb. "Which is what we hope the First Ones have done by now back in the Milky Way," he said. "Well, *we're* the First Ones here, and it's not going to help matters to waste the ship's resources by going off on a wild goose chase to the end of the Universe."

Most of the others at the table nodded in agreement at that and went back to placidly eating their dinners.

By the time Joorn got back to his quarters, the relay satellite had risen over the horizon and his screen was blinking impatiently to tell him that his call could go through. Alten picked up almost immediately.

"What's up, Father?"

"Can you get back to the ship before the weekend rush?"

Alten's voice was reluctant. "Well, we're not quite finished here, but I suppose I could leave Daryl in charge. Why? What's happening?"

"I'd like you to be here for the Council meeting on Freeday. Karn's up to something, and I'd like you to hear what he says."

"I'm just a lowly engineer these days, Father. Karn's still the big cheese in the astrophysics department."

"You were quite a Karn disciple in your youth, as I recall. His protégé, in fact. You're capable of following his thought processes much better than I can. Besides, as an astrophysicist yourself, you could clear up any confusion he might stir up at the meeting."

Alten laughed. "I'm still a youth, relatively speaking. And no longer an astrophysicist. That part of our hegira's over, and it's time to get down to business. We're here, and the daydreams are over."

"You sound like an Endgamist," Joorn said reproachfully.

Alten grew serious. "I'd like to return to Earth too, Father. At least to its former neighborhood. You know that. But it isn't practical. Earth'll be gone—its charred remnants taken out of the baking oven and the oven left to cool off. And the neighborhood will be gone to hell. This is what we've got now, and there are things to do here."

"Don't you think I know that?" Joorn snapped. He got himself under control again. "I'm resigned to following the will of the majority, but until they've finished nibbling away at *Time's Beginning*, I'll continue to advocate for turning it over to the Homegoing party. But Karn's up to some mischief."

"There's nothing he can do, Father. His faction's smaller than yours."

"I'd like you to come anyway. If Karn succeeds in swaying any of the Council members to his way of thinking, it can only hurt our cause."

There was a pause at the other end. "All right, Father. I'll book myself on the shuttle for tomorrow's flight."

The meeting hall was still unfinished. In ten or fifteen years there would begin to be lumber from actual trees, but until then the colony was making do with composites formulated from feeder stock provided by the local carbon-based vegetation, gigantic fernlike fronds that hadn't yet developed woody stems. There were stacks of new panels waiting to be installed, scaffolding everywhere, and irregular rows of folding chairs cannibalized from one of the habitats still in orbit. There was a lingering smell of synthetic resins, which together with the slightly higher oxygen content of Rebirth's atmosphere, gave one a mildly heady feeling.

Joorn and Alten were seated with several committee members in the front row, while the Council was arranged on a makeshift platform. Karn, sitting opposite their table, was holding forth.

"To answer that," he was telling one of the Councilors, "I'd like to remind you why we ended up here in the first place."

With his legs crossed, Karn looked quite relaxed and in command of the situation. But then, Karn had always been a bit of a con artist at meetings. It was one of the reasons he had risen so quickly in the scientific community when he was young.

"There he goes," Joorn whispered, nudging Alten.

"Remember that the original idea behind *Time's Beginning* was to chase down a quasar at the so-called edge of the observable Universe, dating from the era when the first galaxies were being formed. That's where the name of our ark came from in the first place, isn't it? The reasoning, at least of the politicians who funded it, was that, according to what was known as the First Civilization hypothesis, in a very young galaxy intelligent life had not yet had a chance to evolve—remember, it took a couple of billion years for that to happen on Earth—and that human beings had a chance to become the Firsts in a new galaxy."

He had the Councilors nodding. He smiled pleasantly and went on.

"Of course the reasoning was fallacious. But try to explain that to a politician. It was the early years after the discovery of the First Ones, and there was a lot of public hysteria. We weren't alone in the galaxy, it seemed. In fact, we were being crowded out of the Milky Way by a prior race that already owned it."

He uncrossed and recrossed his legs. He was still smiling. "It was quite a shock. It was only fifty years since the Higgs drive had made human starships possible, and we were full of ourselves. We were going to conquer the Universe. We'd already planted a tiny outpost on a planet of Tau Ceti, and another on a quite Earthlike planet of Delta Pavonis, a full twenty light-years away. The Milky Way was our oyster."

"Here it comes," Joorn whispered.

"But it turned out that someone else had won that first toss of the dice some thirty million years earlier. While mankind, if you want to count the early hominids, had only been around for a couple of million years. The First Civilization hypothesis says that the earliest intelligent race to emerge in any galaxy gets to own it. The calculation is that it takes only thirty million years of logarithmic expansion to fill a galaxy, and the race that starts first wins.

"Humans, unfortunately, started second. By the time we were capable of interstellar travel at relativistic speeds, there was no habitable real estate available in the Milky Way. The First Ones had already made an alien suburb out of virtually every F-, G-, and K-type star system in the galaxy. Our little bubble had a radius of only about twenty light-years when the wave front of the First Ones' diffusion reached us. They left us alone. There's no conceivable profit in interstellar war, not at the distances involved. And there can be no such thing as a galactic empire, not when communication at the speed of light would take sixty thousand years to cross the galaxy. There's a twenty- or thirty-light-year limit for any imaginable kind of politics. So they stopped short of our little bubble. And we were boxed in."

The Councilors shifted uncomfortably in their seats. It was an old bedtime story, one nobody liked. Karn went on relentlessly. He wasn't smiling anymore.

"Of course there was a lot of public nonsense about alien invasions and alien attacks and alien takeovers. The pundits fed the hysteria, and the politicians catered to it. In the meantime, the First Ones simply ignored us. Neither trade nor conquest had any interest for them. We were simply an unimportant bump in their road."

One of the Councilmen cleared his throat. "Excuse me, Professor Karn, but where are we going with this?"

"I didn't mean to try your patience, Councilman Brego," Karn said nastily. "We're only talking about the fate of the human species in the Universe."

The other members of the Council didn't like that. They exchanged glances. Brego had acquired two ruddy patches on his cheeks.

"That did it," Joorn said to Alten. "Karn never learns."

Karn went on, oblivious. "As I was *trying* to say, you don't populate a galaxy the way you populate a planet, increment by straightforward increment. The distances just grow too great for meaningful communication, even at twenty or thirty light-years. Instead, it has to become a process of diffusion. When a colony's grown enough to have the resources to send out starships of its own, each new colony becomes a focal point in itself, and so ad infinitum. The process can be described mathematically, and it was so described in the late twentieth century by scientists at Princeton and Cornell—two institutions that were still going strong two hundred years after *Time's Beginning* left Earth and that were instrumental in choosing the quasar 3C-273 as our target.

"Their conclusion was that it takes thirty million years of logarithmic expansion to fill a galaxy—if the species hasn't gone extinct by then. The dinosaurs didn't last that long, but then, as we know, they turned into something else. Perhaps that's what happened to the First Ones. They wouldn't have much in common from one end of the galaxy to the other, but they'd have the same genetic heritage."

The Councilors were growing visibly restive. One was tapping a foot. Another was scribbling with his data pad's stylus.

Everybody but Karn could see that they were annoyed at being talked down to. Or perhaps he could. He had a small insolent smile on his face.

Joorn leaned toward Alten. "He's deliberately trying to provoke them," he said. "What's he up to?"

"He *wants* them to turn him down. He knew they were going to do it anyway."

"The man's crazy. He's sabotaging our chances too." He started to get up. "I'm going to ask the Council if I can speak."

Alten grabbed his sleeve. "Don't. You'll only make matters worse."

"But this may be the last chance to make a case for the Homegoers!"

"They're going to turn you down too, Father," Alten said. "Face it."

Karn seemed to be enjoying himself. "But I digress, gentlemen," he said. "And lady," he added negligently, with a nod to the Council's sole female member. "We were talking about public hysteria, weren't we? About the media-induced panic that ensued when the hoi polloi discovered that we were being crowded out of our home. So we turned our instruments on the nearby galaxies. We'd never detected signs of life at those distances before, but lo and behold, funding was suddenly found at a level that had never been available for the search for intelligent life within our *own* galaxy.

"Bad luck. Andromeda, our nearest neighbor at only two million light-years, proved to have evidence of intelligent life, after the data were analyzed with the new techniques and instruments. A hundred years earlier we would have been delighted. Now it was bad news. The emanations didn't come from just one or two stars; they came from the entire galaxy, and they were suggestively uniform. It seemed Andromeda had its First Ones too. So did the Magellanic Clouds, and every galaxy out to the Virgo Cluster, fifty million light-years away.

"But we had the Higgs drive. We'd had it for twenty years by then. It had already taken us to Alpha Centauri, Epsilon Eridani, Delta Pavonis, and the other interesting candidates in our little sphere. And it had done so at a constant one-G acceleration because it provided what amounted to unlimited fuel. The Higgs boson generates the masses of all the fundamental particles, and consequently, as virtual particles wink into existence, mediates the energy of the vacuum. When we learned how to manipulate the Higgs field, which exists everywhere, a starship could create its own fuel as it went along, in much the same way virtual particles are created in the vicinity of a black hole.

"So by being able to maintain a constant one-G acceleration, it was now possible to reach the nearer stars within a human lifetime. But what about *intergalactic* distances, at *millions* of light-years?"

Karn was in full lecture mode now. "A funny thing happens on the way to the speed of light. As you pass ninety-nine-point-nine percent and begin to add more nines after the decimal point, relativistic values rise steeply. Incredibly steeply. So while it took twenty-two years of ship time at one G to reach our own galactic center thirty thousand light-years away, a paltry investment of another *five* years would take us to the Andromeda galaxy, two million light-years away. An additional five years would take us to the Virgo Cluster of galaxies, at a distance of fifty million light-years."

He paused dramatically. "And in less than another thirty years of lifetime, one could reach the edge of the visible Universe."

"He's reached the sales pitch," Alten whispered. "But he's too late. They're out of patience."

Karn had let his hands drop to his sides. "That was the idea anyway. But with the existence of the human race at stake, the petty bureaucrats in Brussels and Beijing and Suprawashington lost their nerve—"

"We know the story, Professor Karn," Councilman Brego interrupted. "The visible edge of Creation was fourteen billion years away at the time. It still is for us here in 3C-273— we're barely keeping up with the expansion of the Universe. The infant galaxies might have been prebiotic as we saw them, but by the time we'd get there, life might have evolved, become extinct, and evolved again many times over."

"But . . . " Karn began.

Brego raised a hand to stop him. "So they very wisely opted for a closer, younger quasar. A second-generation quasar. The odds were better. After all, in our own case, life didn't arise for more than ten billion years, when the sun—a second-generation star, by the way—was in its third billennium. The First Ones preceded humankind by only a few tens of thousands of years. The odds are that the same rule will hold true for 3C-273."

"Brego's no fool," Alten said in a low voice. "He may be a

Neocreationist, but he knows his astrophysics."

Karn didn't like being interrupted. He tried to stare Brego down. "I was about to say that I have no quarrel with your settling here. It's done, isn't it? We've planted our colonies. The rest is up to time. Thirty million years of it. I never had any interest in dropping off a load of jolly colonists in your hatchery. *My* people are after knowledge. And maybe, just maybe, after another fifteen billion years, we'll still be around to be humanity's hole card in a dying Universe. Carry humanity past the end of everything. Or into a new beginning."

His voice rose and became strident. "We're asking again for you to let us have *Time's Beginning* before it's too late. Let us keep just one habitat. That's all my little band of truth-seekers needs. You can have the rest."

He stood, offering each of them a challenging stare in turn.

"We'll take it under consideration, Professor Karn," the chairman said. "We'll let you know."

They caught up with Karn outside. The people attending the meeting were dispersing and returning along the manicured walks to their various jobs. It was a beautiful autumn day in Rebirth's northern temperate zone. A golden sun—a G-4 that still had a couple of billion years to go before it used up its hydrogen and grew into a red giant that would swallow its children—shone brilliantly in a nearly cloudless azure sky. The air was fragrant with the perfume of terrestrial wildflowers that were slowly winning a battle with Rebirth's native vegetation, and somewhere in the middle distance a meadowlark was singing its heart out.

"I hope you know you blew it, Delbert," Joorn said. "The

Council's decision isn't going to be favorable."

Karn didn't seem to be at all perturbed. "Hell, I knew that going in," he said. "I'm not going to wait for a decision. I just wanted to make it absolutely clear that I gave them one last chance."

"If you think—" Joorn began.

Karn interrupted him. "How many people do you have in your party whom you can absolutely depend on?"

"Depend on? What are you talking about? So far I've got over four thousand signatures from dedicated Homegoers on our petition to the Council, and—"

Karn gave him a pitying look. "Petitions!" he snorted. "You've got twice as many dreamers in your little coalition as I have in mine, but mine have more fire in their bellies."

"I don't see what—"

"And more discipline."

Joorn and Alten exchanged apprehensive glances.

"I've made a young fellow named Miles Oliver my deputy," Karn said. "With his military experience, he's been whipping them into shape. Miles made a name for himself in the Dissolutionist Wars of the '80s. Almost got himself hanged by the Corporate Nations League. Came out of it alive and went back to school. Brilliant student, with degrees in astrophysics and Brane Theory. He'll inherit my mantle when I go." He looked sorrowfully at Alten. "That could have been you, my boy."

Alten said, "I'm sorry, Professor Karn. I—"

"No apologies necessary. We go where life takes us. I'm sorry too."

"I don't like where you're going with this, Delbert," Joorn

said. "You can't just—"

"All I ask is that you come to a little meeting back at the ship. Both of you. We have something to discuss."

"I don't—"

"It concerns you, Joorn. Be there. Everybody can come out of this a winner."

As Joorn hesitated, Alten said, "We'll be there, Professor."

"Good." Karn turned on his heel, and started walking away rapidly. Joorn saw him take the path that led to the primitive spaceport across the meadow.

"I don't like this," Joorn said.

"Neither do I," Alten said. "But if Karn means to involve us in something shady, we need to have our eyes wide open."

CHAPTER 7

The habitat where Karn maintained his quarters still had several thousand people living in it, mostly diehard Endgamists who were putting off moving to Rebirth's surface until the last possible moment. Joorn had long been aware that the overwhelming majority of them were young people who had been born during *Time's Beginning*'s long journey and who never had known what it was like to live on a planet. As disciples of Karn, they tended to cluster around their guru.

"It's about a quarter-mile down this corridor," Joorn said as they floated along with the sparse traffic. "He's meeting us in the old physics classroom. He's still giving lectures there."

"I know the way, Father," Alten said.

Joorn glanced at him sharply, looking for guilt or defiance, but saw only the usual matter-of-fact expression on his face.

They passed a couple of security patrols along the way. But they weren't wearing the modest identification badges usually sported by the Council's security people. Instead they wore makeshift tabards inscribed with a stylized infinity symbol. All of them were young toughs identically armed with lengths of titanium pipe. Despite their unprofessional appearance, they obviously served some sort of unauthorized security function. As Joorn and Alten were passing, one such ragtag group had stopped an elderly couple for questioning. The man was indignantly protesting. One of the young thugs paused long enough to give Joorn a hard stare. Joorn couldn't tell if the fellow had recognized his captain.

"What's happening here?" Joorn asked Alten with a frown.

Alten didn't answer. He continued to look straight ahead, aiming his little hand fan to pull him along.

"Here we are," Alten said, braking himself to a stop and swiveling in midair to plant himself upright on a stickymat.

Joorn tried the knob and found that the door was locked. He rattled the knob, and after a moment, someone on the other side opened the door.

Two young men wearing the infinity tabards put out their hands to stop them from proceeding, and one of them, to Joorn's amazement, made as if to frisk them.

"It's all right, Pfyfe," an unfamiliar voice said from the other end of the room. "Let them through."

Karn's desk was slanted catty-corner in front of a blackboard covered with scribbled equations and Feynman diagrams. A hollow-cheeked man who looked to be middle-aged was sitting in a chair drawn up next to the desk.

"That's him—Miles Oliver, the guy Karn was talking about," Alten whispered. He stepped forward, leaving Joorn to follow.

"Glad you decided to come," Karn said without getting up. "Your cooperation is going to be vital. I'm going to offer you a bargain, Joorn. With it, both of us have a chance to get what we want. Without it, the Council will have their way, and *Time's Beginning* will be dismantled for its junk value."

He nodded to the bully boys at the door, and one of them, the one named Pfyfe, hurried up and, with a resentful look at Joorn and Alten, dragged a couple of chairs forward for them to sit in, though the microgravity provided by the ship's central core was barely sufficient to keep the seats of their pants in contact. Joorn noticed that Pfyfe had one of the ubiquitous titanium pipes tucked under his belt.

"Sorry about that little misunderstanding at the door," Karn said. "We can't be too careful about security. We don't want the Council getting wind of this meeting."

"What's this about, Delbert?" Joorn said. "And what do you mean, you're offering me a bargain?"

Miles Oliver spoke for the first time. He extended a hand with the fingers spread out and said, "It's like these fingers, see. When they're separated, they can't do much." He abruptly clenched them. "But when you put them together, you have a fist."

Karn smiled. "You'll have to excuse Miles. He's been making a lot of speeches lately."

"And what are we going to do with this fist?" Joorn said.

"Why, we're going to hijack the ship and its remaining habitats, Joorn," Karn said. "Then we're going to drop you and your sentimentalists off at the Milky Way, see you settled, then take the ship and its Higgs drive, together with the last habitat, build up its relativistic velocity to the edge of the Sanger limit, and continue on to the birth of time."

His eyes were blazing, and Joorn could plainly see the hidden fanatic that Karn had always been. "We're not prepared to use force against innocent people, Delbert," Joorn said gently. "We accept that the Council speaks for the majority."

Oliver spoke up glibly. "We're not going to use force, Captain. Only the threat of force. And our combined numbers to back it up. You and your crowd of collaborators don't have to do a thing."

Joorn turned to Alten. "Did you know about this?"

Alten avoided looking at him. He stared straight ahead and said nothing.

"We offered him a chance to come in with us," Karn said. "I think deep down he's tempted. But he's loyal to his father."

"We don't need him," Oliver said.

"But you need me, don't you?" Joorn said. "To run the ship."

"We could use your help," Karn admitted. "But Miles is fully competent to do that."

"He's still in training, isn't he?" Joorn said, and was rewarded by an immediate flash of resentment on Oliver's face.

"He can handle it. He might need your backup when we start out."

"They can't do it without us, Father," Alten interposed. "It takes a lot of manpower to maintain a starship like this for years and decades. You know that better than anybody. And he needs our numbers to give him legitimacy. Otherwise they're just a small band of malcontents committing piracy."

"I promise you no one will get hurt," Karn said. "And Alten's right, in a way. Between your constituents and mine, we're a significant minority in the total human population. We deserve to have a say in how the resource represented by *Time's Beginning* gets used."

Joorn scratched the stubble on his chin. "No rough stuff?" he said.

"I promise you. We're going to temporarily inconvenience the relatively small number of settlers who still remain in orbit, but no one will get hurt. When we have control, we'll ship them down to Rebirth in one of the habitats. Those who want to join your returnees or my little band of explorers will be allowed to stay. In the meantime, I suggest that you round up as many of your followers who are already down below as you can and get them up here on some pretext or another. In small groups, it goes without saying."

Joorn hesitated.

"Think about it," Karn said earnestly. "You get to go home, albeit to a very changed home, and start the human race all over again in the Milky Way. I get to see the Universe at its birth, just seconds past the inflationary epoch. And maybe take the human race past the final collapse to a new beginning. And as for those intrepid Endgamist pioneers down below"—he couldn't keep his lip from curling in contempt—"they get to seed this late-term galaxy with our species while the Universe, Brego's God bless it, still has a few billion years to go. Everybody wins."

"He's right, Father," Alten said.

"Thank you, Alten," Karn said without taking his eyes off Joorn. "Maybe during the long detour back to our"—his lip curled again—"ancestral nest in the Milky Way, I'll be able to persuade you to throw your lot in with us. I might not live long enough to see the birth of time, but you will." His voice grew vibrant. "You have it in you to be the Aaron to my Moses, my boy."

Joorn glanced at Miles Oliver long enough to see a flicker of envy cross his face. It was gone almost before he registered it.

He avoided looking at Alten. He turned back to Karn and said, "All right, Delbert. It's a bargain."

CHAPTER 8

6,000,000,000 A.D.
The Oort Cloud

Torris wasn't ready to die. Knowing it was futile, he managed, with a convulsive effort, to contort his body upward and grasp the rope above his trapped ankle. Even as he felt the snare loosen—too late—he had an upside-down view of the woman's face through her clouded helmet as she drew back the bow-string and revised her aim upward. She was shaking her head sadly, as if to reproach him.

Before she could loose the arrow, there was a commotion in the leaves above. A flutterbeast had been lurking there, probably hoping to snatch any prey caught by the web spinner.

Startled, the woman spun around and let the arrow fly just as the creature swooped to rake her with its claws. Her aim was off, and the arrow went clear through one of the outspread wings. But it had thrown the flutterbeast off too, and she was able to duck in time. The beast sailed past her, brushing against Torris in the process. It collided with a section of branch and twisted around to launch itself again from the new platform.

By that time, Torris had his feet under him and turned himself into a projectile that bowled the woman over and sent her weapon flying. He had a close-up look through the faceplate at a striking face, dark eyes huge with surprise, and features sharper and more angular than those of the women of his own tribe.

And then, without a moment to spare, he rolled the two of them into a crevice in the branch and squeezed them as deep into the cleft as was possible.

It was barely deep enough. The creature's claws scrabbled at them, only inches away. The huge flat snout pressed against the opening, and the creature had edged a bulbous eye in place to peer malevolently at them. Torris stabbed at it with his knife, and it withdrew.

They huddled together for what seemed like hours before the flutterbeast decided to give up. Even so, they waited another long interval before they risked emerging. The dark-eyed woman surveyed their surroundings with the painstaking thoroughness of a hunter, then crept out on the branch to retrieve her bow. Torris did nothing to stop her.

Torris found his own spear and bow and donned his backpack again. The woman retrieved her kit from where she had stowed it. They exchanged a wary look, then started climbing together to a safer neighborhood.

Her name was Ning. She was a huntress, a concept that Torris at first found hard to grasp. But she made him understand that in the Tree that she came from, women hunters were not uncommon. They banded together in sororities of five or six women and generally hunted in pairs or small parties. They were women without men, or women whose men were lazy, or incompetent or abusive, or whose men had died. The hunting parties included girls as young as nine or ten who were taught by their mothers or grandmothers and taken along on hunts to help with the butchering or carrying the kill home. Ning was unusual in that she had been taught to use a bow at an early age by her father, who wasn't too stiff-necked to partner with his mate and who was proud of his little girl's prowess. When Ning's father was killed by a flutterbeast, her mother and grandmother had taken her with them into a hunting association. She was only a little older than Torris, but she already had a reputation as an extraordinarily gifted hunter who often hunted alone, as a few men did.

The inhabitants of Ning's Tree had been watching the slow drift of the two Trees toward each other for years, and their young men were just as eager as those of Torris's tribe for a chance at a bride raid. It would be years more before the Trees were close enough to make the leap possible.

But Ning was audacious enough—or reckless enough—to brave the deadly gap. Game had been scarce lately in the upper branches of her own Tree. She announced, to much shaking of heads and not a little resentment from the young men, that she was going to make the attempt.

Torris gathered that she had launched herself from a springy branch in the upper reaches of the Tree, timing its slow rotation to give her an extra boost, with no witnesses to see her off. She had taken along a large sack of explosive seed pods and a bladder of heat chemicals from a slaughtered stovebeast to trick them into bursting.

Even so, she had spent days adrift in the void without food or water, having decided to trade them for extra air, judiciously setting off a seed pod from time to time for a course correction or additional thrust.

But she'd won her crazy gamble. She landed, weak and hungry but still alive. She replenished her supplies, and after a day's rest started hunting. She bagged a wild meatbeast right away and without pause started hunting again. Like Torris, she took the butchered carcass with her in a sling between her forays. Her lunatic plan was to tie four or five carcasses together and catapult them toward her Tree with a gigantic slingshot spliced together from lengths of animal sinew. She actually planned to ride the carcasses back. This time, she told Torris, she'd have something to eat on the way back.

They made camp together, still a little wary of each other, and spent what was left of the red starlight with their heads pressed together, exchanging helmet talk. Her dialect was different from that of Torris's tribe, but they found that, with a little patience, they were perfectly able to make themselves understood. By the time they made camp, Torris had already grasped the basic outlines of her story through nothing more than finger talk and a little lip reading. Interestingly enough, though the spoken words often differed, their finger talk was almost identical.

Now she was telling Torris that she had realized after a few days that someone was stalking her too.

"I thought you were my stalker," she said in her faint helmet voice. It sounded as if she were talking to him from the other end of an ice cave.

"And I thought you were *my* stalker," he said with a laugh. Then, more soberly, "I think I know who it is."

"When I caught a glimpse of him in the distance, he had a

suit like yours, with patterns of beads instead of embroidery, and it was insulated in squares like yours instead of being sensibly padded in triangles. One night when I was asleep, he stole some of my supplies, including a spare airbag and one of my carcasses. What he didn't steal, he wantonly destroyed."

"That's him all right," he said.

"I sent an arrow after him," she said fiercely, "but I missed. But I scared the lifelight out of him from the way he danced. Now he knows I'll kill him. He won't bother us again."

They shared a hasty meal in a joint shelter, then set up their sleeping sacks side by side—back to back so that they could keep a lookout in both directions. Ning seemed to fall asleep almost immediately, as far as Torris could tell. At least he felt no movement after a minute or two. Torris himself tossed uncomfortably, beset by confusing thoughts. He tried in vain not to think about Ning. For one thing, she was about the same age as Secondmother. That was troubling. She was not from his tribe, which made her fair game, yet he couldn't seem to sort out his feelings.

In the morning, she was cheerful and he was glum. They joined their air sacks together for another shared meal, collected their gear, and resumed their climbing. Torris wondered if being in the company of someone else during a Climb was a mortal sin, even if the other person was not another Climber pursuing a Tree dream, was not a male, and was not even a member of the tribe. It was indubitable that being with someone who could share food, survival chores, and hunting was a help within the meaning of the taboo. In the end, he decided to leave the question to Claz. There might be some kind of penance or purification rite.

It occurred to him that he could choose not to tell Claz anything, but he dismissed the idea. He also could separate himself from Ning, but he found he didn't want to do that. Ning herself seemed to take it for granted that they would stay together. She was headed to the top of the Tree herself, hoping for better hunting. And besides, there was the problem of the stalker. They hadn't seen him again, but that didn't mean anything. There was always the danger that he was watching from a distance, waiting for a chance to separate them.

They climbed for another two days without incident. Ning bagged another meatbeast, a big torpedo-shaped male with vestigial fins and oversized tusks that made it especially valuable, and Torris was given the job of dragging it along.

She was the one who raised the question of the Tree dream. "Why do you climb, Tor-ris?" she said during one of their rest pauses. "I climb to find better hunting, but that is not what drives you, right? You are content to let me do the hunting, but at the same time, I think you would be happy to live on mushrooms and hoppers while climbing, and there is something that bothers you about accepting help from me."

Reluctantly, not knowing if he was violating another taboo, he explained that the Climb was a rite of manhood and that each Climber must face it alone.

"But not a rite of womanhood, is that not so?" she said with a peculiar smile that had a hint of mockery in it.

For some ridiculous reason the question made him feel defensive. "No," he admitted.

She knew all about Tree dreams, but the ritual was different in her tribe, she said.

"The Dream is for boys, yes. But it is a joyous occasion for his kin, and we have a Dream ceremony in which even the women and girls are allowed to share. We don't believe that a boy should be left to have his Dream alone, helpless in his delirium, when any predator—animal or human—can come along and harm him. At the very least, he is accompanied by his father or an uncle or some trusted older man who can watch over him, and to whom he can tell his Dream when he returns to his senses. More often, his family makes the Climb with him." Again there was that mocking smile. "Sometimes there is even a woman or two along to take care of the men's comfort and feeding."

He tried to digest the strange new ideas but failed. He felt a vague sense of unease.

"The Trees give us our laws, and we know these laws by our Dreams," he finally said lamely, quoting the catechism that Claz had taught him.

"Don't trouble yourself about it, Tor-ris," she said. "Soon I will have enough meatbeast carcasses and I will leave your Tree and go back to my own people. Perhaps we will meet again one day when our Trees come closer and you can join your young men on a bride raid." She gave him a smile, a mischievous one this time. "Unless our young men go on a bride raid first. For now, Tor-ris the Pious, you are welcome to your Dream, and you can return to your cave to tell it to your priest." He didn't know how to reply to that. She didn't seem to be angry with him. He settled for saying, "We still have an hour of light left. We'd better start climbing again."

[HAPTER 9]

3,500,000,000 A.D.
Quasar 3C-273

The klaxon hoot of the emergency override woke him up. Joorn glanced bleary-eyed at the clock face on his personal screen. It was about an hour too early to get up.

"Permission granted," he said, and the screen blinked to show him the close-up features of an elderly man who seemed to have a bloody nose. He recognized the face of one of his older shipmates—Stefan, the man's name was, the one who'd been awaiting a housing assignment down below in the growing residential area of New Brussels. Of course! Stefan would be one of those who knew his code, and someone who wouldn't abuse it.

"Captain," he said, "you'd better come quick. Something's happening here, and it's . . . "

Then there were rough hands yanking Stefan away from the screen, and Joorn got a longer view of a shipboard double cabin, with Stefan in disarrayed nightclothes being manhandled by somebody wearing an infinity tabard over his shirt. Over by the bulkhead, two more men in tabards were restraining Stefan's frightened-looking wife.

A large hand appeared, and Joorn's screen went blank. He tried to revive it and found it wasn't working anymore.

He dressed quickly and went out into the corridor. People in their nightclothes were milling about and being systematically rounded up and herded in groups by more young men in tabards toward the passages leading to the public facilities. Some of them were brandishing the titanium pipes or using them to poke and prod, but Joorn didn't see anyone actually being struck.

No one molested him. He'd had the foresight to snatch his old uniform jacket from the hook by the door where it had been retired, and perhaps they had no orders concerning him.

He headed down the corridor where he knew Stefan was billeted. He was challenged only once by a young bully-boy who detached himself from his compatriots and floated into his path with his hand up.

"Hold it right there, mister!"

He drew himself up as well as anyone could while hanging in midair and used the sharp-edged voice of authority he'd honed in some forty years of giving orders.

"What's your name, fellow?" he barked. "Who do you report to? Don't you recognize your captain?" For a moment, he was afraid it wasn't going to work, but then, after a doubtful glance at the jacket and its insignia, the young cockerel backed down.

Joorn continued, and when he found Stefan's corridor, it was already clear of people. A door hung open halfway down, and Joorn aimed himself for it. He landed feetfirst inside the doorway and found Oliver waiting for him along with a trio of bully-boys.

"Glad you could make it, Captain," Oliver said.

"What's going on, Oliver, and where's the person who lives here?" Joorn demanded.

"The old man is fine. He's been taken to a holding area, where he'll be safe until it's over. When the boys here saw that he'd succeeded in contacting you, they thought they'd better let me know. I shouldn't have overlooked you."

"Where's Professor Karn?"

"He's in the comm center, negotiating with the Council. They get their people back, and we get ours. Including yours. The professor insisted on that. I told him you could only get in the way, but I guess that you and him go way back. We should be ready to leave this system within a week."

Joorn turned to go. One of the enforcers stepped in his way. The other two closed in on either side of him.

"Don't do anything foolish, Captain," Oliver said.

"I want to see Karn."

"All in good time, Captain. For the time being, we're going to lock you in your cabin for your own safety."

The two henchmen took over. One of them gripped him by the upper arm. Joorn shook him off, but the man only grabbed him again, more firmly this time. They escorted him unsmilingly through a maze of corridors that were already emptying, as more and more of the habitat's occupants were caught in the roundup. Some of the people recognized him, or recognized the uniform, but were too intimidated to call out to him.

When they arrived at his quarters, one of his keepers went inside to make sure the cabin was empty. Then they thrust him inside and closed the door. Joorn heard an electronic click. He tried the knob, but it wouldn't turn. His comm screen wouldn't work either, and he was unable to rouse it. He poured himself a drink and sat down. After a couple of hours, the door opened. A pair of briefly glimpsed men in tabards pushed Alten inside and closed the door again.

"So they got you too," Joorn said.

Alten smiled crookedly. "I saw Karn himself. He apologized but said we'd be a distraction. He said to tell you not to worry; it would all be over soon. Enough Homegoers have already been repatriated to make us the majority. He needs them for grunt labor during the trip, if nothing else. You'll be released as soon as we're under way. He'll need your help with the Higgs drive."

"Do the geniuses doing this realize that if they turn on the Higgs drive before we're clear of the inner system, they'll kill everything on Rebirth's surface, including the colonists?"

Alten looked genuinely shocked. "They're not that crazy."

Joorn unclenched his teeth. He hadn't realized how tightened up he was. "You said something about making 'us' the majority," he said. "Does that mean you're with us?"

"Father, I was never against you. And I still think Karn is a great man."

"A great physicist, maybe. As a leader of men, he has his deficiencies. Especially in the honesty department."

Alten was rummaging through Joorn's kitchen alcove. "Have you got anything to eat around here? I don't think the commissary's going to be open for a while."

An invisible sea of Higgs bosons surrounded *Time's Beginning*, stretching out to infinity. Matter/antimatter pairs winked in and out of existence—an illusion caused by their restless jiggling back and forth through the extra dimension at the intersection of the Universe with an adjoining brane. The Higgs field had detected the sea but had not yet begun to trap the antimatter particles before they could disappear. When that happened, there would be limitless fuel, stolen from the energy of the vacuum. It would violate the bookkeeping of the Universe, but that would be the problem of the adjacent cosmos.

Joorn was standing in front of a bank of instruments, Alten beside him. Karn was standing well back, giving them space.

Farther back, next to a bulkhead, Oliver had stationed himself with some of his young men. They didn't seem to be the same contumelious types as the bullies who had rounded up the habitat dwellers, and none of them were wearing the infinity tabards. There were no titanium pipes visible. Instead they were wielding data pads and paying close attention. One skinny fellow with an intense manner was taking notes on paper, on a loose sheaf that kept getting away from him.

Oliver was showing his impatience. "What are you waiting for? We've had the Higgs field focused on the decay products and ready to zap hadronic photons for at least five minutes now."

"Shut up, Miles," Karn said.

"But—"

"Don't distract the captain."

Oliver simmered silently, his narrow face darkening, but he subsided. The apprentices stopped tapping at their data pads, looking uneasy, then resumed after a moment.

Joorn took his time, his eyes darting from one display to another, comparing streams of data, then, at measured intervals, punching in a command.

"Okay, we've got our Higgs parent particles," Joorn drawled, "and the Feynman diagrams say they're decaying into two protons faster than you can blink. Now the trick is to freeze them before they can disappear and bat them one hundred and eighty degrees to bounce them off the mirror assembly. *Voilà!* Hadronic photons! Photons with actual mass, billions of times heavier than they ought to be."

The skinny fellow with the pencil was scribbling as fast as he could. The others were peering earnestly at the blur of symbols streaming by on the displays.

"The God Particle," Karn said with mock reverence. "That's what they called it in the twenty-first century. And what Neo-creationists like Brego are still calling it. Remember the old bull sessions in the dorm, Joorn?"

"Don't knock it, Delbert," Joorn said. "Hawking didn't." He kept his eyes on the displays.

"Jackass," Karn said. "Brego, I mean. He was still making threats even after we took the ship. As if he could possibly organize his dullard clods into an effective force and—"

"Alten, start focusing the mirror assembly," Joorn cut in.

"Right," Alten said. The skinny fellow stopped scribbling and stared worriedly at the screen that showed the patch of sky they had come from. Rebirth's sun was just a star like any other now, a little brighter than most.

"Don't worry, Daniel," Joorn said without taking his eyes off the screens. "We're safely out of range."

His fingers moved over the keys like a pianist playing by ear. The floor gave a shudder, and then everyone's weight, which had been only about a tenth of Earth-normal during the outward swing, began to increase.

It would be a year at constant one-G acceleration before

they reached the upper limit, brushing the speed of light itself. By then the ship would outweigh whole galaxies, and eons would pass in hours. The stars ahead and behind would have dopplered into blind spots as the rainbow hoops of the starbow compressed themselves first into a thin halo, then squeezed themselves out of existence.

And a mere thirty years later, they would be home.

CHAPTER 10

6,000,000,000 A.D.
The Oort Cloud

Torris methodically piled his gear in the fork of two twigs next to the calyx. He topped the pile with his bow and quiver after a short regretful pause. The only thing he retained was the little stovebeast, because it was inside his airsuit and he would freeze to death in minutes without it.

"I'll camp nearby where I can see the Dream nest," Ning said. "Don't worry, Tor-ris. Have a good Dream, and may the Tree give you wisdom."

"The Tree does not speak to everyone," he said. "Sometimes the Dream makes no sense, but the old men always say they have never forgotten it."

She laughed, then remembered that this was supposed to be a solemn moment. "Yes, some of our young men have Dreams like that too, but then the elders try to interpret it, each with his own opinion. I've noticed that the opinions are usually opinions they've had all along."

Torris tried to give her a stern look, but that didn't work with Ning. He turned his attention to the calyx, a swelling green structure three times the height of a man. It was ready to receive a Dreamer. Small pollinating creatures were already swarming around the flaring invitation at the top.

"Here, Tor-ris," she said, handing him a small woven bag. "It is a gift of pollen from our Tree."

He took the bag, giving her a quizzical look.

"Our priests gave me the offering when they knew I was going to attempt a crossing. They say it is a pious act to give a gift of pollen from one Tree to another. And the Tree thanks the donor with a more powerful Dream for a more ordinary dusting from a few grains received at random from insects."

Torris had already dusted his suit from another calyx growing on the branch, but he took the bag and thanked her. Then, impatient to begin, he took a nicely calculated leap to the calyx's portal at the top.

The pollinating insects scattered, scurrying in all directions. He carefully pried the portal open, wide enough for him to squeeze himself inside, following the instructions that Claz had given him. It occurred to him, in an unseemly instant of amusement, that he had become a pollinating insect himself. The portal closed above him, but there was still a dim haze of green light seeping through the fleshy walls.

He worked his way downward to the tiny chamber below. He could tell at once that it was warm inside and that there was air—moist air, he could surmise from the moisture that condensed on his faceplate. He overcame an unworthy moment of fear and raised the Face to take a sniff. The air was rich and fragrant, thicker than the kind of air you got from drilling for air pockets in the cambium.

He squirmed out of his airsuit and set the stovebeast free. The furry little animal immediately started climbing upward on its stubby limbs. It was going to have a feast on the insects swarming outside.

He dusted himself with the pollen that Ning had given him and settled down in the nest made by overlapping sepals. He was already beginning to feel sleepy.

He was the Tree. He didn't know how long he had been the Tree; he seemed to have existed for eternity, in a swirl of stars and blackness where stars grew and shrank and changed their colors and sometimes exploded. He was aware of commensal life on and within himself, fluttering in his branches, flourishing on his bark, burrowing shallowly to drink his air and water and the heat of his growth. But their microscopic needs were hardly noticeable in his vastness. He had hosted them as long as he could remember.

Down below, where he drank the ice that nourished him, was a new kind of life that lived between his roots, tiny creatures that had arrived less than a million years ago. One of them was within him now, in the ovule where he gave birth to his seeds. It had brought him a surfeit of pollen—pollen from a Brother Tree—and it was hastening meiosis. He and his brothers had taught these odd new mites from beyond to do that when they had first arrived out of the void, rewarding them with hallucinations that they seemed to find pleasurable.

He turned his ponderous attention to the mite that had climbed from his roots and entered his calyx. He could see it clearly from a height, stretched out on a bed of sepals, having removed its skin, which was made from the skins of other commensal animals, and it had lost its own consciousness and entered his.

To his mild surprise, it seemed to be himself, too dizzy with hallucinogens to sort out the mingled perceptions. He saw himself through an undulating haze. He tried to get back to his body, but the Tree wasn't through with him yet.

He woke up suddenly and completely, perfectly aware of where he was. He had no idea of how long he'd been unconscious, but he was weak and very hungry. The pale light seeping through the pellucid walls had a pinkish cast, so it had been at least a day, maybe more.

At last he was able to move. He got up stiffly and looked around. A central bulge on the receptacle floor seemed to have grown thicker while he slept, and the sweetish smell that had put him to sleep was fading, and that was all. There was sudden movement above and an occlusion of light. He looked up and saw a stovebeast inching its clumsy way downward. Whether it was his or another he couldn't tell.

He swept the little beast up, and it quickly attached itself to the small of his back. He could feel its warmth spreading through his aching spine. It seemed chubbier than before. He climbed into his airsuit and sealed its Face. When he poked his head through the calyx into airlessness, the Treescape was suffused with pink and the first of the Sisters was rising. So it was daybreak of whatever day it was.

His belongings were where he'd left them. He bundled them into his sleeping sack and slung it over his shoulder. For some obscure reason, he didn't feel like stowing his bow away with the rest of his possessions and strung it, carrying it along with his spear. He still had one of his original arrows with Claz's rune on it, along with three more he'd whittled during the Climb, and he was pleased with himself for this evidence of his frugality.

He looked around for Ning's camp and saw what looked like a low-hanging bundle of meatbeast carcasses through the leaves. He set off in that direction with a low-gravity shuffle.

The hanging bundle came into view, with Ning's sleeping sack under it. At first, focused on the sleeping sack, he didn't see the airsuited figure standing off to the side. Then, with a shock, it penetrated his consciousness.

It was someone from his own tribe. Even at a distance, he could tell that it was Brank's airsuit, with its splash of ostentatious beadwork spread across the upper shoulders and down the arms. Brank's back was to him, but Torris could tell that he had an arrow trained on the shadowy form visible through the translucent integument of the sack. Brank had caught Ning during her morning wash, when she was out of her airsuit and unable to emerge into a vacuum. Otherwise she would have had an arrow through him.

Brank seemed to be enjoying himself, taunting her by moving his bow around, aiming the arrow at various parts of her body and pantomiming what he was going to do.

Torris saw it all in a horrified flash and started running forward without thinking. He realized his mistake instantly as he lost contact with the branch and found himself levitating helplessly. It seemed an eternity before his feet found purchase again and he was able to push himself forward with an occasional one-handed assist from a reachable stem.

Brank wasn't aware of the motion behind him yet. At any moment, he could turn his head and get off a quick shot. But he was preoccupied by the game he was playing with Ning, who didn't dare move. She wouldn't have been able to get into her airsuit quickly enough anyway. It was part of the game.

Torris's bow was already strung. He was able to reach around and draw an arrow out of his quiver and fit it to the bowstring without slowing the shallow shuffle that was moving him forward.

He burst through some trailing leaves and branches, bringing the bow up. In the same instant, Brank must have become aware of the minute vibrations that had reached him. He whirled around and loosed the arrow he had been saving for Ning.

Torris would have been unable to dodge, but Brank's aim had been bad, or perhaps he hadn't had time to aim at all. The arrow whizzed past Torris's head, only a finger's width away, and buried itself in a branch.

Torris raised his bow, took deliberate aim, and shot Brank through the chest. Brank took a few teetering steps, his arms flailing, and fell over the edge of the branch he'd been standing on. Torris, feeling weak and drained, fell to one knee and looked down. Brank's body was twisting, falling with nightmarish slowness in the negligible gravity of the comet. Somewhere in the first few miles of its descent, it would probably lodge in a clot of branches. Something prompted Torris to look into his quiver. The arrow he'd drawn had been the last of the ten marked and sanctified arrows that Claz had given him.

He tottered on unsteady legs to Ning's sleeping sack. She was naked and struggling in its cramped interior to get into her airsuit. More quickly than Torris would have expected, she heaved herself out of the sack and was standing before him, her bow cocked and an arrow pointed at his heart.

"Have you killed him?" she said in lip talk.

"Yes," he said.

She lowered her bow and slid the arrow back into its quiver. "He came early, before I was clad against the vacuum," she said. "He told me with his arrow for a pointer that I was not to move. He kept me thus while he thought things over. I know that he was trying to think of how to get into the air sack with me and use me for his pleasure. But he did not dare. He knew I would kill him as soon as he was out of his own airsuit. So he decided on this other way. He told me that he would have as much pleasure from it. There are such men. He was tiring of his amusement when you arrived. But I thought I would try to stay alive as long as possible, in case something might distract him. I might be able to scramble into my airsuit quickly enough to get to him with my knife, even with an arrow in me."

"He's gone," Torris said. "Food for the scavengers."

"Show me," she said.

He took her to the place where Brank had fallen. Together they peered over the edge. Brank's body was floating some tens of man-lengths down. It still hadn't picked up much speed. His bow hovered over him like a judgment.

"You have done well, Tor-ris," she said. "Why so glum?"

He could not share her fierce joy. He stared after the drifting corpse in horror. He was damned forever. He had violated the deepest of taboos. He had killed another Climber. When he returned to his tribe, he would be an outcast, a pariah.

CHAPTER 11

4,250,000,000 A.D.
Galaxy 3C-295

Time to start losing weight, is it?" Joorn quipped.

"Almost," Alten said. "There's still a few more days till turnaround. I'd better go over the numbers one more time."

Joorn patted his belly in mock dismay. Not that he had much of a belly to speak of. At the age of ninety-five—almost halfway through a normal human lifespan—his stomach was still as flat and hard as it had been at eighty.

"Again?" he said. "Last week you told me I personally out-massed the entire Virgo Cluster. I can't imagine what the ship and all its people weighs by now."

Alten frowned. "There's something fishy about Karn's data. According to my original calculations, turnaround time should have been a week ago."

Joorn became serious. "Did you adjust for the new estimates for the expansion of the Universe in the last one and three-quarter billion years?"

"Yes, of course."

"And the rate of increase of the expansion discovered by Karn's bright young men?"

Alten showed his exasperation. "Father, be serious."

"Well, then, it's the zig zag."

"We don't zig zag. You know that. We'd keep losing gamma. We have to keep accelerating in a straight line, with one course correction at the halfway point to allow for the change in position of the Milky Way relative to our signposts."

"So our signposts do the zig zagging."

"You could put it that way. The galaxies rush apart not because they're rushing apart but because the Universe is expanding. And expanding faster than the speed of light at the magic boundary—something that Karn and Oliver choose to ignore, brilliant as they're supposed to be. Relativity still holds at the local level. The Milky Way and the Local Group remain gravitationally bound to the Virgo Cluster, as distant as they are from it—or, as some of the ancient diehards liked to put it, the Local Group was actually a 'part' of the greater Virgo Cluster."

Joorn glanced at the forward viewscreen. It was filled with a Doppler-adjusted representation of a brilliant galaxy, 3C-295, less than two hundred thousand light-years away, closer than the Magellanic Clouds had once been to the Milky Way.

"Let's take a look at our flag post galaxy the way it really is," Joorn murmured. "Right now, we're seeing it as a co-moving object."

His fingers danced over the console, and the screen showed them a vertical smear of mashed multicolored light that was squeezed between the two blind spots that almost filled the screen fore and aft. "I'm cheating a little bit," he said. "We're seeing it as a rattlesnake might see it—otherwise the red shift would be too extreme."

Alten nodded. "From here we draw a straight line to the

Milky Way, which we can see now. After more than four billion years of expansion and galactic drift since we left Earth, the signposts we started out with are scattered on either side of the line, so we ignore them. The Milky Way itself has drifted along with its co-moving companions, of course, but I'm allowing for that, and we can make another small adjustment when we're within spitting distance."

"So what's your problem?"

Alten frowned. "There's something wrong. We should have passed 3C-295 a week ago. I tried to tell Karn about it, but he just told me to recheck my figures. I did that and got the same answer. Karn told me you can't argue with the navigation data and to talk to Oliver about it."

"And?"

"I got the usual runaround. A ship can't have two captains and two navigators and all that. Karn has his team of dedicated cosmologists, and they're fully competent. You've got only me. Maybe it's time for you to retire as captain. After more than twenty years of running ship operations, Oliver can handle the final run."

Joorn's lips tightened. "Karn might have something to say about that. We had a deal."

"I'll talk to some of the new cosmology grads. They're the new generation. Karn's 'young men' are all middle-aged now and ossified in their thinking. Their idea of how to arrive at a truth is to get a pronouncement from Karn. Maybe it's time for that whole crowd to retire and let the new generation take over."

"Except me, of course," Joorn said with a smile.

"Father, they worship you. The legendary captain who led the exodus to the promised land, planted the human race in another galaxy, and now is leading them back to the galaxy of their fathers."

"That's a little fulsome, my boy," Joorn demurred. "The Universe is winding down; the galaxies are flying farther and farther apart, isolating themselves; the skies everywhere are getting darker. Fewer and fewer stars are being born, and more of the remaining ones are turning into cinders or black holes incapable of contributing to the rebirth of a stellar population."

He looked Alten squarely in the eye. "But there's life in the old cosmos yet, a few more billion years of it. And the human race is going home."

Alten grew thoughtful. "I'll talk to some of the new people. The demographics of the ship are changing. The generation that's grown up on board knows nothing about Rebirth or 3C-273, or the half a lifetime it took to get there. It's just legend, like Earth itself. They grew up with the notion of returning to the Milky Way, not settling 3C-273 or joining Karn on a wild goose chase. Politically, they're likely to side with us old-timers in the Homegoing movement. We still outnumber Karn's aging disciples—they were just more ruthless than us. But the new people aren't intimidated by them. Neither are the Endgamists they kidnapped when we took off in such a hurry. Karn's tough guys don't look so tough anymore."

"And if it turns out that we've really overshot our turnover slot?"

"We can still make it up at this point by adding another fraction of a G to our deceleration mode." He grinned. "We'll all just be a little overweight for the rest of the trip."

"You better make it soon. If we've miscalculated, we'll shoot right past the Milky Way on the way to infinity."

Alten got up. "I'll get on it right away. Get ready to cut off the Higgs drive at short notice."

"Don't overlook Karn's people either. They've had over twenty years to become disaffected. You might seek out that cosmology apprentice who was so worried about sterilizing Rebirth with the Higgs exhaust—what was his name? Daniel something."

Alten paused on the way out to take a last look at the distorted galaxy on the display, squeezed to a thin line between the fore and aft blind spots compressing the narrowing starbow. To an observer in 3C-295, if such a thing were possible, *Time's Beginning* and everyone in it, including himself, would seem to be a wafer-thin disc in the direction of its flight. The thought never failed to astonish him. He didn't feel at all like a paper cutout. Funny, but he felt normal. Yet eons were ticking by in mere seconds as he paused to look back at his father, fiddling worriedly with dials at the console. Once the ship turned over and began to decelerate, the blind spots would start to shrink and the rainbow hoops of stars would expand again. By the time they reached the vicinity of Sol, the Universe would have regained its multicolored glory.

The display abruptly disappeared. His father had found it too unsettling. Alten couldn't blame him. It was a reminder that the ship had been pushed to within a sliver of its limits and that Karn wanted to push it still further.

"Keep her on course, Skipper," he said at the door.

Joorn yawned and rubbed his eyes. It was ship's night, and all the interior lights had dimmed themselves hours ago. He had been at the console for fourteen hours straight.

"Why don't you knock off and get some sleep, Skipper," said his first officer, a young physics apprentice named Chu. "I can handle it."

Chu was a promising aspirant from the ranks of the new generation who had been born during the homeward flight, and he was both bright and impatient. He had been twiddling his thumbs for the last two hours.

"Alten should have been back by now," Joorn said. "And I can't seem to raise him on his talkie."

"He's wise," Chu said. "He probably has it turned off."

"What do you mean?" Joorn had confided in Chu, telling him all about Alten's suspicions and about what they were going to have to do if they proved correct. He was grooming Chu to captain the ship himself someday, and in any case, with turnaround almost upon them, Chu needed to be au courant.

"Oliver's guys have been acting antsy the last few days. As if something's up. They broke up a meeting of the physics club two days ago. They'd been eavesdropping on our chatter, and something was making them nervous. Those antiquated tough guys and the silly tabards they wear! They even roughed up a couple of our guys for talking back. We couldn't believe it! It was sort of like the way my dad describes the old days, when we started out from Rebirth. I get hassled once in a while too. Oliver Twisty—that's what some of our guys call him—isn't too happy about my being first officer. He wants to put in his own man."

"I wonder if Alten made contact with Daniel," Joorn said.

"Oh, the guy you mentioned? Daniel Petrocelli, one of the Old Guard physicists who doesn't dance to Oliver's tune anymore. I don't know if that was a good idea. They might be watching him. I think he was starting to come around. He was coming to the physics club meetings for a while like some of the others that age, the tired-out gaffers who want to stop gallivanting around the Universe with Karn and settle down. Then he stopped coming. Maybe he just got scared. Or maybe he's a fink."

Joorn tapped in to the running estimate of the deceleration needed to come to a stop at the Milky Way if Alten's original estimate was correct. It still was only a hair over one gravity, but as he watched, a digit four places past the decimal point ticked over.

"I think we'd better . . . " he began.

The door to the control room was flung wide open, and a dozen men crowded into the compartment. Chu started to get up, but he was immediately surrounded by shadowy figures.

"Stay where you are, and don't move, Mr. Chu," Oliver's voice ordered. One of the figures brandished a pipe for emphasis.

Joorn didn't try to get up. He swiveled around in his seat and said, "What do you want, Oliver? And where's Alten?"

"Alten's locked up where he can't cause any trouble," Oliver said. "He won't be harmed as long as he behaves himself. I can't say the same for that turncoat, Petrocelli."

"What's going to happen to Petrocelli?" Joorn said evenly.

"He's going to be hanged when we get around to it," Oliver said. He smiled humorlessly, a flash of white teeth in the dim lighting. "Fortunate that we're going to maintain our one-G acceleration, isn't it?"

"On what charge? And who made you the law aboard my ship?"

"What charge?" Oliver savored the question. "Why, consorting with the enemy."

Joorn had trouble containing his fury. "Enemy? My son? Me?"

"Control yourself, Captain Gant. Captain no more, I'm afraid. I'm captain now."

"What does Professor Karn have to say about this?

"Professor Karn will be informed in due course. At the moment he's busy, thinking great thoughts."

Joorn put all the authority he could muster into his voice. "Professor Karn and I made an agreement when we left Rebirth. He'll have the ship when we disembark at Sol."

Oliver laughed. "The professor never intended to keep that agreement. He's not willing to lose the built-up gamma factor we've reached so far. He's an old man, and he's afraid he won't live to achieve his dream if he does. We've been feeding you doctored data for two decades. You would have figured it out sooner or later. Now it's too late."

"Not yet!" Joorn heaved himself out of his chair and lunged for Oliver. A titanium pipe caught him in the midsection and drove the air out of him. He sank back in his chair, gasping and nauseous. He was dizzily aware that Chu had tried to get up to help him and that Oliver's thugs were beating him senseless.

"Careful, Captain," Oliver said. We don't want to hurt you. Professor Karn wouldn't like it. We might need you again."

Chu was being dragged from his chair now, limp and bloody, but conscious. Oliver nodded at one of his cohorts, a middle-aged, pot-bellied man who'd been standing to one side while the others worked Chu over.

"Okay, Shenk, why don't you try the second seat on for size?" Oliver said. "I'll be with you in a minute. Don't touch anything. We're still at one G. I don't think the captain here did anything yet to start the turnover procedure."

A pair of Oliver's aging thugs had a rubber-legged Chu on his feet, supporting him on either side. Two others bracketed Joorn and started to pull him upright. He shook off their hands and stood up by himself. Oliver motioned, and the two started herding Joorn toward the door after Chu and his captors.

"Put them in the lockup with the others," Oliver said. "Nobody talks to them. If anybody gets too curious, lock them up too."

The passageways were practically empty this time of night. The few people they passed, most of them solitary or in twos, glanced at them, but nobody tried to approach the odd procession. Joorn thought there was a kind of hush in the atmosphere, but perhaps he was imagining it.

Wherever they were taking him, it couldn't be too far; Chu was in no condition to stay on his feet long, and he doubted they'd want to carry him. He kept looking around, but he saw no way to get control of the situation.

Then he thought he saw an opportunity—a slim one, but maybe the only chance he'd get. They were headed toward the door of what looked like a storeroom, and for some reason a small crowd had gathered there—not more than twenty or thirty people. A big redheaded young fellow, with two or three other youngsters of his generation joining in, was arguing with the tabard-bedecked quartet who were stationed in front of the door.

"We demand to see them!" he was yelling. "You had no right

to lock them up!" There were mutters of agreement from the crowd. The quartet of guards, beefy men from Oliver's generation, were looking uncomfortable and fingering their titanium pipes.

By that time, some in the crowd had become aware of the approaching entourage. Several of them recognized Chu and yelled out to him. Chu raised his bloodied head and responded with what was evidently a slogan of the younger generation: "Screw the Trogs!" Joorn assumed it meant troglodytes. The crowd started to take up the chant, and things began to look ugly.

It was now or never. Joorn eyed his guards. They were thoroughly distracted, not paying any attention to him. All four were of Oliver's generation: overweight, jowly, and out of shape. Joorn was older than any of them, but he had kept himself fit. He whirled and pushed one of his unwanted escorts with both hands as hard as he could. The man toppled over and hit the floor. Joorn didn't wait to see if he'd hit his head. With the momentum of the same whirling motion, he chopped the other man in the face, just below the nose, with the edge of a clenched fist. The other two dropped Chu and were on him in a second. The titanium pipes came out, and Joorn never saw the one that hit him alongside the head.

Joorn came to, his head throbbing and his vision blurred. He was lying on some kind of hard surface—the lid of a plastic crate. A woman was sponging his head and the side of his face. He was aware of blood trickling down into the collar of his uniform.

"Don't try to move yet, Captain," the woman said.

He ignored her and sat up. It was too quick, and there was a moment of dizziness. It passed, and his vision cleared.

He was in a dim, smallish room crowded with irregular piles of goods. About two dozen people were interned with him, sitting on crates or standing around. The men were mostly young, with close-cropped beards or scraggly attempts at them. The women, fewer of them, were in the same age group but more kempt.

Alten's face swam into view. He leaned over Joorn and said, "Take it easy, Father. How do you feel?"

"Rotten. What happened?"

"After they dumped you and Chu inside with the other unreliables? They started arresting people outside and shoving them in here with us. They stopped that business pretty quick. I think they're afraid to open the door now. The crowd's growing."

The redheaded agitator who'd been haranguing the Karnites loomed behind Alten. He moved closer. He had a black eye and a split lip. "They're spreading the word outside. We're not going to let the Trogs get away with this, Captain. Not this time. Their day is past." He grinned and his lip started bleeding again. "We've even got some of them on our side."

"Like Petrocelli," Alten said grimly.

Joorn raised himself on one elbow and looked around. "Where's Chu?"

"He's right over there, Captain Gant," said the woman who was sponging the blood off his contusions. "We think he has a couple of cracked ribs, but he'll be all right. No, don't try to get up."

Joorn craned his neck to see Chu. The first officer was lying on a crate a short distance away. His head was wrapped in makeshift bandages that looked like ripped-up sheets. A couple of women were attending to him. They had his shirt off, and one of the women was winding a bandage around his torso.

"What did they do to Petrocelli?" Joorn said.

"They roughed him up pretty good," Alten said. "Then they took him away someplace. They kept telling him he was going to get a one-gravity necktie. They must have had a tag on him all along because they were all over us about five minutes after we met. So he didn't have a chance to say too much, and he was very nervous. But I got the impression that he wanted to come over to the Homegoer side."

"Yeah," the big agitator put in. "That's what we thought too. He was very cagey with us after the physics club raid, but we thought he was one of those who'd come around in the end. He was one scared little guy, but he had guts."

"This is Leonard Ryan," Alten said. "His specialty is multi-verse theory. When he's not busy stirring up trouble."

Ryan grinned at Alten. "I'm working with your boy on a paper on quantum chromodynamics. We're going to stir up a lot of trouble there too."

"We're applying QCD to the problem of the Higgs boson and hadronic photons," Alten explained.

"Karn double-crossed us," Joorn told them. "He never had any intention of dropping us off at Sol. Oliver and a flunky named Shenk are up in the control room right now. They're kidnapping us all over again."

Ryan grew serious. "I know Shenk. He tried to present some

kindergarten version of string theory at the physics club, and when the reviewers turned him down, he got Oliver to force a presentation. He doesn't know a black hole from a hole in the ground, and he doesn't know anything about the Higgs field except that it works when you press the right button."

"He especially doesn't know what would happen to a planet if a Higgs drive got within sneezing distance when a ship was decelerating," Alten said grimly.

"Nothing that hasn't already happened to Earth during the sun's red giant phase, Alten," Ryan reminded him.

"That's moot," Joorn said. "Oliver doesn't plan to decelerate. We may zip past the Milky Way altogether if we don't make a course correction now. The question is: How do we stop them?"

"We can take them, Captain," Ryan said.

"We're locked up," Joorn said savagely. "Besides, we may outnumber them, but we're not exactly a fighting force, are we?"

He looked around pointedly at the people in the storeroom. There was Chu with his bloody bandages, not to mention himself. There was a preponderance of young men and women, most of them students—impractical and idealistic, some of them showing signs of mistreatment by the thugs outside and doubtless intimidated by them. And there was a handful of bewildered oldsters, would-be Earthbound returnees who'd been swept up in the confusion of Oliver's takeover.

"Listen," Ryan said urgently, "by now those goons out there have sent for reinforcements. The crowd's getting out of hand."

Joorn listened to the noise outside. It was getting louder. There was a dangerous rumble, punctuated by angry shouts.

They were throwing things now. Joorn heard a thunk as something breakable hit the storeroom door. After a moment in which the beleaguered guards must have done something retaliatory, there was a surge in crowd noise.

"They're getting panicky," Ryan said. He turned his head and called, "Any moment now, people! Take your positions."

Joorn watched in amazement as a number of the young people, including the two women who'd been doing the nursing, separated from the prisoners and flattened themselves against the bulkhead on either side of the door, as if they'd rehearsed. To his further surprise, a couple of the Earthborn oldsters conferred briefly and joined them.

After a minute or two, the door handle rattled and the door sprang open. A couple of people from the crowd were propelled inside with enough force to send them sprawling. The men who had pushed them followed, brandishing their lengths of pipe. On their heels came the other two guards, manhandling two more struggling protesters.

There was no time for them to react. They were immediately engulfed by the people who'd been hiding on either side of the door. Their titanium pipes were plucked from their hands before they knew it, and they found themselves face down on the floor with enough feet on their backs and necks to keep them from getting up. The mild young woman who'd been nursing Joorn was holding one of the titanium pipes and eyeing it speculatively when Ryan reached her side, saying, "No, Maryann, no."

In moments the room was flooded with people from outside. There were lots of hugs and a few tears. Ryan's voice cut through the din.

"Come on, people, we've got to get out of here before the reinforcements arrive!"

The crowd broke up and swirled through the door. Ryan was nodding to people here and there, and Joorn saw a couple of them improvising a stretcher from the lid of a storage bin and loading Chu onto it. Then Ryan was at Joorn's side.

"Can you walk, Captain?"

"I can walk," Joorn said tightly.

Ryan nodded again, and a couple of his stalwarts helped Joorn to his feet and supported him. They joined the crowd that was now pouring out the door.

"Where are we going?" Joorn said.

"The control room," Ryan replied.

The corridors were filling with people as the crowd went swarming by. The corridor lights were still dimmed for the night, but doors to living compartments were opening as they passed and bleary-eyed people, some of them still struggling into their clothes, were adding to their numbers.

"The word's out," Ryan said.

It wasn't far to the control room, and they only encountered one of Oliver's corridor patrols. There were only three of them, sloppy fellows with their best years behind them, if they had ever had any best years. They were deep in some halfhearted argument raised only to dispel after-hours boredom, and when they saw the mob surging toward them, they looked at each other and took off without further discussion.

The door to the control room was locked or barricaded, but a couple of Ryan's hefty young stalwarts kicked it open in short order. Some kind of advance squad rushed with them into the control room, while others held back the crowd.

Joorn tried to break loose from his attendants, but they held on to him. "Not yet, Captain," one of them said. "Wait till we know it's safe."

There was the sound of what might have been a scuffle inside the control room. Joorn thought he recognized Oliver's voice before it was abruptly silenced.

Then he saw Alten being escorted inside by one of Ryan's tough-looking physics students. Immediately afterward, Oliver and his hapless assistant, Shenk, were led out by more of Ryan's men. Their hands were tied behind their backs, and they looked very angry. Shenk had a honey of a welt on his forehead.

A roar went up from the crowd. A few people tried to get at them, but Ryan's men cleared a path and bore them off down the corridor. Then the goons who had beaten Chu appeared, also with their hands tied behind their backs. They were being handled more roughly, pushed, pulled, and prodded by their captors. One of them, who had evidently put up too much of a fight, was unconscious or otherwise incapacitated, and was being dragged unceremoniously along.

Another angry roar came from the crowd, but Ryan's men got their prisoners safely through the crowd and disappeared down the corridor with them.

"What's happening?" Joorn said, and tried again to break free.

"Wait a minute," one of the men said. "We'd better find something to hang on to." The two of them helped him to a side wall and saw that he had a support to grasp.

And then he didn't have to ask what was happening, because

all of a sudden he had no weight. Around him, people were floating off the floor and hovering like a cloud of gnats. Others were doing their best to cling to the floor.

The cloud had itself sorted out after a minute or two. "Okay, Captain," one of his escorts said. They carried Joorn expertly between them on a midair trajectory that got them through the door without brushing against anything.

Alten was sitting in Chu's seat, busying himself with the control panel. Joorn's attendants deposited him carefully in the captain's seat and strapped him in.

Alten turned to him and said, "Shenk didn't have time to bollix anything up. He and Oliver were still arguing about what to do when our boys dragged them out of their chairs. We'll get our weight back in a couple of hours, when turnover's complete and we can turn on the engines again."

He brought up an image on the screen. It was a computer fiction showing a beautiful spiral galaxy—the Milky Way as it had looked nearly five billion years ago when his father and a shipfull of hopefuls had left it to find a new home for the human race elsewhere in the Universe. The computer added crosshairs to show that *Time's Beginning* was on target.

Alten replied to Joorn's unspoken question. "No, we didn't slip too far past the turnover point. A fraction of added G on the last leg of the trip should compensate for it. We'll hardly feel it."

He tapped keys again, and the image shrugged and became distorted. Now it was an elliptical galaxy, bright with the combined stellar populations of the Milky Way, the Andromeda galaxy, and the Magellanic Clouds.

"We'll only be a few million years late," Alten said. "The Sun will have swallowed the Earth long since and begun to regurgitate what's left of it. It'll be late in its red giant phase. But there'll still be hundreds of millions of years till it shrinks to the white dwarf stage, and more years still till the white dwarf cools enough to stop giving useful heat. Plenty of time for life to start again. Particularly if there's already terrestrial life in the outer system to reseed a solidifying Earth. Surely human beings would have brought life with them past the orbit of Jupiter—if only inadvertently—in the centuries after *Time's Beginning* left. And I'm not just talking about microbes. If I remember my ancient history, when you and Karn set off on your hegira there was already talk of growing bioengineered trees on comets to provide lumber for habitats and other space construction. Wasn't there a scientist named Bernal in the early twentieth century—long before they knew about DNA—who pointed out that trees adapted to vacuum could grow to heights of hundreds of miles in microgravity?"

Joorn had stopped listening. He was studying the new Milky Way that would be born sometime in the next billion years. His face showed something like bliss.

"Home," he said.

[HAPTER 12

Torris found it hard to get used to the idea of sharing a sleeping sack with another, as pleasurable as it might be, but he was learning the hard way not to mention it to Ning.

"What, Tor-ris the Pious," she said, snuggling up against him, "do your people mate in the open, like beasts?"

"Of course not," he said, offended. "People have their niches and corners, and sometimes hang skins over them, or even build a shelter of wood and foliage there, with their own fire or tethered stovebeast to supplement the heat from the communal fire. But men and women don't go hunting together, and so we don't have that custom."

She continued to tease him. "And don't you have the custom of privacy either?"

There was no word for privacy in Torris's language, but he was learning to use Ning's. It seemed to mean something like being out of the sight or hearing of other people.

He took another tack. "I'm just used to keeping my airsuit on when I sleep. In case there's a leak in the night. Or some danger, like a Brank sneaking up on you. You of all people should understand that. You almost died."

"But Brank is dead," she said, tracing the stubbled outline of his jaw with a fingertip. "And the large beasts are too stupid to find a way to get at us in this little hiding place we hollowed out for ourselves."

He gave up. "The red star has long been up. We should get moving."

They struggled into their airsuits, a tangle of limbs in the enclosed space. "We didn't hunt all day yesterday," Ning said, as though it was his fault. "And the day before that there wasn't a trace of game."

"This place is hunted out," Torris said. "We've stayed in one spot too long. We need to start climbing again."

"Ah, Tor-ris, are you so anxious to be rid of me?" she said accusingly. "A few more kills and I'll have enough carcasses to leave your Tree."

Torris didn't know how to reply to that. He knew that he should have started the climb down the trunk long ago, but a part of him wanted to keep things the way they were forever. Besides, though he tried not to admit it to himself, he was afraid to face Claz. "Don't be ridiculous," he said gruffly. "Here, let me borrow your bone-scraping adze. I'll whittle some more arrowheads along the way."

They climbed for the rest of the day still without seeing any large game, though there were signs that a herd of meatbeasts had passed that way some time ago. Torris occupied himself during their rests by scraping away at a dried meatbeast scapula with Ning's adze, and by nightfall he had produced the first of the new arrowheads for her.

They spent the night in an abandoned treehopper burrow after enlarging the opening so that they could fit through it. It was a snug fit, but it had a satisfactory bend to keep them out of the reach of any large predators, and there was a little rill that the hoppers had drunk from, mostly dried up but still producing a trickle of sap. It could not compare with their previous nest, but it would do for a temporary stopping place.

In the morning it was Ning who wanted to go on, and he who wanted to stay and rest for a few days.

"Oh Tor-ris, my lazy one, you are just trying to put off the day of my leaving," she said, "but there is no point in setting up a camp here. It is no better than the last spot was for finding game. They have wisely gone on to the great savannah at the top of the Tree, where you can see for miles around and where they can see predators coming and we can see them from a distance. You can have your love camp there just as well."

His ears burning, Torris packed up their belongings and prepared for the upward trek. In the end, it took four more days, with an unsatisfactory stop each night, three of which they slept practically in the open, back to back in their own sleeping sacks.

He knew he was getting close to the top of the Tree when the light filtering through the overhead canopy started to get brighter and he could catch an occasional glimpse of a patch of sky through gaps in the branches. Ning must have come to the same conclusion. She started to climb faster, leaving him farther and farther behind, dangling the unwieldy bundle of carcasses— now bulking several times his own mass—beneath him.

Suddenly he realized that she had stopped climbing. She had come to an abrupt stop, her body above the waist hidden by a swath of leaves. Her feet were doing an impatient little dance, searching for a place to stand. He had the impression that she was shouting within her helmet, but of course he couldn't hear anything. Her excitement was revealed by her feet; she was shaking a boot at him—the only way she could communicate.

He dropped the bundle of carcasses, after first hitching the end of the tether to a branch. He levered himself upward to stand beside her. When he poked his head through the canopy of leaves, he saw splendor.

They were near the center of a vast, flat circular expanse that went on for miles and miles. There was the illusion that it was one continuous solid surface when the eye strayed beyond the immediate area. Within a few arms' lengths, though, you could see that it was a carpet composed of countless twigs and leaves that had been grazed level to look almost like a flat landscape—a kind of landscape that Torris had never seen before.

For there were animals aplenty to graze it. Torris gasped at the fantastic sight. There were hundreds—no, thousands, if Torris had been able to put words to such a concept—of wild meatbeasts and other large grazing animals dotting the plain, another concept that was beyond his vocabulary. The meatbeasts that his tribe pursued in its hunting grounds just a few miles above the root caves where they lived were isolated prey that had strayed from the small herds they belonged to. Or at most, there might be a chance stumbling on four or five beasts together. But these animals numbered more than the stars in the sky—the only way he had of expressing large numbers. Moreover, they were fatter and more complacent than the scrawny beasts that sustained Torris's people. Their great numbers had made them unwary.

He touched helmets with Ning. She must have been holding her breath too because he heard a sharp intake of air before she was able to speak.

"Tor-ris, so many, so many. Just there for the taking."

He knew what she was thinking. With a few hours' work, she would have more carcasses than she ever dreamed of to take back to her Tree.

And she knew what he was thinking too. She laid a gloved hand on his arm. "Don't be sad, Tor-ris mine," she said. "There is much to do before I leave. You must help me build my cata-pult—an even bigger one than I had thought of making before. That will take many days. And we must learn how to move among them without alarming them."

"We're not the only ones who see easy hunting here. Look!"

In the distance he could see a black speck that resolved itself into a flutterbeast emerging from the foliage below. It was handicapped here in this open space without a tangle of branches for it to career off of, with no way for it to get above its prey. It chose its victim and began flapping awkwardly along the ground toward it.

The herd didn't seem to be particularly alarmed. They moved aside without haste to clear a path for the floundering monster. It made a final clumsy leap and engulfed the cho-sen meatbeast with its great membranous wings. Torris had thought that here in the weak fraction of gravity so far above the Tree's comet, the meatbeast would have time enough to scoot from under its attacker, but the flutterbeast had managed to get only a few feet above its prey and was able to get its wing claws hooked into the animal in mid-hover.

The flutterbeast settled down to gnaw at its catch. The rest of the herd gave it a moderately wide berth and continued placidly grazing.

"I think we've already learned," Torris said.

They crawled up the branch they were standing on and pulled their feet through the top layer of vegetation. Torris cautiously stood up and found that the surface growth supported his weight. He might have expected as much; the meatbeasts in the distance seemed to have no trouble walking around without breaking through, and they weighed many times more than he did. For that matter, even the flutterbeast, huge as it was, had managed to skate over the top growth on its belly.

Ning spoke to him in finger talk. "We had better make camp before dark. That grove over there looks like a likely spot."

She pointed at what looked like a cluster of small trees, no taller than a dozen men standing on one another's shoulders would have been. It was one of a dozen such clusters that dotted the plain, places where growing branches, following the Tree's imperative to grow straight upward, had burst through the surface layer of growth and somehow had escaped being clipped by the grazing beasts until they were tall enough to escape being munched on.

She helped him haul up the bundle of carcasses that he had left hanging on the tether. It had grown enormous by now, the dozen or so slaughtered animals outweighing even a flutterbeast. Torris could have hauled it up by himself; he'd been climbing for days while managing to cope. Its weight was no problem—things tended to keep going in the microgravity, even in an upward direction, once you got a rhythm going of strategic tugs. It was its mass that made the bundle so awkward.

The thing breached the surface in a shower of broken twigs

and leaves that hung in the air before starting imperceptibly to settle. They managed to drag it a few feet, and then, the underlying fuzz being too fragile to support its weight, it sank out of sight. They hauled it up to the surface, got it nicely balanced with great effort, managed to drag it a little farther, and the same thing happened again.

"This isn't going to work," Torris said. "It's past the weight limit for this scrub."

"You give up too easily, Tor-ris. It's just a question of dividing it into two bundles. Or four. Or whatever it takes. Men always want things to be easy."

She helped him untie the packed carcasses and make smaller bundles. In the end, dividing the mass into four parts turned out to be enough. But it was Torris who saw that the trick was to spread the carcasses out to make flat bundles so that there would be more area supporting the same weight. "Yes, just like a man, always figuring out a way to do less work," she said dismissively. "It will not be so easy to improve the catapult I have worked out in my head, you will see."

But even two trips to the grove, unsnagging the bundles as they went, was enough to wear them out. "I think that little group of four trees is shelter enough for tonight," she said. "Tomorrow I will show you how to use them as a support to make a little cave out of animal skins."

He was startled. "Will it hold air?"

She laughed. "Yes. And the heat from two stovebeasts. And both of us."

The dwarf trees were good for one thing: they kept curious meatbeasts from investigating the sheltered space and trampling them. And they protected Torris and Ning from the improbable event of some errant flutterbeast somehow dropping on them from above. But Torris resigned himself to sleeping in the open for tonight. Alone.

In the morning, Ning wasted no time. After a hasty breakfast of thawed raw meat in her sleeping sack, she emerged and made preparations for a foray into the thick of the herd. It was possibly an hour's difficult hike, given the insubstantial footing.

"You will help me butcher them when I return," she said. "In the meantime"—she measured a space in the circle of trees with her eyes—"skin five of the other carcasses. You will have to take them one at a time to thaw their outer surfaces in your sleeping sack." She cocked her head. "Does your tribe know how to skin a carcass in one piece?"

"Of course," he said indignantly. "We are not savages."

"No," she said. "Perhaps in some ways you are not savage enough."

With that she gathered up her bow and quiver and set off at an easy lope. Torris followed her with his eyes, admiring her grace and marveling at the ease with which she gauged the ability of the fragile gorse to resist the impact of her boots and hold her trifling weight.

She returned a few hours later, balancing a dead meatbeast on top of her helmet, its legs waggling skyward. Her progress was slower coming back because she had the meatbeast's added weight pressing on the soles of her boots. A foot would disappear into the gorse every once in a while. When that happened, she would stand stock-still, balanced on the other foot. She'd free the trapped boot very carefully, then place it flat on the supporting furze and resume walking with a deliberate, flat-footed gait.

She dumped the dead beast triumphantly at his feet. "How many animals have you skinned?" she asked.

"Three so far."

"Skin this one too, while it's still warm. We'd better butcher it right away. It will save time and heat later."

They took the time to seal themselves into a sack and eat a quick meal of scraps. Ning was ravenous. That done, she sat cross-legged and began to sew skins together. She was delighted to use the spool of web beast silk he gave her. "It makes a better airtight seal than animal sinew," she said. "They spin cocoons for themselves and their young with it. If one one is lucky enough to kill the creature inside and recover the material intact, it is a very useful piece of gear."

No one in Torris's tribe had ever done such a thing. "A dangerous enterprise," he said, impressed.

"Not if you know what you're doing," she said.

She sent him down beneath the gorse to gather wood for the frame while she sewed skins together. He had a serrated arrowhead that was adequate to the task of sawing off branches. The branches didn't have to be particularly thick, she explained, but they had to be the length of a man. And they had to be straight; that was important. She would need eight of them, she told him, counting the number off on her fingers as if he were a child.

Torris had never seen a cube, and there was no word for it in his language. He marveled that she could be so exact in advance about the number of supporting pieces she would need for the frame. It smacked of the kind of wizardry Claz could do. But Ning could not be a numberer—not this maddeningly irreverent young woman who had earned the resentment of the men of her tribe because she was a better hunter than they were. Numberers were mumbling old men like Claz who lived in their heads.

He made three trips below the gorse until the rotation of the Tree brought the face of the dark too near. He'd brought back only six of the stripped branches she required. She sighed and put down her awl and thread. "I'm not quite finished either," she said. "I still have some stitching to do, and then there will be the resin to apply. We will have to wait until tomorrow, my poor impatient Tor-ris."

She spread the skins on the ground to show him her work. She had sewn four of the skins together, end to end, to make a long strip more than four times Torris's own length. Two more squares jutted out, one on either side. She showed him how they would be folded. He understood at once and cried out, "Yes, like a cave!"

She finished the sewing the next day and spread sealant liberally along the seams. Like Torris's, her tribe's sealant was the same resin used to cast Faces, except that something dark had been added to make it opaque. When he tried helpfully to point out that a transparent sealant was better because it could always show the condition of the stitches underneath, she became impatient and said snappishly, "Have you nothing better to do than sit around and watch me work? Find something useful to do. You could gather leaves and stems and make a soft bed for us. Or finish assembling the new arrows you promised."

"Or I could hunt meatbeast and bring back a carcass or two to add to your insane hoard!" he shot back angrily, and was immediately sorry. The last thing he wanted to do was to hasten her departure.

"Do you think it's so easy?" she retorted. "This is a new kind of hunting, and you are not an experienced hunter. You don't even know how to move on an open surface without a solid branch to grab hold of. You could fall through and start thrashing and start a stampede. Run off all that meat. And as if that wasn't bad enough, you could get yourself kicked to death in the bargain. Or you could launch yourself into the sky by mistake and then, while you're hanging there like a fool waiting for the Tree to kindly draw you back to it, get yourself snapped up by some hovering flutterbeast who's learned how to hunt under these conditions."

For emphasis she pointed to the sky above the teeming greensward. The three or four black dots hovering there were opportunistic flutterbeasts that had managed to launch themselves to heights that would not alarm the grazing beasts below. It took them a long, long time to drift down to an altitude where they might represent a threat, and of course, while out of contact with the ground, with nothing to push against, they could not circle or otherwise maneuver. Every so often one of them would essay moderate lateral movement by spitting reaction mass, but their downward drift was so slow that it was easy for a watchful meatbeast to keep track of them and avoid being directly underneath when they landed.

But sometimes the meatbeasts were not watchful enough or were lulled by the slowness of the descent. And flutterbeasts were a lot smarter than they were. As Torris watched, one of the black shapes, timing it just right, spat a gob of reaction mass and managed a last-minute course adjustment. A quick push of a wing sent it scooting sideways to snare a meatbeast that hadn't retreated quite as far as its fellows when they moved aside to clear a safe landing zone.

"One of them tried to get me that way," Ning said matter-of-factly.

Torris shuddered. Across the plain, the frantic flurry of motion had stopped as the flutterbeast engulfed the unlucky animal in its wings and settled down to devour its feast. The other meatbeasts went back to their grazing. They had nothing to worry about now.

"Stop gawking," Ning said. "We have a lot of work to do."

Torris stood back and surveyed the odd contraption that he and Ning had been working on for the last four days. Ning's catapult was taking shape now. He had been sawing wood to length for her, shaping dovetails, splicing and winding animal tendons into thick cables while she whittled notches into oddly fashioned pieces that were supposed to fit together somehow.

He could see now that it was a sort of gigantic bow that was braced against one of the underlying branches beneath their feet. The strength of a dozen men could not have drawn it, but Ning had explained that it could be bent little by little by a kind of winding thing that could be cranked back over and over again by one person at the long end of a staff. Each pull would advance the mighty bowstring by only a finger's width, but one of the wooden things she was carving would catch it while the staff was pushed back to its starting position. When the bowstring was fully drawn, you could release it by leaning sideways on the staff.

Torris marveled at the complexity of the device. He had made traps that sprang suddenly to ensnare small prey, but he had never imagined a contrivance of such power.

"Does your tribe make such things?" he said wonderingly.

"No," she said. "There are legends that they were used long ago by a race of giants that lived before man. There are pictures carved on ancient slabs of wood that show them. The slabs are held sacred. But I think they were just people like us who thought big and dared greatly." She paused in her work to give him a challenging grin. "Perhaps they used them to venture to more distant Trees on bride raids. And they could go as an armed group instead of landing singly and have a greater chance of overpowering a defending clot of men."

"So you don't believe in giants?"

Her expression grew fierce. "The carvings are very clear and detailed. You can tell from them how these great bows must have worked. I think they must have been used to pass on the knowledge of how to make them to their artificers."

"Have you ever made one of these before?"

She blushed behind her faceplate. "No." Then, after a moment: "It would not have been allowed."

"Didn't you talk to your elders?"

She scowled at him. "The old men laughed when I tried to tell them what I thought. They said I was just a woman and didn't know anything. Then, when I wouldn't back down, they became angry. They said I was being blasphemous. That I would be punished if I persisted in my apostasy."

Torris wanted to ask her if she really thought her strange

contraption would work, but he thought it best not to pursue the subject. "I think we need one or two more carcasses to balance that bundle of meat if you intend to ride it back to your Tree. You don't want it spinning when you're trying to hang on to it."

"All right," she relented. "You can go hunting with me tomorrow. We'll get another couple of animals first, then finish up here."

It took another eight days of hard work to finish assembling Ning's giant sling. Then there was an unexpected problem with the intricate catch. It tended to slip prematurely. They tested it by hurling a massive log at the stars. But they did not dare to position the mound of dressed carcasses in the basketwork cup they had made for it until Ning was mounted and ready to fly; they were afraid that the oversensitive trigger might send the cargo of meat soaring into space without her.

But at last Ning pronounced them ready. "You have been a good pair of hands, my patient Tor-ris," she said. "You have earned the rest you shall have tonight." She peered at the sky, where the tiny green dot that was their target had already set. "Tomorrow, when the world has made another full turn and we face the Sisters again, our giants' bow will again be aimed at my people's Tree. We must wait until the orange star has merged with the red Stepsister, and you must pull the trigger at the precise moment when orange Sister appears again. I will show you how you must count. If you miss the moment, we will have to wait a whole day before we try again, and then I will have to change the counting to account for a slight sideways shift."

Torris could only gape at that. Ning sounded for all the

world like Claz making one of his mysterious pronouncements, and she sounded just as sure of herself.

She laughed when she saw the expression on his face. "Don't look so worried, my mighty hunter. Tonight you will be sleeping with a woman, not a priest."

[HAPTER 13

Ning was straddling the enormous mound of frozen carcasses that Torris had painstakingly tied and retied until he had a solid, secure mass that would not fly apart from the stresses to which it would shortly be subjected. With one hand she was holding on for dear life to the improvised harness in front of her. With the other hand she was tightly grasping the sack of explosive seed pods she would need for minor course corrections. She wasn't worried about running out. She had all the extra reaction mass she might need in the form of the haunches of frozen meat she was sitting on.

Torris stared at the spectacle with misgivings he knew in his heart were unworthy. There was enough meat there to feed his own tribe for an entire season. Any member of his tribe would have told him that it was his duty to kill Ning and drop the packet of meat to the foot of the Tree where it could be retrieved. He could imagine what Claz or his father would say about his perverse scruples. Now he had a new lie to tell. He shifted his eyes to her face. She paid no attention to him. Her gaze was fixed on the sky, waiting for the Sisters to emerge from their brief occlusion. Through her transparent faceplate he could see her lips moving as she counted off the moments. Perched atop her prize at last, she was wound up as tightly as her fantastic invention. He kept his hands assiduously away from the trigger staff, as she had told him to do. She was taking no chances on a premature release.

His eyes strayed momentarily to the patch of sky she was concentrating on, and he almost missed her signal. When he flicked his eyes back to her face, her lips were mouthing a frantic command in no-air talk.

"Pull, Tor-ris, pull!" she was screaming soundlessly. She added a few choice words of invective as he sprang guiltily to obey.

The recoil from the staff knocked him off his feet and sent him flying. When he picked himself up, Ning and her frozen cargo were gone, and the catapult, which had seemed so sturdy when they were putting it together, was in shambles. The violence of the launch had been too much for it.

When he raised his eyes to the sky, Ning was already a dwindling figure among the stars. She had managed to retain her grip on the harness, so that was all right.

As he watched, he saw a few hovering flutterbeasts take notice of the eruption and turn their narrow heads toward the miraculous bundle of flying meat. They had been lazing aloft, hoping to snare one of the unwary meatbeasts that had been grazing too close to the edge of the circular meadow and, inattentive to the gentle push of the Tree's rotation, had slid over the brink into the sky. The ability to spit mouthfuls of reaction mass had been good enough to let the waiting flutterbeasts maneuver close enough to these involuntary snacks to engulf an unfortunate animal or two, but Ning and her cargo were already out of reach. But not so out of reach for those grounded flutterbeasts that could push against something solid. Several of these raised curious heads, sensed food, and launched themselves with enough force to have a chance of intercepting Ning.

There wasn't much Torris could do. He ran for the bow he had left on the ground some distance away, took hasty aim, and managed to put an arrow through one of the creatures as it sailed overhead. It writhed in agony, spurting globules of blood. That diverted one of the pursuing flutterbeasts, which turned its attention to this easier prey.

Another couple of the black-winged monsters hadn't launched themselves forcefully enough to intercept Ning, and they too gave up the chase. That left three or four flutterbeasts with enough initial momentum to overtake Ning. And they were gradually closing the gap.

Torris stood by helplessly as they drew nearer to Ning. The two that were closest to her were already spreading their huge clawed wings in anticipation of a capture.

Ning was a tiny figure at this distance, but Torris could see that she had let go of the harness and was standing up, her long body streaming outward. She would be an easy snack for one of her pursuers if she started drifting away from her hurtling missile. But then he saw that she must have hooked her feet under the harness and was securely anchored.

Now she was fitting an arrow to her bow. Taking cool aim, she shot the flutterbeast that was closest, then calmly drew another arrow from her quiver and shot another one. One of the following beasts caught up with the nearer of its two wounded fellows and started chewing on it despite its vigorous objections. That left one more pursuer. Its slightly oblique vector wouldn't allow it to catch up to Ning's other victim, so it spat a quick course correction and slammed into the feeding flutterbeast to counter the feast.

Torris watched with relief as Ning's miniscule figure drew itself in, and she was once again seated securely. Her arrows had reduced the momentum of victims and victors alike, and the gap between Ning and the squabbling flutterbeasts slowly began to widen. Squinting with one eye, he assured himself that Ning's flying larder was eclipsing the green dot that was her Tree.

He stared for a long time at the ruins of Ning's wrecked contrivance and finally shook his head. He picked up his bow and scattered belongings and trudged slowly toward the shelter where he and Ning had spent their last night. He had a lot of thinking to do.

By morning he had made up his mind. There was no point in lingering here in this strange land of plenty, where game was to be had for the asking and where the Tree ended and naked space began. A person was not a person away from his tribe.

He had finished his Climb. He had had his Dream, and it was a good one. Claz would be pleased. Perhaps Torris's Dream would even go into the annals to be recited by future priests.

That was the rub. He could tell his Dream but not the rest of it.

Ning had argued and argued with him about that. "Torris, my virtuous simpleton," she'd finally said in exasperation, "you simply cannot tell your priest or anyone else that you have killed another Climber. This Brank of yours was a plain murderer who would have killed me and gone on to kill you when you were still helpless in your Dream, or so he thought. You had no choice. If he were the one on trial before your tribe, he would be the one to be sentenced to be cast into the darkness for stealing from another Climber if for nothing else. He is not worth risking your overscrupulous neck for."

"The Climb is a sacrament," he replied piously. "And to lie is blasphemy."

"Tor-ris, Tor-ris, what am I to do with you?" she'd said, rolling her eyes. "You wouldn't be lying; you'd only be leaving things out."

"And what else am I to leave out?" he'd asked hotly. "That I paired with you, and that we spent days and days climbing to the land at the top of the Tree, where game abounds and where people go when they die? And that we made a bow of the giants to send a gift of meat to the people of another Tree—a Tree that our bride hunters will be raiding someday?"

She knitted her brows. "You can tell them about the land at the top of the Tree," she said judiciously. "I have no doubt that there will be some that call it blasphemy and that you will have to endure being lectured by your priest and your elders. But in the past, there must have been hardy souls in your tribe who climbed to the land at the end of the Tree and brought back tales. And that is where your legends come from. One day, other youths making the Climb will break through, then more, and it will be legend no longer. Your tribe will know abundance, and the legends will be about you. But you must not tell them about me. That would make you a traitor."

In truth, Torris had already come to the same conclusion, but he could not admit it to himself. It was easier to blame it on Ning and to make himself angry. But he knew in his heart that he was unworthy. And that he would be a coward.

He took a final look around the nest that he and Ning had shared. She hadn't left much behind. She'd taken the arrowheads he'd carved for her, and in some bittersweet fashion, that made him happy. There wasn't anything there that he wanted, and he couldn't have explained some artifact from another Tree anyway. There was a fresh stovebeast that he and Ning had caught the night before, tied in the corner, and he exchanged it for the one he'd been harboring for the last few days. The furry little fellow he'd been using was at the airseal as soon as he opened it, and it scampered away as fast as its stubby legs would carry it.

He walked to the edge of the circular plateau and followed its perimeter for some distance until he came to a spot where there was a clear drop of at least a mile, with no branches in the way to slow his descent. Like all the life forms that had evolved on the Tree, he had an exquisite sense of gravity no matter how feeble it might be, and he could feel the infinitesimal pull of the comet's mass far below. It would be a long fall from paradise. Clutching his bow and spear, he stepped off the edge.

CHAPTER 14

The first group he encountered, with still a few hours of descent ahead of him, was a party of hunters in the lower branches. There were five of them carrying one pathetic prize among them—a starveling meatbeast that must have been the cull of its herd.

They stopped and stared at Torris but did not try to approach him. One did not speak to a returning Dreamer until he had poured out his Dream to Claz and had undergone the proper rituals. They conferred briefly among themselves, then one of them scrambled downward and disappeared among the low-lying boughs. To spread the news, Torris supposed.

He saluted them wryly and continued his descent. By the time he got to the cave mouth he was exhausted. Climbing down was just as tiring as climbing up, except that it didn't take as long, with intervals of dropping free alternating with threading one's way through the branches. He was hungry, too, not having stopped often enough to forage or to hunt.

The usual handful of people in airsuits were loitering on the trampled ground outside the entrance to the ice cave. They made way for him but kept their distance. He traversed the twisting downward tunnel and let himself through the triple animal-skin airlock into the big common chamber. The usual perpetual fire was going, keeping the place almost warm enough to melt ice, and there were perhaps two handfuls of people taking advantage of it, mostly mothers with small children. They looked at Torris, then looked away. He could hear them whispering as he passed on his way to Claz's niche, his helmet under his arm.

The priest was not there, but he could hear voices from behind the curtain of skins that covered the entrance to Claz's personal space. "Claz?" he said, announcing himself hesitantly, and let himself through.

Three heads turned in his direction as he entered. The other two scowled at the interruption, but Claz recognized Torris immediately and said, "So you're alive, boy. We lost three Climbers this turn of the stars, and when you didn't return for so long, we thought the Tree had swallowed you too."

The two visitors frowned in concert. Torris had hoped to see Claz alone, at least through the welcoming ceremony, and their presence was disquieting at the least. They were the two recognized elders of the tribe, old enough to have streaks of gray in their beards. Torris acknowledged them with the necessary nods of deference, but his heart was sinking.

One of the two was Cleb the Chronicler, Brank's long-suffering father. Torris's heart sank still further.

"Did you see my boy Brank?" Cleb asked harshly. "Was he by any chance still alive?"

Claz thumped his walking staff. "Later, Cleb, later," he said. He turned back to Torris. "First, Torris-postulant, did you bring me a Dream?"

"I did," Torris said, following the ritual.

The two elders bowed their heads in compliance—Cleb unwillingly, the other in stolid conformance. Torris knew the other man well. He was Igg the Spearmaker, and Torris had endured his share of cuffs and blows from him while he was growing up. Igg had been a mighty hunter in his day—the tribe's best—but that had ended after a kick from a wounded meatbeast had lamed him. He eked out a living by making spears for the tribe and by instructing the young boys in the use of the spear. Torris had complained to his father about Igg's treatment, but his father had belittled his bruises and the other abuse. "That's just his way," he'd said. "How would it look if the son of the Facemaker got special treatment?" Then, after a moment, "Perhaps he treats you a little worse than the other boys because he resents me. Nobody has the special skill needed to cast a clear Face, so they must come to me. But anybody can make a spear, and so there are many who choose not to let Igg tithe them."

"You may tell your Dream," Claz said. "Leave nothing out."

Torris began hesitantly but soon was caught up in the telling of his Dream. Claz listened impassively, but the two elders exchanged frowns as Torris struggled to describe the strangeness of both being himself, living the Tree's slow thoughts, and somehow being the Tree itself, looking down at the tiny naked creature sprawled unconscious in its calyx, a parasite like the other life it hosted but a specimen of a promising species it had conditioned over the millennia to bring it gifts of pollen from its Brother Trees.

"Blasphemy," Igg muttered.

"Overweening conceit, at any rate, to claim to be in some sense the Tree itself," Cleb said in the doctrinaire tone of voice he affected when he was making his pronouncements as Chronicler.

"Do not interrupt," Claz said sternly. Then, with a sideways glance at Torris, "I have heard such things before from some of the more imaginative returnees. And I can remember describing my own Dream in a similar way when I was a young postulant. And how can it not be? The Tree created us long ago, and how can a god not have powerful thoughts, thoughts that we cannot understand or find words for?"

He turned to Torris. "Go on, boy. You said something about bringing a bag of pollen as a gift—pollen from a Brother Tree. But did you not scrape the pollen from a calyx of the Tree itself?"

At that moment Torris realized he had made a mistake. He had been so caught up in the memory of his strange transformation that he had let that slip.

"I . . . er . . . no . . . that is, there was this bag of pollen that . . . " He trailed off. He had hoped incoherently that he could somehow imply that he had found a bag of pollen that some other Climber had left behind, but now he was entangled in his own words. How could he know that it was the pollen of another Tree? Torris, like all the primitive people who had ever been, was not used to telling outright lies. In fact, there was a term for such a person—*web talker*—and once a person had been so labeled, nobody ever took him seriously again.

Claz was looking at him oddly.

Torris blurted out: "The pollen was left by someone from the Tree-that-draws-closer." He stopped. That would not be enough. He knew, miserably, that he had simply provided more questions for Claz to ask.

Igg, at least, had been misdirected. "A bride raider!" he exclaimed excitedly. "By the Tree of Trees, it's some impudent bride raider from a Tree we've had our eye on for half a lifetime!" He became alarmed. "There may be others! We're in great danger! I'll get the men together. We may have to fight . . . " Now he was perplexed. "But how was he able to cross? It's still too far!"

"Calm yourself, Igg," Claz said. He turned to Torris. "Perhaps you had better explain yourself, boy."

Torris's head was spinning. "It was a woman," he said, forcing the words out unwillingly. "She brought the pollen from her own Tree. But she . . . "

This was getting harder. He gulped and went on. " . . . but she gave the pollen to me because she thought the gift would be more pleasing to our Tree than the usual scrapings and that It would reward me with a more powerful Dream. I . . . I . . . " He stopped, lost in confusion.

Cleb was indignant. "You *connived* with this . . . this *woman*?" he sputtered. "Why did you not kill her?"

Igg couldn't restrain himself either. "She was sent by the people of her Tree to spy on us so that their bride raiders could kill us all and take our women! They sent a woman because it was doubtful that anyone could survive such a crossing, and it was not worth risking one of their men!"

Claz kept his composure. "That seems a fair question, Torris," he said gently. "Why did you not kill her?"

Torris's ears burned. What had he gotten himself into? "She . . . she caught me in a trap," he confessed. "But she spared me. And then . . . and then she saved me from being eaten by a web beast. She came with me on my Climb, and we . . . we helped each other."

Claz seemed sad rather than angry. "Tell the truth, Torris," he said. "Did you violate your vow of chastity as well?"

He couldn't meet Claz's eyes. "Y . . . yes."

Cleb took a new tack. Using his orotund Chronicler's voice, he said, "It's becoming clear. They sent her to steal our seed. She is a witch, and that is how she survived the crossing."

Claz ignored him. "Tell me, Torris. How did you help this woman?"

It was over for him now. The last of his resistance crumbled. He'd have to tell Claz everything. Everything except killing Brank. He steeled himself not to let that spill out. But he raised his eyes to meet Claz's steady gaze, and the words tumbled out.

"She . . . she wasn't here to spy. Times are lean on her Tree. The game has been failing there. She came here hoping to score a huge kill and send the meat back to her Tree. To help her people and prove herself as a hunter."

That was too much for Igg. "A woman hunter? This is disgraceful, Claz. Wholly unnatural, and as a participant, this boy has sunk to the lowest depths! It's an offense against all men! Word of this must never get out! It would threaten our whole way of life!"

His hand strayed toward his knife, but a glance from Claz quelled him.

"And did you hunt with this unnatural woman, Torris?" Claz continued calmly, almost kindly.

"N . . . no, not exactly," Torris said. "I . . . snared some small game to help feed us on the way, but Ning wouldn't let me come with her on the meatbeast hunts. She said . . . " He blushed. " . . . I wasn't an experienced hunter."

"So you made camp for this Ning and snared hoppers and such for food along the way, like any small child taken along on a hunt," Claz said.

Torris realized too late that Claz was goading him for a purpose. He briefly flared with suppressed anger and said defensively, "I helped to make the giants' bow by which she returned to her Tree."

Claz pounced. "What is this giants' bow?"

So Torris had to explain about Ning's catapult in detail. Claz questioned him closely and seemed to grasp some of the fine points of construction, though Torris was often at a loss for words to make his meaning clear. Claz was particularly interested in the fact that Ning was able to measure things in her head without trying them out first, and he pressed Torris hard on the details. He seemed to know what Torris was talking about when Torris described the ancient slabs of wood with pictures on them. It made Torris wonder if his own tribe had once had such slabs, and if they had been destroyed for their impiety or if were hidden.

When Torris told Claz how Ning had used the movement of the stars to take aim at her approaching Tree, Claz became inordinately interested. "Is this Ning a numberer, then?" he asked with a show of indifference.

"N . . . no," Torris said. "Everyone knows a woman cannot be a numberer."

Igg nodded, his expression hardening. "She's a witch," he said.

Cleb was looking at Torris with distaste. "That's no excuse," he said to Claz. "This is a clear case not only of impiety, in violating the canons of the Climb by soliciting help from another, but of making a mockery of them by pairing with an enemy of the tribe to do so. And a woman at that—a sacrilege in itself."

Torris longed to be able to tell Cleb that his own son, Brank, had violated the sacred canons of the Climb by stealing from another Climber, and that one of the reasons he and Ning had formed their alliance was for protection. But he knew that to mention Brank was to condemn himself to perdition.

Claz looked at Torris sadly. "Wait outside, boy. I will tell you my decision when I have mulled these things over."

The common chamber was filled with people when Torris emerged. It was the hour of the main meal now, and even many of those who had fires of their own in a niche or lean-to within the cave and did not have to depend on the central fire for cooking their food had joined the others for camaraderie. Perhaps some were there out of curiosity because word had traveled that one of the returned Climbers who had been thought dead had been with Claz and the elders for an inordinately long time. That the returnee was the son of Parn the Facemaker added spice to the curiosity.

The chatter stopped and all eyes turned to Torris. But no one spoke to him and no one would meet his eyes. He made his way to an unoccupied spot against the wall and squatted down, trying to make himself as inconspicuous as possible. After a while they went back to their eating and chatter.

Torris looked around the cave for his father or one of his mothers but saw no sign of them. Parn must have known by now that his son had returned, but he was being strict about not speaking to him until the priest had collected his Dream—and not letting Firstmother and Secondmother out of his sight either.

He waited for what seemed like a very long time. At last

Claz appeared at his niche and searched for Torris. He found him immediately, and everybody else looked at Torris too.

"The postulant will return to hear the judgment," he announced, and disappeared behind the skin curtain.

Torris made his way across the chamber, feeling all eyes on him. This was not the usual order of things. He let himself through the curtain and found Claz and the two elders seated on the gnarled root that was used as a bench for formal judgments.

"It has been decided," Claz said. "You are guilty of heresy. You are to be Shunned."

CHAPTER 15

5,999,900,000 A.D.
Local Group

The Milky Way was a blaze of glory against the black of a near-empty sky as Joorn and his family watched the projected view in the observation gallery unfold. But it was no longer the beautiful spiral it had been when Joorn had left it two and a half billion years ago. It had been deformed and elongated by its encounter with Andromeda and was now an elliptical galaxy, and a rather distorted one at that.

"It's beautiful, Grandpa!" exclaimed eleven-year-old Nina. "But it doesn't look like the pictures. Is that because of the collision with Andromeda? And it isn't as colorful as I expected. Is that because so many of the larger stars turned into white dwarfs or black holes after all these years?"

Joorn tousled her hair fondly. It was pretty obvious by now that Nina had decided to follow in her father's footsteps as an astrophysicist rather than become an anthropologist like her mother, despite the growing popularity of anthropology as a career choice among girls in her age group now that they were nearing the ancestral cradle of humanity. Her brother, Martin, ten years her senior, was caught up in the practical aspects of quantum physics and the Higgs field, and he would probably end up as an engineer in the Higgs drive department.

"Well, er . . . " he began.

Alten took over. "Right on the button, baby," he said. "But it wasn't exactly a collision. Galaxies are so big, and the stars so far apart, that Andromeda simply passed through the Milky Way with only a few million individual collisions of stars. And yes, when two stars whose mass adds up to more than eight solar masses collide, or even get too close, they merge—quite quickly—and become a black hole. So galaxies of a certain age tend to have a lot of black holes, and eventually the holes merge and become one great big black hole at the center."

His wife, Irina, nudged him. "Alten, you're lecturing again."

"I know, I know," he said good-naturedly. "Just let me finish." They'd been married for more than twenty years now, having met shortly after *Time's Beginning* began its homeward hegira. Joorn thought the world of his beautiful daughter-in-law and never missed an opportunity to tell Alten how lucky he was.

"But," Alten continued while Nina gave him her worshipful attention, "there's a lot of dust in a galaxy, and it exerted a gravitational force powerful enough to pull the Milky Way out of shape. And yes, a lot of stars that are too small to become black holes eventually burn up their hydrogen, swell up into red giants, then end their lives as white dwarfs—hot dwarfs that after a few billion years cool into cinders."

"Stars like Sol."

"Yes, baby, like Sol. We all get old, even stars. Sol should still be a red giant when we get there, though it will already have started to shrink. But it'll take at least another few hundred thousand years or so before it becomes a white dwarf, and even then it will still be giving off light and heat as it cools because of the gravitational shrinkage."

Martin had been fidgeting and now he interrupted. "Father, do you mind if I take off for the control room? Chu promised me he'd let me watch when he started to feather down to half a light, and we're smack in the middle of one of the nebulae that didn't get dragged along with the rest of the Large Cloud of Magellan."

Nina cut in. "The Tarantula Nebula in Nubecula Major," she said, showing off.

"Don't interrupt your brother, Nina," Irina said. "It's not polite."

"Can I?" Martin said.

"I don't want you bothering Chu," Alten said. "He's got a lot on his mind now that he's about to start decelerating."

"Oh for heaven's sake, Alten, don't be a stick-in-the-mud," Joorn said. "Chu and the boy are as thick as thieves."

"He lets me help him sometimes," Martin said. "When he needs somebody to run through his numbers."

Alten pretended to think it over. "Okay," he said, "but don't touch anything unless he tells you to."

Martin scurried off happily. Joorn and Alten looked at each other and laughed. "He'll have Chu's job one of these days," Joorn said.

Alten became suddenly sober. "I hope so," he said. "Would you believe it: Oliver's been lobbying for the job."

"Oliver? But he and Karn are still under restrictions."

"The restrictions have been loosening the last few years. Oliver and Karn still have a lot of friends aboard, even though that crowd is getting older and tamer. Besides, a new generation is growing up, one that doesn't remember our departure or the attempted mutiny."

"They'll never rehabilitate themselves, not as long as Ryan is ship's president. And *he's* the one with all the followers these days. He's in his fourth consecutive term as ship's president, and *that's* where the politics of the ship stand." Joorn shook his head, continuing. "Ryan's been too lenient with them. He's mellowed since the early days when he was the firebrand activist who led the counter-mutiny. I was never easy with the decision of Ryan and the ship's council to give Karn teaching privileges again. That's how he built up his band of disciples in the first place."

"I wouldn't worry too much about it, Father," Alten said. "Ryan knows what a pair of snakes they are. He's keeping an eye on them. But we can't afford to waste a mind like Karn's. He was the most brilliant astrophysicist of your generation back on Earth. He still is, in our little traveling bubble of a society. We need teachers like him if we're going to repopulate the Milky Way."

"I know, I know," Joorn said. "Delbert was my friend. That friendship's still there, in a way." He gave Alten a wry grin. "I seem to remember that you were his disciple once upon a time."

"I still am—in a way," Alten said. "And Martin's attending his classes in Higgs field theory. I can't object to that, can I?"

Nina tugged at Joorn's hand. "Are you talking about Uncle Delbert?" she chimed.

Joorn tried not to show his surprise. Alten was not as successful. "What is this 'Uncle Delbert' business?" he said.

"He said I could sit at the back of his class in quantum point motion if I was quiet." She giggled. "He calls it quantum jitters.

And afterward he stayed to explain quantum field theory, and he gave me a copy of his book. He said that he and Grandpa were best friends when they were Martin's age."

Joorn and Alten exchanged a worried look, but Nina was already lost in dreamy contemplation of the Milky Way again.

"I don't trust him," Alten said. "He's up to something."

"What could he do?" Joorn shrugged. "We reached our terminal velocity a long time ago, and we've been coasting ever since, albeit at almost the speed of a photon. We did it just in time to avoid zipping past our target as Karn had planned. Now it's just about time for Chu to start decelerating so that we can enter the Sun-Alpha Centauri system at nonrelativistic speeds. There would be no point in Karn and Oliver trying anything after we shed enough delta-v."

"Karn's had a long time to brood."

"He's bitter," Joorn agreed. "He's still lobbying the council to live up to my original bargain with him and let him and his followers have the module with the Higgs drive after we get settled. But Ryan won't have any of it. He's said more than once that Karn's mutiny when we discovered Oliver's deception back at the 3C-295 flag post canceled his original bargain with me."

"The trouble is that half the council is too young to remember the mutiny. To them it's just an old story told by their fuddy-duddy parents—probably nothing more than an exaggeration of a policy dispute with the Homegoing faction. Karn is playing on their sympathy. He's presenting himself as the bold dreamer once again, the iconoclast who's being deprived of his dream by his political enemies. And some of them are buying it. They have no memory of Earth. Or of Rebirth, for that matter. *Time's Beginning* is their Universe. And I'm sure that some of them even entertain secret fantasies of going with Karn on his journey to nowhere.

"We won *Time's Beginning* fair and square," Alten continued. "Karn and Oliver lost, and they'd better get used to it. Lord knows, we can put all the ship's resources, including the Higgs drive, to good use. After we find a congenial world—hopefully in the Sol-Centauri system itself—and don't see any need to go star-hopping again, we might decide to give him the Higgs module anyway. Then, for all we care, that whole bunch could take off for the end of the Universe in any direction they choose. The so-called edge is the same distance from anywhere, if you subscribe to the theory that the Universe is just a three-dimensional skin of a brane that's a closed system, like a higher dimensional version of a sphere. So there'd be no need for them to use up more lifetime by retracing their steps to our former starting point in 3C-273. They'd have to start building gamma from scratch here in the Local Group, true, but that was the bargain they made with you on Rebirth, like it or not."

"Karn may not see it that way. He's obsessed about getting old. He lost a big chunk of lifetime getting to 3C-273 and back. He's afraid he'll die before he gets to see his Valhalla."

"Nonsense. I spoke to Dr. Hahn at the parole committee just last week, and Karn's telomere treatments are going just fine. He'll live to be two hundred, like everybody else. And if he doesn't—well, that was the same chance he took when we started out six billion years ago."

"I'd better have a talk with Karn before this gets out of hand. There's no way I'm going to accept Miles Oliver as my first officer. Chu's perfectly willing to go back to his old job, and we've still got some tricky maneuvers to go through before we're home free. I don't like this business of Oliver lobbying the council. And I don't want him thinking that there's the slightest chance that we'd ever trust him again."

"I'll get together with Ryan," Alten said. "Have him speak to the council's younger members."

At that moment, they suddenly became weightless, and everybody automatically grabbed for a handhold. Irina reached for her daughter's shoulder and steadied her. Joorn was abruptly aware that the subtle thrumming of the Higgs drive had ceased.

"Chu's preparing for turnaround," he said.

Nina wriggled free of her mother's grasp and found a handhold of her own. She turned to her grandfather and said hopefully, "Are we there yet?"

Karn hadn't aged well. His face was gaunt and wintry, and he was starting to acquire a stoop. When Joorn entered he was sitting at a keyboard facing a hugely magnified display that was splashed over an entire wall. As soon as he was aware of Joorn, he stabbed at his keyboard and the wall display winked out. "It's been quite a long time since you've deigned to visit me, Joorn," he said. "What brings you here today?"

"We need to have a talk, Delbert."

"What for? The last time I saw you, you made it painfully clear that we no longer have anything to talk about."

Joorn's retinal memory retained the flash of enlarged numbers he'd seen in the fraction of a second before Karn succeeded in erasing the display. It was a star table of some sort, and he'd managed to catch the labels "Tau Ceti" and "Epsilon Eridani," two of the sunlike stars that were closest to Sol, where Earth had planted colonies before mankind had discovered the existence of the Others. What was interesting about them was that they obviously came from a table of relativistic time dilation values for travel from Sol at a constant one-G acceleration and deceleration. Joorn had made trips to both those stars as a young starship pilot in the early years after the Higgs drive made starflight possible. The figures were roughly the same for travel to any nearby star—about a year to boost to near-lightspeed and another year to deboost, with the sliding scale that got you to those velocities amounting to only about three years of lifetime for a trip to any star within a hundred light-years. Any star at all. The subjective time added after reaching terminal velocity was insignificant for any of those destinations.

"Planning a trip, Delbert?" he said.

"What are you talking about?"

"Estimating how much lifespan you'll spend if you maroon the rest of us on one of the habitable planets of our former neighbors. Habitable six billion years ago, that is. Of course both Tau Ceti and Epsilon Eridani have the virtue of being somewhat smaller than Sol, and so are below the mass threshold for turning into a red giant that swallows its children."

"Can't an old man dream? Or isn't that allowed either?"

"Don't try to play the self-pity card, Delbert. It doesn't become you."

"No self-pity, just realism. I've always faced facts, and the fact is that you and that Ryan crowd have the upper hand. Even if you somehow had a change of heart and decided to live up to our original bargain after getting your flock safely settled on the available real estate, it would be too late for me. I'm resigned, Joorn. I'm just playing make-believe here."

"Miles Oliver doesn't seem to think it's make-believe. He's acting as though he thinks he has a realistic chance of replacing Chu as first officer. Supposedly to hone his piloting skills in case we ever change our minds about letting your crowd have the ship. I suspect *his* daydream is to make the Homegoers walk the plank so he doesn't have to slow down for us."

"Miles Oliver!" Karn almost spat the words. "That insolent puppy! I think he's become unhinged. He thinks my grand vision of reaching the end of time belongs to *him* now, and he's surrounded himself with the most unsavory elements of the old party. They treat me as a sort of mascot and don't listen to anything I have to say. I gather I'll be allowed along on the trip if I behave myself." The contempt in Karn's voice was palpable.

Joorn was startled at Karn's vehemence. "Are you trying to tell me that you and your star pupil have had a falling-out?"

"Miles has become a megalomaniac. It's now a psychopathological condition. Twenty years of frustration will do that. And the dullards he keeps around him only encourage his fantasies."

"What about you, Delbert? Wasn't there a touch of megalomania about your scheme to hijack the ship when the majority voted to settle down at Rebirth?"

"Maybe. It was a gamble. Maybe I was ruthless. Maybe I overreached. But I never lost sight of the realities. When the majority took back the ship, I knew it was all over. All that lovely accumulated velocity was gone. Paid back to the cosmic accounts. And now I'm resigned to being a doddering old physics teacher."

"You, Delbert? Doddering? Never. What are you really up to?"

"Joorn, I swear . . . "

"Are you proselytizing Nina?

"I'm just nudging her along in physics. She's a bright little girl. She has real potential. And maybe someday she'll be fired by a grand vision of her own. I have no control over that. And neither do you."

"And what about Martin?"

"He attends my classes, period. He knows I'm the best teacher of Higgs field physics around. He needs my help to achieve his ambition of being chief drive engineer. He's a nice boy, and he's very smart, but he was born with a monkey wrench in his hand."

"If I thought for one minute—"

"Relax, Joorn. I have no designs on your grandchildren. Alten was another matter." He shook his head sadly. "He could have been my intellectual heir. Instead of Oliver."

"You be careful, Delbert. I'm keeping an eye on you."

"You'd be better advised to keep an eye on Oliver."

Karn swung back to his keyboard. The wall display sprang back to life. He was making no effort to conceal it. The relativistic comparisons were gone. It was all visuals now, a breathtaking close-up of one of the Milky Way's spiral arms, still recognizable despite its distortion. Karn was zooming in on one of its star systems now. It was dominated by a bloated red giant, but there was a healthy-looking orange star too, possibly a K-5, and two white dwarfs. Joorn searched and after a moment found a dim outlying red dwarf that had to be Proxima. He watched the image a few moments more, then turned and left.

CHAPTER 16

5,999,999,999 A.D.
The Oort Cloud

Ryan had posted a couple of guards outside the door to the control room, a pair of hefty fellows of his own generation who were perhaps showing a little bit of bulge at the waistline but otherwise looked quite fit. One of them smiled at Nina and said to Joorn, "Bringing the young lady along for a firsthand look, Captain?"

"Try and keep her away," Joorn said. "Why all the security, Talbot? I thought we'd agreed that we were past the need for all that now that we're down to less than a tenth of a light."

Talbot shrugged. "I guess Ryan doesn't want to take any chances at this stage. The intelligence boys may have stumbled onto something. There are still Karnite fanatics around, and they're not exactly rational people."

"I'm sure their teeth are pulled, but of course President Ryan has to consider all the possibilities," Joorn acknowledged.

The door slid open in response to some kind of a signal from Talbot, and Joorn and Nina stepped through. There were two more guards just inside, and Joorn was dismayed to see that they were equipped with wooden billy clubs from the homegrown forest maintained in an adjacent habitat by the carpentry shop. Joorn remembered the earnest debate at the last general ship's meeting.

There were those who thought that clubs fashioned from wood were an extravagance when there was plenty of cheap titanium pipe available. And an opposing side with long memories who wanted no reminder of the kind of tactics employed by the Karnite thugs when they had seized the ship years ago. Then there was the civility crowd who thought the ship's security unit should have nothing to do with any kind of clubs, wood *or* titanium.

"Morning, sir." A sandy-haired young man wearing a grad student's chevron offered a sloppy salute that he must have copied from one of the old Earth videos.

"You've got things well in hand, I see," Joorn said.

"Yes, sir. Security thought it would be a good idea to secure the control room before the Higgs drive was turned off. You see, the thought was that some opposition elements might get to feeling desperate when—"

"Yes, yes, Talbot filled me in. When did the order come through?"

"First dog watch, sir."

"Very good. Carry on."

Nina caught sight of Chu and ran across the control room to where he was seated. She stopped short of him while she decided whether he could be interrupted. When he held out his arms for a hug, she gave it to him and slid into the adjacent seat, her hands in her lap away from any knobs or buttons.

"Are you going to tell me about the trees, Uncle Chu?" she asked.

"You bet, sweetheart," Chu said. "There's one only a few light-months away—just as soon as I can zoom in on it."

Joorn studied his granddaughter with approval. She'd shot up quite a bit in the ten thousand years since deceleration had begun. She was now a composed young lady of thirteen, taking her first formal classes in astrophysics, well ahead of her classmates, and promising to overtake her brother, Martin.

He slid into the captain's chair and, after a nod from Chu, started to punch himself in.

"Where do we stand?" he asked.

"Everything's nominal," Chu said. "The program's ready to go. We'll switch to the secondary drive without a hitch."

"Where's Martin? I'd have thought he'd want to be here."

"He's babysitting the conjugate mirror assembly with the engineering crew. He thought he ought to be there when it goes off-line."

Joorn nodded. "Good boy."

"Boy no longer," Chu said.

Nina was fidgeting. "What about the trees?" she asked.

Chu's hands flew over the keys that operated the imaging system. On the viewscreen blurred specks bounced and jiggled until one of them grew into a recognizable shape as the focus seemed to race toward it, technically faster than light, though that was an effect of the computer choosing successively from millions of foci per second.

"Ah, there we are. Do you know where that is, Nina?"

"Yes, of course," she replied with thirteen-year-old certitude. "That's in the Oort cloud."

"Right. Actually two Oort clouds mingled together to become one. The Alpha Centauri system had its own Oort cloud, just like Sol, extending outward a couple of light-years. The two Oort clouds may actually have brushed against each other at their boundaries."

"It was Oort all the way, pussycat," Joorn offered, quoting the tired old classroom joke.

"I know all that!" Nina said scornfully. "It's from Astronomy One."

Chu reprimanded Joorn with a cocked eyebrow and continued. "Then, a couple of thousand millennia ago, the net drift of the Centauri system toward the solar system resulted in a quadruple star system, with the three Centauri stars and our sun doing a complicated dance together. And the two Oort clouds became one huge Oort cloud, an enormous egg-shaped cloud containing trillions and trillions of comets surrounding the quadruple system."

"Yes, yes, I know." Nina was impatient. "Egg-shaped, not spherical, because it would become gravitationally stretched when the clouds interpenetrated. And because the clouds are counter-rotating in relation to each other, there'll be a tremendous confusion of the cometary traffic." She tossed an unruly mop of dark hair. "But not a lot of comets colliding or capturing one another because on average they're so far apart. *Please*, Uncle Chu!"

Joorn grinned proudly at Chu over Nina's head.

Chu ignored him and went on patiently. "Now we come to the trees. In the very early twentieth century, the 1920s in fact—"

"Six billion years ago," Nina interrupted.

"Yes, six billion, more or less," Chu said dryly. "Give or take a few years, of course. In the 1920s, a scientist named Bernal speculated that if you could breed trees to live in vacuum and plant them on comets, they could grow to an enormous size. In fact, in the absence of any appreciable gravity, they could grow to heights of hundreds of miles. Quite a stretch . . . " He paused to give Joorn time to groan. " . . . at a time when his fellow scientists were arguing that space travel itself would never be possible! There were plenty of comets, and they could provide the growing Trees with all the water and trace elements they needed. What was especially remarkable about Bernal's fantastic vision was that nothing was known about DNA at the time. Genetic engineering, as we understand the term, hadn't even been imagined. Bernal was talking about good old-fashioned Gregor Mendel–style plant breeding."

Nina's agile imagination had already made the leap. "So the Oort cloud is actually one huge forest in space."

"By now it is," Chu said. "The trees have had six billion years to grow and evolve. By now they've had an eternity to spread throughout the entire Oort cloud. And, probably, the Oort clouds of all the nearby stars as well—Barnard's Star, Sirius, Tau Ceti, Delta Pavonis, and beyond. In the fullness of time, I don't doubt that they'll fill the entire galaxy."

Nina's young face showed that she was trying to digest that. "Sort of like the Others did," she said in a hushed voice. "Except that trees don't think or communicate with each other."

"Oh but they do, in their own way," Joorn submitted. "Didn't you learn that in your biology class? Biology's just as fascinating as astrophysics, you know."

"Listen to your father," Chu said.

"What do you mean, in their own way?" Nina said, subdued now.

"Even on Earth, trees and other plants had the ability to share information and plan for a common defense against their enemies," Joorn said. "If a tree was attacked by bark beetles, for example, it could warn its fellow trees to thicken their bark or produce appropriate toxins or repellents by sending chemical signals through the groundwater or the air."

"There's no air in space, let alone groundwater," Nina protested.

"In an Oort cloud filled with trillions of living things, there'd be plenty of exudations, no matter how thinned out," Chu pointed out. "Stray water molecules from the trees' metabolism, plant hormones, individual grains of pollen. It wouldn't take much. One molecule per every cubic meter or so would constitute a medium for transmitting chemical messages, though perhaps at a rate imperceptible to us fast-living humans."

"But why would people plant trees in space in the first place?" Nina asked. "The colonists on Rebirth are planting forests there, and we've got our own little forest for whatever wood we need right here in the ship."

"Chu's too young to remember," Joorn said. "He was born on Rebirth. I was raised on Mother Earth less than a century after our expansion into space began. The answer is that lots of wood was needed for construction out there, and, just as important, in the tremendous sizes provided by Bernal's trees. It dawned on our brave planners that wood was the ideal construction material for our new space age. It didn't deteriorate like plastic under ultraviolet bombardment. It didn't have to be boosted into space at great expense, let alone mined at even greater expense. And even better, it provided greater protection against killer radiation than the tin cans we were using for habitats and spaceships before then."

Joorn paused reflectively. Chu maintained a respectful silence.

"I'm old enough to remember when the first space habitat was constructed out of vacuum-grown wood. There was a lot of hype about it, enough to fire the imagination of a small boy who wanted to be a starship pilot. And it wasn't even made of comet-grown wood under conditions of negligible gravity. The first Oortian trees hadn't matured yet. This one was carpentered together out of wood from the still-experimental lunar forests, under conditions of one-sixth Earth gravity. Those early trees only grew to a height of about half a mile.

"The construction of that first habitat was crude. It was polygonal rather than toroidal. They hadn't yet thought of those enormous planters that rotate an increment at a time to make the tree grow with the proper curvature as it keeps striving toward the vertical under one-sixth gravity. So they started with eighteen straight joists made into six equilateral triangles that were about three thousand feet on a side and as wide as a football field. Then they framed the habitat by joining the triangles to make a hexagon and went on from there."

He smiled reminiscently. "I visited the habitat when I was a young man in training. It was in orbit around Jupiter, at a relatively safe distance beyond the orbit of Himalia. It was a little disconcerting. Gravity seemed to be straight up and down when you were standing in the center of one of those football fields, but as you walked toward the next triangle, it began to feel like walking uphill. Your eyes told you that you were walking on a flat surface, but your inner ear disagreed. It kept getting steeper and steeper till you reached the next triangle, then you were walking downhill till you reached that segment's center. People got used to it."

Chu nodded vigorously. He was a great history buff and had always been fascinated by the romantic era of wooden habitats and wooden spaceships. His captain was a living relic, a first-hand witness of those bygone days, and whenever the duty roster made it possible, Chu enjoyed whiling away the long hours of his watch by listening to Joorn's oft-told tales.

"The day of the wooden spaceship vanished when the Higgs drive came in," Chu said sadly. "Just as the age of sail vanished when steam power began to replace wooden sailing ships. But change was inevitable."

"Not quite," Joorn said. "The first starships to Alpha Centauri and Tau Ceti, which were launched before the Higgs drive with its built-in radiation shield made wooden spaceships obsolete, were made of wood. A thickness of fifteen feet of wood was safer than a metal skin. Energetic particles were absorbed, not bounced around to create killer secondary radiation, and it was more practical than embedding the living quarters inside fifteen feet of water, which did the same thing. It could handle anything from solar flares to the sleet of gamma rays you got from interstellar travel." He chuckled. "When the first Higgs ship made it to Alpha Centauri after a five-year trip, some sixty years after a maiden expedition had been launched in one of those old wooden ships, the would-be colonists were still less than halfway across. A rescue mission was mounted to intercept the First Centauri Expedition and transfer the colonists to a Higgs ship, leaving the old wooden hulk to drift for eternity. When the original colonists arrived at

Alpha Centauri, they were surprised—and a little miffed—to find a settlement already flourishing there."

He became serious. "Of course it was only wooden spaceships that were made obsolete by the Higgs drive," he said soberly. "Wooden habitats were still more practical than aluminum and titanium and man-made plastics. And a lot cheaper. When your grandmother and I left Earth, the habitats orbiting Mars and the gas giants were still being constructed of giant timbers harvested in the Oort cloud and the Kuiper Belt. In the fullness of time, our colonists on Rebirth will be harvesting lumber that's come to maturity in *their* Oort cloud."

"The fullness of time's already come to pass," Chu reminded him. "Six billion years of it. "The human race in that galaxy has long been supplanted by whatever evolution does to a species in six billion years."

"Yes, of course," Joorn said. "Forgive an old man. Time tends to run together at my age."

"On the other hand," Chu said, "the engineered trees, or whatever they've evolved into, have probably filled 3C-273 and all the galaxies in our supercluster by now."

"Our supercluster is—was—a hundred and fifty million light-years across," Nina said, showing off. "How could randomly drifting trees disperse through an area like that, even in six billion years?"

"Good question," Chu said. "The answer is that they didn't randomly drift. Your grandfather can tell you about that."

Joorn obliged. "They had light sails, and they had their plantlike volition," he said. "All plants are phototropic, each in its own fashion. The poplar trees that these immense growths were derived from were no exception. But, with an assist from the genetic engineers of the day, they could utilize parts of the electromagnetic spectrum that ordinary plants can't—from the long radio waves below the infrared to the x-rays and gamma rays at the top. It didn't kill them, because they had reflective leaves that bounced the dangerous stuff back and forth till it was usable. And more to the point, the tropisms that made this possible turned their leaves into little light sails to seek promising sources of light—including supernova flashes in nearby galaxies. Trees are patient. They could build up their acceleration through light pressure over periods of hundreds of years, maybe even attaining modest relativistic speeds."

Chu couldn't restrain himself. "Those early genetic engineers speculated that by the time of the Big Crunch—they believed in it then—Earth life in the form of those wandering trees could spread through the entire Universe."

"And that's not all," Joorn said. "Don't forget that all trees harbor commensal life—even those early moon-nurtured trees that first seeded the Oort cloud acquired it one way or another. You saw it on Rebirth and even in our little shipboard forest. Insects. The spiders that feed on insects. Moths—you can't escape them—and the bats that hunt moths. Tree snakes. Fungi of all types. Parasitic plants and symbiotic plants. Every tree has its own rich ecology, and the Bernal trees were in effect self-contained planetoids that provided water, nutrients, and the internal atmospheres that they manufactured for their own use out of cometary ice."

Joorn could see that Nina was getting caught up in the speculation. "And the people who harvested the trees in the Oort cloud must have lived there while they worked on them," she offered. "They would have brought plants and animals of their own."

"Good point, princess. The lumberjacks they sent out from Earth would have had to live there for years at a time while they trimmed branches and operated the sawmills that made the giant boards, and otherwise prepared to send their products sunward. And of course they would have had to be fed. That means cattle and other meat animals. Chickens and turkeys—"

"Little dinosaurs at first," Chu interjected.

"Of course that would have been hundreds of years after my time," Joorn said. "There's no telling what might have developed afterward. But even before I departed Earth, they'd begun to employ dolphins as safety engineers on space habitats to search out leaks and cracks with their sonar and such. And they're awfully good at holding their breath, aren't they? As a lumber industry grew in the Oort cloud and Kuiper Belt, there must have been a need for dolphins among the personnel."

"That's where I draw the line," Chu said good-naturedly. "Their sonar would be no good in a vacuum. And no matter how long they could learn to hold their breath, they have no legs. Out of their tanks, how would they get around?"

"Six million millennia of reverse evolution," Joorn retorted. "All cetaceans once were land animals, like hippos. They'd crawled out of the sea to become mammals, then, after some millions of years, crawled back and lost their legs. Did you know that whales have vestigial leg bones?"

Nina giggled. "Can you picture Jonah or Triton running around on legs? Wearing little booties? The two dolphin safety engineers were Martin's colleagues on his outside maintenance rounds, and Nina had become fast friends with them, even joining them in their tank for an occasional swim. Their ancestors would have populated Rebirth's seas long ago.

Chu shrugged. "We're getting a bit fanciful here. I'll grant you the bugs and spiders. We'll soon find out. We're well within the Oort cloud now, and that object in the viewscreen is within planetary distances. Let's have a closer look."

He fiddled with the banks of keys, and the jiggling image jumped in size as it sprang into sharper focus.

Nina gasped. It was a tree all right. Just like the pictures she'd seen of trees on Rebirth and vanished Earth, or the tamed thirty-footers in *Time's Beginning*'s forest compartment.

But not quite. It was a real tree, with the unmistakable natural shape of any plant responding to its environment. But it was designed to grow in the absence of gravity. It was almost perfectly symmetrical—two flattened spheres joined by a thick trunk, like a dumbbell. The green spheroid was the tree's crown. The balancing brownish spheroid, clutching an outmatched globe of dirty ice that had to be a comet, was the tree's root ball. But the root ball, too, was streaked with green—adventitious leaves that the tree had grown to take advantage of any quantum of electromagnetic energy that came its way.

"It's a rather conflicted tree, sweetheart," Joorn lectured. "It knows that it's supposed to respond to gravity by growing straight up. Our ancestors chose poplar trees for their experiments. They're fast-growing, and they grow straight—good for lumber. But the comets didn't give them much help. Their gravity's too feeble. The tree's strategy was to use its rotation as a growth guide. Centrifugal force is a good substitute for gravity, right? The trees rotate along their vertical axis, and those two oblate spheres respond by growing into matching symmetrical shapes."

Nina's face was glowing. "Grandfather!" she exclaimed.

"This is where a really, really dull subject like botany becomes an actual branch of astronomy!"

"Precisely, princess. Bear that in mind when you go back to class. Biologists are scientists too. And watch those puns."

"I wish Martin were here to see this," Nina said.

"He's getting a better view," Chu said. "Or will be. Hanging by his heels from one of the dolphin pods."

Some of the color drained from Nina's face. "Uncle Chu, you won't . . . "

"Don't worry, sweetheart. The Higgs drive will be turned off while Martin's working outside, the way it always is. We'll coast without gaining any gamma. What's a few hours out of a billion and a quarter years, right?"

"You mean losing, not gaining," Nina pointed out tartly. "We've been decelerating since midpoint."

"Touché, little genius," Chu said. "That's what I meant to say."

"We ought to be switching to the fusion drive soon anyway," Joorn said. "We're in the outer fringes of the Oort cloud now, but we'll be within planetary distances before you know it. We didn't come all this way to sterilize the planets of Sol and Alpha Centauri, assuming that some sort of bacterial life survived. And now, with these trees . . . "

"We don't want to sterilize the comets either," Chu finished for him. "I'm way ahead of you, Skipper. I've already warmed up the deuterium-helium-3 reaction, and it's on standby." He checked the figures unreeling on his screen. "And weren't we lucky that Rebirth's oceans turned out to be full of deuterium?"

"And that the deuterium-helium reaction turned out to

be a lot less lethal than deuterium-tritium fusion. What's our gamma now, Chu?"

"We're down to about one-tenth of the speed of light, Skipper. We're practically in real time now."

"All right. Keep track of our distance from that tree. I don't want to get any closer than twenty astronomical units with the Higgs drive still on."

"You've got it, Skipper," Chu said.

"What's happening, Uncle Chu?" Nina said.

"We're about to get a closer look, sweetheart," Chu said. He punched in further instructions, and the image bloomed again. You could see that the smooth ball of the crown was actually composed of individual branches.

Nina gasped. "What are those things like midges hovering over the edge of the green ball?" She squinted. "They look like they're sort of . . . *flapping*! Like bats."

"That's crazy, Nina," her grandfather said. "Nothing can fly in a vacuum."

"There! Look at that one down near the rim! It's after some kind of little speck that I can't make out! It is too! It's flapping!"

"We're about to find out, sweetheart," Chu said. His hands flew over the board. The deep thrum of the Higgs drive stopped abruptly. Weight disappeared, and Nina grabbed for her armrests.

Chu tapped at the keys again. Weight returned. "It's all yours, Skipper," Chu said. He turned to Nina. "Hang on to your hat, sweetheart," he said. "It's going to be a downhill ride."

CHAPTER 17

6,000,000,000 A.D.
The Oort Cloud

A small boy in a skinsuit that was too big for him threw an iceball at Torris as he headed for the cave mouth. He ducked without haste, and it missed him, but then two or three of the other children who were playing outside joined the sport. Another iceball grazed him, dangerously close to his airbag gasket, but by then the mothers were hauling their children back to keep them from becoming contaminated by Torris. Being Shunned meant not being noticed by other people at all, either for good or ill.

He shifted the towering load of firewood on his back for better balance. He was not banned from the communal fire, but nobody made way for him either. He'd also been lucky enough to snare a couple of fat stovebeasts, which were trying to escape from a sack dangling from his waist. Other than that, he hadn't had much luck on his foraging expedition: a few bark hoppers that would barely fill his stomach, a small pouch of thin syrup from a worn-out stretch of root that the tribe no longer bothered to tap, and some edible seed pods from the vegetation growing on the lower branches.

He could smell roasting meat as he made his way down the

main passageway, his helmet tilted back as he breathed the communal air. His mouth watered as he thought of the feast his father would be having at this hour. His father, particularly, made a point of avoiding him. He understood that, but it bothered him all the same. Neither Firstmother nor Secondmother would dare try to sneak food to him; it would be too dangerous. He understood that too.

A group of rowdy young men was blocking his way. They made no attempt to move aside for him, but some sneaked glances as he edged past them. He heard someone whisper "heretic," followed by a whispered reply about "a woman" that sounded envious.

They resumed the loud discussion they'd been having. They were talking excitedly about the coming bride raid and the approaching foreign Tree, speculating about when it would be close enough for Claz to give his approval. All of them were armed, and they were comparing weapons and boasting about their prowess.

He longed to tell them that the people of Ning's Tree were far more advanced than their own tribe and would probably prove to be formidable adversaries. The talk that would be generated by Ning's return would probably spur the young bloods there to launch their own bride raid sooner than Torris's tribe would dare risk it.

Torris wondered if Ning would be in the vanguard, if she would come looking for him, as a man might target a particular woman. He shook his head to rid himself of the insane thought. A thought as far from the natural order of things as wishing for a world without caves, where you could walk around on the surface and yet somehow breathe.

He pushed aside the translucent gut curtain that sealed the third of the three airlocks and stepped through into the communal chamber. Nobody noticed him at first; they were all gathered around the big central fire, busy eating, talking, minding the children, and jockeying for places closer to the warmth, so he was able to catch fragments of the evening's chitchat.

" . . . and this new star is bright enough to cast its own shadows. So it is clear that the Tree has created it as a fourth holy object to be worshipped and propitiated in its name. . . . "

"Nonsense, it's only a wandering star like those we've seen before, and one day it will be gone. It's not like our own stars that move, which never vary from their fixed courses, showing that they each have a holy purpose. . . . "

"Still, it moves. . . . "

"Not anymore," a new voice cut in. "It suddenly stood still in the sky five sleeps ago and changed its color. Now it grows brighter and brighter every day. . . . "

"I've been telling you, it's a Sign. . . . "

A few people had begun to notice him as he made his way across the cave. He was supposed to be treated as if he were invisible. As if he didn't exist. But people couldn't help themselves. The talk stopped, and an uneasy silence took its place. People unconsciously moved a little closer to one another, barring access to the fire. They studiously avoided looking at him. Torris was doing the same. He looked straight ahead, as if they were the ones who were invisible. But he couldn't avoid hearing the person who lost all self-control and burst out, "It's an omen, that's what it is! A Sign that we must propitiate the Tree by offering the heretic as a sacrifice."

There was a low muttering of agreement. "Cast him into the outer dark," someone said.

Torris tightened his lips. Claz had stopped short of that. The prescribed penalties for each degree of heresy had been passed down through the ages and were law.

He hurried his steps a little and escaped down the dank passageway, where he had found a cramped hollow to sleep in.

His little fire still flickered, sending greasy smoke into the corridor. He'd cooked his meager supper of bark hoppers on it and tethered the two captured stovebeasts nearby. He piled more wood on the fire and was debating with himself whether or not to sleep in his airsuit when a sodden sleep overtook him.

He woke in the middle of the night, hearing voices down the corridor coming closer. Angry voices.

They stopped outside his cubbyhole. A hand thrust aside the skin he'd hung to conserve heat and ripped it down. The small space was suddenly crowded with a half dozen men, all of them shouting at him.

They hauled him violently to his feet. A fist smashed into his mouth, catching him unawares. He only had time to think, *They can't do that; you're not supposed to touch a Shunned person.*

They hustled him down the passageway, handling him roughly. One of them was leading the way with a torch. Someone growled, "We're taking you to see Claz, murderer," and Torris, confused, could only think, *You're not supposed to talk to a Shunned person either.* His mouth was bleeding, and his head was spinning. He tried to wipe away the blood on his chin, but two young bruisers were pinning his arms.

He could recognize some of them now. They were all unattached young men of an age to band together for a bride raid. A couple of them were part of the same catechism class that had made the ill-fated Climb with him and Brank.

People usually slept at this hour, but the commotion had roused a couple handfuls of the curious. More people were straggling into the common chamber, staring after Torris as he was dragged toward Claz's cubicle.

Claz was waiting for them, along with two elders—Igg the lame Spearmaker and Cleb the Chronicler, Brank's father. All three of them were looking grim and bleary-eyed, as though they'd been roused from a sound sleep and weren't too happy about it. A few small objects were spread across the horizontal root Claz used for a table and bench: some scraps of quilted fabric from an airsuit, a bone toggle for fastening a helmet, and a glove. Claz was holding an arrow, and Torris could see that the arrowhead was flecked with dried blood.

"His skeleton was picked clean," Claz said without preamble, "but this was lodged between the ribs."

He held out the arrow as if it were something distasteful. Torris could see that it was his, one of the arrows that Claz had inscribed with a blessing for success in the Climb.

"What was left of him came to rest at the bottom of the Tree in the middle of the night. The body must have been caught in the branches many miles above, until the carrion creatures that were feeding on it finally dislodged it. It was Brank, no question about it."

He gestured at the scraps of airsuit fabric, and Torris could see that some of them were festooned with the colored beads that were Brank's trademark. Cleb made a wordless sound in his throat, but Claz ignored it.

"And this," Claz continued with naked fury, "is your arrow. No question about that either!"

Torris stood dumbstruck. There was nothing he could possibly say. One of the surly guardians who was holding him gave him an angry shake.

"If it hadn't been for Uz here," Claz was saying with a nod at Torris's captor, "the murder might never have been discovered." He'd mastered his anger, and now his tone was merely severe. "He happened to be wandering about in the middle of the night with his idle companions, for what purpose I don't know, and I will have a talk with them about that."

"We were just . . . " Uz started to mumble, but a glance from Claz silenced him.

"You are not needed here," Claz said. "Go."

Reluctantly, the two who were holding Torris released him and left with their friends. Claz stared at Torris for a long time in silence as if he were something strange and remarkable, like a two-headed tree snake. Finally he spoke one word.

"Why?"

Torris struggled to say something, but nothing would come out of his mouth. What was the point? He could tell them that Brank had been stalking him, but then he would have to tell them that Brank was stalking Ning too, and where would that lead? Nowhere. Or could he reveal Brank as a criminal who had violated every sacred precept when he stole another Climber's supplies and destroyed what he couldn't carry off? That Brank had attempted to kill a Dreamer freshly emerged from his calyx, when one of his judges was Brank's enraged father? Or try to explain that Brank was attempting to rape and kill an impious woman from another Tree? That wasn't even an offense. What did all that count against an arrow with his name on it in the rib cage of a murdered Climber?

Claz and the two elders whispered together in a corner for long minutes while Torris stood and stared at the ice walls with their network of root filaments. At last they turned and looked at him impersonally, the way one might regard a used-up stovebeast that had to be gotten rid of.

His knees went weak, but he managed to stay upright. Claz said sorrowfully, "I expected much from you, Torris. My disappointment is all the greater."

"Get on with it, Claz," Igg said impatiently, breaching protocol.

Claz thumped his staff on the ground twice. "You have committed an unspeakable murder," he said. "It is the will of the tribe that you be expelled from the Tree."

There were three days of purification rites. Torris was confined to his little cubbyhole, with two or three guards always stationed just outside, as much to keep impulsive people from getting at him as to keep him from getting out. His guards would not talk to him, but they'd talk at him when hostility and frustration got the better of them.

"I'd like to put my spear through you, unbeliever! Brank was a friend of mine."

"Shut up, Uz. Claz said not to talk to him. He's still Shunned."

"Igg said it too," Uz grumbled. "He told me he'd like to talk to him with his spear."

He was fed once a day, an undercooked haunch of meatbeast or a bone with enough scraps of flesh still on it to make a meager meal. He had to be kept alive until the day of his expulsion, he heard one guard explain to the other, so that his sacrifice could proceed properly and remove the stain of apostasy from the tribe. There were rules about that handed down from priest to priest since time out of mind.

They didn't bother to provide him with water; the cloudy drippings he was able to lick from the ice walls of his niche were considered to be sufficient to sustain him.

The traffic past his little cul-de-sac was uncommonly heavy for this little-used branch of a side tunnel. Everyone wanted to get a look at the heretic who was to be sacrificed, the first casting-out in years. The guards kept them moving, but Torris noticed that when Uz was on duty he tended to be lenient to those who had come to heap abuse on the heretic.

His father and his two mothers were not among those who filed past. His father's tenure as Facemaker would be shaky now, and a couple of likely aspirants for that position had already declared themselves—younger men whose qualifications Parn had always dismissed. He could not risk having Firstmother lose her self-control and attempt to speak to Torris as he hustled her past.

On the third day, they let him put his airsuit on and gave him a skin of air. He took the more robust of the two stovebeasts with him; it was near the end of its endurance now, but it would last long enough to see him through till his air gave out.

They prodded him with the butts of their spears and herded him down the corridor without speaking. The common cave was strangely deserted; they'd left some children behind to tend the central fire, but everybody else would be waiting out by the launch point to witness his expulsion.

It was the same low hillock that was traditionally used by departing bride raiders. There hadn't been an expulsion since Torris had been a small child. A lone flutterbeast was hovering motionless in the sky, too far away for arrows. It couldn't possibly know what was about to happen, but some instinct had brought it here, perhaps from its hunting ground at the crown of the Tree.

The ground was trampled for many man-lengths around the hillock, the packed snow turned into dirty ice by all the footprints. The hillock itself was barely a man-length in height, but it was the highest point around.

Torris's jailers hustled him forward. The crowd parted easily to let them through. If any of them was shouting imprecations at him, Torris couldn't hear it; all sound was damped by the eerie silence of Outside.

The scene was lit by the unnatural brightness of the new star, now brighter than either the red giant or the white dwarf. It hung motionless overhead, in the same spot where it had stopped abruptly a dozen sleeps ago, burning fiercely against the black sky. It was a frightening sight, and perhaps that was the reason the crowd seemed so subdued.

Torris tried to drag his feet, hoping to see his father and mothers somewhere in the crowd yet knowing that they wouldn't be there. His guards pushed him along relentlessly.

Two of the tribe's biggest men were waiting with a fur blanket at the crest of the hillock. Claz and the two elders were there too, but Claz didn't attempt to address the crowd in finger talk or no-air talk. He'd probably done that earlier.

He nodded at the blanket men, and they stretched it tightly between them. They held it as close to the ground as possible; there could be no swinging it back and forth in the low gravity to build up momentum.

Torris's captors pushed him down on the blanket, holding him down briefly to prevent him from bouncing. When all motion was stopped, they stepped back. Torris had a moment to contemplate the ominous new star overhead. He spotted the hovering flutterbeast, which seemed to have taken an interest in the proceedings. Then someone handed him an arrow. His hand closed unwillingly around it. It was the bloodstained arrow that had killed Brank. It was an unclean object and was to be sent into eternity with him. Torris lay there rigidly, and then someone gave him his bow, forcing his hand around it when he was slow in taking it. The bow was an unclean object too.

Claz nodded again. The blanket men gave a mighty heave, and Torris went sailing into space. He twisted his head to see the scene below, which was rapidly dwindling. He could not make out individual people anymore, just a circular muddle against the snow. He turned to locate the flutterbeast. It was moving now, spitting reaction mass to try to intercept him.

Then the new star suddenly winked out, and he was plunged into darkness.

CHAPTER 10

6,000,000,000 A.D.
The Oort Cloud

Okay, the drive's off," Chu said. "We're coasting. Don't worry, Nina. Your tree's safe. We're still a couple of astronomical units away from it. Let's have a look at your bat."

He zoomed in on the fluttering midge until it filled the screen, still blurry but its shape plainly visible.

"You're right, princess. It does sort of resemble a bat, but of course it's not flying. Those appendages that look like wings are just twitching reflexively. *There!* That's how it maneuvers in a vacuum! Did you see that little jerk when it changed trajectory? It somehow jettisoned a blob of reaction mass. What kind, I can't guess."

A gasp had escaped Joorn. "Life!" he breathed. "Some kind of animal life in naked space!"

"Let's have a look at what it's after," Chu said. He jiggled verniers on his board until he captured the other speck. This time they all gasped. Magnified, the speck had the unmistakable shape of a human being.

"How . . . " Joorn choked. "After six billion years! How could they survive as human beings? The early hominids came and went after only a few million years. After six *billion* years . . . "

"A space-dwelling hominid?" Chu suggested.

"He's a man," Nina said firmly. "And he's not adapted for space. At least not completely. He's wearing some kind of homemade spacesuit. It looks quilted, and I think I can see embroidery on it. And his helmet's not rigid—it's sort of like a hood, with a glassy mask. And that thing that looks like a bat is going to eat him."

They watched in horror as the winged creature adjusted its course several times to intersect the man's trajectory.

"He has nothing that he can use for reaction mass to throw, not even an air tank," Joorn said grimly.

"That thing on his back that looks something like a bagpipe must be where he gets his air," Chu said. "Very primitive."

"Isn't there something we can *do*?" Nina pleaded.

"Not from here, baby," Joorn said. "We're still planetary distances away."

"What's that he's holding?" Chu asked. "It looks like a stick. What the . . . He's bending it. It's a bow!"

The distance was too great for them to see the flight of the arrow, but there was a jolt that stopped the beast's motion as something invisible impacted it and sent it spinning. Gouts of what must have been blood spurted into space, contracting into a swarm of perfectly spherical globules that followed the twisting creature as it disappeared into the void.

"Well, he can take care of himself, but he can't breathe in a vacuum," Joorn said. "How long will it take till we get to him?"

The computer matched trajectories and velocities. Chu read

the answers off his board. "About six and a half hours, if his air holds out that long. There'll have to be a forty-five second burn at eight G's at the end. The ship can't take that, and neither can the passengers. We'll have to deploy one of the lifeboats. They can do an easy eight G's on a chemical burn."

Joorn started to get up. "I'll get Martin," he said. "We'll get a boat ready. Nina, you better find your mother. We're finally going to have work for an anthropologist. She'd never forgive me if she missed out on first contact."

Chu stopped him. "Stay where you are, Skipper. You're needed to take the helm. You can't do eight G's, and you know it. I'm two generations behind you and still as fit as an ox. Martin and I will take the boat. And Irina can wait here with you till we deliver her first specimen. Bringing an armed aborigine back might be dicey."

Joorn reluctantly acquiesced. "Don't take any chances, Chu. And that includes your last-minute burn. Irina can line up her assistants and figure out a first contact protocol. I think the best she was hoping for was some kind of surviving six-billion-year-old algae in the ruins of an asteroid settlement."

Chu closed out his board and got up. "Where will I find Martin?" he asked.

"He'll be with the dolphins," Joorn said. "They'll be getting into their excursion pods now that the drive's off. But the outside inspection can wait. I'll let them know."

"Okay," Chu said. "He's probably already in his spacesuit by now. Ring him up and tell him to meet me in the boat lock next to the dolphin pool." He hurried out, with a nod to the guards at the door.

Nina slid out of her chair. "I'll go find Mother."

Joorn was absorbed in his control panel and indicator displays. Without looking up he said, "Tell her she can watch the show from the observation deck. I'll have a larger-than-life feed going on there, and if Chu transmits any close-ups from the boat, I'll include those too."

Nina was already at the door. A guard opened it for her and said, "Do you want an escort, miss?"

"What for?" she said, and hurried off down the corridor.

[HAPTER 13

He was tumbling, with no way to stop it except to vent air, and he wasn't going to do that. Torris watched the stars swoop by in great circles—the two little sisters, the red stepsister, and a sprinkling of the lesser stars that ordinarily wheeled by in a stately circle that marked a full day. The red star looked different from out here in the void, away from the thin miasma provided by the Tree. He could see now that it was not merely a brilliant point of light like other stars but a tiny circle, and that frightened him.

The tumbling wasn't bad enough to make him dizzy. It had resulted from the fact that the arrow he had loosed was several hand spans above his center of mass. He hadn't wanted to risk trying to aim it from waist level. But the slight pooling of blood in his head and feet made him feel a little odd.

He could catch a glimpse of the Tree about twice a minute, every time his spin put him in the right position. It was tiny at this distance, like any other Tree he had seen growing out of a passing comet. He could see that Claz had been right; his world was actually a round ball that was dwarfed by the God-Tree that clutched it in its roots, and he could see that someday it would be consumed by the Tree's thirst. When that day arrived, the Tree would spread its reflective leaves and search out another comet to attach itself to, just as he had seen in his Dream when he himself had been the Tree. That thought frightened him too;

the world was not as solid and immutable as he had believed. No wonder the tribe needed a priest to make sense of things.

For the first time, he thought about what it would mean to cease to exist. The last of his air would run out in a few hours. The stovebeast, whose warmth he could feel at the small of his back, would outlast him for a while; they could do without air for longer than a man. Then it too would cease to exist, if it and other animals were at all aware of their own existence.

That thought was more dizzying than the spin. He felt more alone in the void than he had ever felt in his life. The sudden disappearance of the new star had indeed been a sign that was meant for him.

He got ready for another fleeting glimpse of the Tree, suddenly anxious to see it again. This time he could see an even tinier Tree beyond it that must be Ning's home. The young bucks on the two Trees must be in a frenzy by now, preparing for their respective bride raids. It was strange to think of so much life going on without him.

He must have dozed then. He was having strange dreams, almost like his Tree dream. Brank was in it, dead but somehow alive, and Ning, and his father, and Secondmother, holding out a bloodstained arrow and insisting that he take it. He woke, feeling muzzy. He didn't know how long he'd been asleep, but his air tasted stale, and his chest was heaving painfully as he tried to breathe.

He was still slowly spinning, the distant stars swinging around him. He could not see the Tree and its iceball anymore; they were lost in the depths of space. But the three familiar stars that had ruled his life were still there, undiminished, glinting off the clear resin of his faceplate as he turned.

When he saw another glint in the sky, like something reflecting the light of the three stars, he thought he was hallucinating.

A bonfire flared above him, the brightest fire he'd ever seen, and an impossibility in the airlessness of space. He cried out in terror, and in the span of a breath or two the fire disappeared, leaving him temporarily blinded.

As his vision returned, another impossibility happened. A long, sleek shape, like the biggest creature that ever could be, glided to a stop beside him. He had no word for it. It was no kind of animal, except perhaps one like the little shell creatures that crept up the trunk of the Tree munching fungus and leaving a trail of slime behind them.

As he watched, a square mouth opened in its side, an opening as big as a cave entrance. He tried vainly to stop his spin and face it and finally settled for slowing the spin down by stretching his arms upward as far as he could and extending his length. He increased the radius of the spin by holding his bow by one end and reaching upward with it. That slowed him enough so that he could keep an eye on the thing.

Two men floated out of the square mouth, trailing tethers behind them. At least they looked something like men, except that they were smaller, maybe only about two-thirds of Torris's length. They wore spacesuits that must have been made by a wondrous tailor; you couldn't see any stitching, and the fabric had a smooth continuous surface without any sign of quilting. They had no proper helmets or Faces—transparent globes enclosed their heads instead.

Torris reached reflexively for his quiver, then realized that he had no arrows, only his useless bow. But these peculiar little men had no bows or any other weapons that he could see.

He watched helplessly as they floated toward him, propelled by small handheld objects that emitted puffs that looked like frozen breath. They halted themselves on either side of him, trailing their tethers. Torris prepared himself for a struggle. Perhaps he could tear off those transparent globes.

Instead they reached out for him and, with the aid of the little propulsion devices, stopped his spin. One of them was trying to talk to him. Torris watched his lips closely but couldn't make any sense out of it. It was just gibberish. The man—if he was some sort of man—didn't seem to know how to speak no-air talk.

Then the two of them seemed to be talking to each other but without touching helmets. Their lips were moving, but it was just more gibberish. And they weren't particularly looking at each other's lips, so it couldn't be no-air talk anyway.

Nevertheless, they came to some sort of decision, took him gingerly by the elbows, and nudged him gently toward the square opening in their shell creature's side.

Now! This was the time to attack if he was going to defend himself at all. But it seemed pointless. There was nothing he could use to grip those smooth transparent globes, no way to pull them off. He had nothing sharp to puncture their suits with. And there was no way to strike a blow when you were weightless and you had nothing immovable to brace yourself against. The reaction would only propel these strange dwarfs to the ends of their tethers and send him drifting back to eternity. His air was almost gone anyway. Better to die quickly.

He said a prayer to the Tree as they carried him through the opening. Then he had a shock as the opening magically closed itself. He was in a small enclosed space that was somehow lit, though there was no torch, no fire, no opening that could let in light.

He had another surprise as the back wall slid aside and disappeared. He could tell, even with his suit on, that a rush of air had filled the space. The little men urged him forward, and the wall slid back behind them, sealing off the enclosed space.

He was in a larger space now, a place made of something that was neither wood nor stone nor animal hides. He understood that it was some sort of hut but one that was many times larger than the family lean-tos in his own tribe's cave. It was warm here, though there was no fire, and well lit, without any obvious light source.

In the middle of the floor was a sort of container, bigger than any bottle or jar he had ever seen, big enough, in fact, for several men to fit inside. Though these men were dwarfs, they had the utensils of giants.

They were taking the transparent bowls off their heads and, with smiles and gestures, urging him to do the same. He didn't hesitate; he could feel the warmth and air all around him, and his faceplate was starting to fog up.

The air was like no air he had ever breathed before—thick and heavy and full of strange smells. There were no cooking odors or wood smoke, no sweat or smell of unwashed feet, or any of the other odors of human habitation.

He looked more closely at his captors. One was a young man, about his own age, with black hair and the same blue eyes that were common in his own tribe, looking very human, in fact, despite his small stature. The other was an older man with thinning hair and dark humorous eyes whose shape was somewhat altered by a sort of fold in his eyelids.

Then the older man did something peculiar. He started talking his gibberish to the empty air, as though there were someone else in the room. More peculiar still, he acted as though he were listening to this nonexistent person answering him, even nodding as if in agreement. Then he repeated his gibberish to the younger man, who nodded back at him in turn.

The two of them then began talking earnestly to Torris with words and gestures, neither of which he understood. He began to understand when they pushed him toward the gigantic container. They wanted to show him something.

Torris towered over them. They hardly reached his chest. But they seemed to be very strong, and they were politely insistent, so he didn't resist.

The long container was lying on its side, but even so, Torris was the only one who was tall enough to look down on it. The first thing he saw was that it had a square opening covered by a transparent lid that looked like some huge faceplate. The next thing that struck him was that the container was filled with water—more water than Torris had ever seen in one place in his entire life. The lid slid back just as the wall in the airlock had done, and he could see something huge stirring in the water.

Torris jumped back in alarm as a large animal heaved itself up out of the water and supported itself on the rim of the opening with a pair of stubby limbs the way a human might rest on his elbows.

It was as big as a meatbeast but much more fearsome. It had a long tapering snout that was curved upward in the semblance of a smile and two dangerous-looking rows of serrated teeth. It looked as if it could easily bite off an arm or a leg and swallow it whole.

Then it amazed him by speaking.

It was more of the gibberish spoken by the men, but it was squeaky and high-pitched, like a child's voice. As it continued, its voice rose higher and higher, full of pops and whistles, until it could no longer be heard by human ears. The younger of the two men held up a hand to stop it, and it responded by diving to the bottom of its container. It surfaced a moment later wearing a sort of necklace with a round medallion made out of some sort of hard material like bone. When it resumed talking, its mouth moved as before, but its voice came out of the round medallion. This time its voice was lower in pitch, sounding more like the humans, and the pops and whistles were gone, replaced by long intervals when the medallion seemed to be speaking on its own.

The three of them were jabbering at him all at once, the men giving him little encouraging pushes. Then it dawned on Torris that they wanted him to get into the container with the beast. They wanted to feed him to the creature!

Torris backed away hastily. The men caught him and held him in place easily with their immense strength. They exchanged jabber, in obvious consternation, and the creature in the tank joined in, its voice getting squeaky again. It seemed upset about the globules of water that had escaped and were floating in the air. It emitted a final burst of agitated high-speed squeaks and submerged itself. The square lid slid back into place, sealing the creature inside.

The men looked at each other and exchanged shrugs. They let go of Torris and stood back, still within reach. Torris rubbed his arm where one of them had squeezed too hard and glared at them. The older dwarf disappeared through an opening into another part of the hut, but the younger one stayed by Torris's side. Torris stared warily at him, ready for anything.

A low rumbling sound filled the hut, and the floor began to vibrate. The dwarf who had stayed with Torris moved his feet apart and planted himself in a wide stance. After a moment Torris did the same.

He became aware that his weight was slowly increasing. In moments he weighed as much as he had ever weighed in his life—the ounces had pressed him down at the surface of the comet.

Incredibly his weight continued to increase. His legs began to ache, until at last they would no longer support him. He went tumbling helplessly, but the little man caught him before he hit the floor. In an easy movement, he picked Torris up as though he weighed nothing and started to carry him over to the water-filled vessel. Torris struggled but found that he had no strength because of the relentless increase of his weight. Even the dwarf was having trouble now. How he managed to stay upright, Torris could not understand.

The floating globules of water splashed to the ground along with a few small objects that had been carelessly placed. His bow, which he had been holding onto stubbornly, slipped out of his grasp and rattled against the floor. He was helpless as a baby, and he didn't care for the feeling.

As the dwarf staggered the last few feet to the vessel, its lid slid open and the animal popped up above its rim to regard them. The creature's long jaw was wide open, showing those frightening rows of sawteeth. The little man who was holding him reached up with one hand and deftly pulled Torris's helmet over his neck ring, where it snapped into place.

From some inexplicable reserve of strength, he heaved Torris over the rim of the opening and gave a final push that dumped him into the water. The lid, all by itself, slid closed and sealed him in with the creature.

But the huge jaws did not close around his head or an arm as he expected. Instead they were delicately manipulating rows of small protrusions under the water, then somehow nudging a tube into place in Torris's depleted air sack. All at once Torris was aware that he was breathing a fresh supply of air, air like he had never breathed before. There was no hint of staleness, no suggestion of all the scents that came from the air that gathered in the cave or that you tapped from the Tree's air pockets, nothing that made you sneeze or have itchy eyes. And it was unusually rich, so that you could breathe more slowly and still have the sensation that it was enough.

There was another effect of being submerged in water. It was almost like being weightless. He could move his limbs again, and though he was still aware of the unnatural mass he had gained, the terrible drag of the new gravity had been nullified.

He looked at the animal that shared the container with him. It had its head above water and seemed to be breathing normally—though through a single nostril on the top of its head! It was a strange sight. He had never seen a large animal breathe before. They all got their air from the Tree, each in their own way, and then could stay out on the branches for as much as half a day to graze or hunt. Except some of the web beasts. Some of them could spin silk cocoons around themselves and stay in vacuum for days at a time.

The animal was studying him too. There was almost a human intelligence in its eyes. It squeaked at him as though it were actually talking. It dawned on him that he could take off his helmet and breathe if he kept his head above water, then submerge himself again when the new gravity got to be too much for him.

The older dwarf who had those queer folds in his eyelids came back from wherever he had been. He climbed several crossbars attached to the side of the water vessel and stared down at Torris through the transparent lid without saying anything. Then he climbed down and conferred briefly with the young dwarf.

Torris could see him through a small round window that would have made a good faceplate for one of Parn's customers. He was laughing.

He turned his head toward the far wall and began talking to the air again.

CHAPTER 20

"I've got another message coming through from Chu," Alten said. "He's a couple of light-hours closer than he was the last time, and he's accelerating at a steady one G."

Joorn looked up from his control board. "What did he say about their passenger?"

"They got him inboard without much resistance. They had to put him in the dolphin tank with Jonah. He couldn't even take the one G."

"That'll be a problem. He'll be okay while we're coasting, but we've got a lot more deceleration to do before we get into the inner system. And then, of course, we'll have to put the ship under spin. We can't function for extended periods under null G."

"We'll worry about that later. He'll either have to live with the dolphins or we can fix him up with facilities at the axis. Damned inconvenient!"

"If he lived on that comet, he's adapted to null G, or close to it."

"Chu says he's about twelve feet tall and probably wouldn't weigh more than a hundred pounds in Earth gravity. Elongated limbs and prehensile toes, from the look of his boots. He's evolved after six billion years. But his equipment is primitive—bow and arrow, no metal of any kind, with fittings carved from some kind of animal bone, a hand-sewn spacesuit made out of some kind of animal gut. About what you'd expect of a Cro-Magnon, if they'd had to survive in space. How he heats the spacesuit is a mystery. We'll have to get him out of it to find out."

"Irina and her team will have their work cut out for them."

Alten frowned. "Speaking of Irina, I haven't heard from her. Nina should have been with her by now."

"Hold on. I'll put you through to her. There, you've got a private channel."

Joorn went back to his piloting. Alten spoke in subdued tones to his communicator. Finally he looked up, concern showing on his face.

"She never showed up. She should have been there long before now. That's not like Nina. She doesn't get distracted. She wanted to be with her mother when our visitor arrived."

There was a sudden crackle of background noise from the speaker. The private channel had somehow been breached. Joorn froze as Miles Oliver's supercilious voice filled the control room.

"Worried about your precious daughter, Alten? She's with me. You'll get her back if you and your doting father do exactly as I say."

The background noise resolved itself into a muffled babble of men's voices. Nina came through faintly. "Don't listen to him, Father! He's crazy!" Then she was cut off.

Alten exploded in a sudden blind rage. "Oliver, what have you done? I promise you that if you—"

"Shut up, bright boy! Or are you bright enough to realize what's at stake?"

Joorn cut in. "What do you want, Oliver?"

"Ah, our eminent captain speaks. You know what we want, Captain. We want you to turn the ship over to us. We've reinforced our numbers with recruits from a new generation, and we haven't forgotten our pursuit of man's greatest adventure."

"Is Professor Karn in on this?"

There was the briefest of pauses. "The professor will come around. You're lucky to have him on your side. He'll see that you and your followers get a habitat or two. They have reentry capability. We're already on the fringes of the inner system, and our gamma is down to a point where the habitats can manage to deorbit on their own. You ought to be able to find someplace to light."

"My granddaughter is right, Oliver. You're crazy. Sol's already expanded past Earth's orbit and might take another million years to shrink. We don't know what's left in the Sol system. You might be condemning a whole human population to death."

Oliver gave a nasty laugh. "Your boy Alten's the genius. He ought to be able to figure something out."

"What's the hurry, Oliver?" Joorn's voice was strained with the effort to sound reasonable. "You waited till now to make your move. It will take years to get all that gamma back. Why not give us time to explore the Sol and Centauri systems, especially since they're joined at the hip now?"

"And give you and your cronies a chance to put us under house arrest for another twenty years? No deal. Now's our hour, and we're not letting it slip away from us this time."

Alten broke in, his voice shaky. "We can talk this over. Where are you holding Nina?"

There was that unpleasant laugh again. "We've just finished

talking it over. The clock is ticking for Nina. Don't take too long to decide, bright boy. We'll be in touch." There was dead silence as the circuit was broken.

Alten turned to Joorn, his face a study in anguish. "What do we do now, Father?"

"First off, we stall Oliver till we get Chu and Martin back. The minute Oliver starts building up gamma again, we lose our ability to rendezvous with the lifeboat. Oliver's perfectly capable of letting them die in space."

"But what about Nina?" Alten cried hoarsely.

"They had to have abducted her somewhere between the control room and the observation gallery. That's a finite distance. And then they would have had to take her somewhere nearby. Some uninhabited nook where they wouldn't be seen."

"She was worried about Martin. She would have passed the staircase leading to the dolphin level. She might have taken a detour to wish him luck before he left."

Joorn called one of the guards over. The man's face was white with shock.

"You heard, Talbot?" Joorn said.

Talbot nodded.

"I want you to find Ryan. *Don't* use your communicator under any circumstances. Do you understand?"

"Yes, sir."

"Tell him what happened. Tell him the war with Karn's on again and to take a large search party to scour the area surrounding the dolphin lagoon—both levels. And tell him to post more guards outside the control room."

"I don't like to leave you alone, Skipper . . . "

"Get going. Oliver isn't going to try anything here for the

time being. He doesn't have enough men, or he wouldn't have tried this fool stunt with my granddaughter."

"Yes, sir!" Talbot fell all over himself getting to the door. He exchanged a few words with the other inside guard and hurriedly left. The door clicked as it locked itself behind him.

"What now?" Alten said.

Joorn busied himself at the control board. "I'm going to talk to Chu." At a look from Alten, he added, "Don't worry. It won't go through the ship's com traffic. It'll be direct laser. No way Oliver can intercept it. Chu should receive it in about three hours."

"Then what?"

"Then I put on the brakes. Hard. Without making a general announcement first. That ought to throw Oliver off-balance. By that point, Chu will have finished accelerating. He'll be motionless in relation to *Time's Beginning*. He can dock with his chemical jets. We'll all be essentially in null G."

"And they'll be home safe then."

"Yes. Our stringbean visitor included."

"Ryan will need to be told."

"He will be."

[HAPTER 21

The bastard!" Martin said.

"We all knew that," Chu said.

"I'd have believed it of Oliver," Martin said, "but not of Professor Karn."

"You weren't born yet when the mutiny happened," Chu said. "Karn deceived us all."

Martin clenched his fists. "If they've hurt Nina, I'll kill them!"

Chu shot him a warning look. "Keep it down, Martin. Our friend will think you're talking about him."

Martin looked over at the strange being they'd rescued. He'd been out of the dolphin pod for about an hour now. He seemed to have gotten along fine with Jonah, and Chu and Martin had come as far as exchanging names with him, though the squeaks and whistles that constituted Jonah's dolphin name were beyond any of them. Currently he was sitting cross-legged on the floor in front of a worktable that he was happily taking apart. It was a spidery pose that put the knees of his long legs at approximately the same level as his shoulders. The floor was littered with things he'd dismantled. Now he was industriously unscrewing the pipestem legs of the worktable.

"Hell on the furniture, isn't he?" Chu said.

"He's curious," Martin said. "He's never seen things made

of metal before, and he wants to see how they're put together. Now he's learning about screw threads." He paused thoughtfully. "Though you can carve spiral threads out of wood or bone, can't you? I wonder how they fastened their arrowheads. Didn't the Cro-Magnons—"

Chu laughed uneasily. "Forget it, Martin. He's not planning to massacre us. We're his friends now, Jonah included. He's a fast learner."

"We can get him to the dolphin pool while the drive's still off," Martin said. "Then we'll have to figure something out. We can't keep the ship in free fall forever."

"Your mother and her anthropology cohorts will have to get used to doing their interviews in the dolphin pool, that's all."

Martin was tightening his fists again. "The question is: What are we going to do about Nina?"

"*We* can't do anything. That's Ryan's job. Maybe he'll have it wound up by the time we get there. If not . . . "

"What?"

Chu became thoughtful. "Oliver will be able to tap into the feed in the observation gallery, won't he? He'll already have seen the transmission I sent when we picked up Mr. Longlegs and when we got him into the dolphin pod with Jonah. When I send the next installment, I can fudge our ETA by a half hour or so. Your grandfather will know the truth because he'll be coordinating the docking. But the hoi polloi on the observation deck won't know until the gravity goes off without warning. And neither will Oliver. Maybe he'll do something stupid."

"Like what?"

"Like showing himself to Ryan."

The elongated man had finished unscrewing the table legs

and placing them carefully beside himself. Now he was holding up the transparent tabletop and inspecting the screw holes. He looked over at Chu and Martin and said something unintelligible in a questioning tone.

"Get your camera," Martin said.

Nina landed a healthy kick on the shin of one of the men holding her and caught him by surprise. He cried out in pain and dropped her arm. She quickly pulled free of the other man, whose grip had finally grown slack, and made a run for the door.

She got about five feet before one of the awful men in the room caught her and roughly dragged her back to her captors. The man she had kicked looked her over, then unexpectedly slapped her in the face. "Little bitch!" he growled.

It was the first time in her life that anyone had hit her. People just didn't do such things, not in her world. For the first few moments, the shock and surprise kept her from getting angry, then the hot rage she had felt when she had first been abducted came back. She got that under control quickly, telling herself that the important thing was to figure out a way to get even. No, she corrected herself, the first thing was to somehow get away. Then her father and grandfather would get even for her.

What made it worse was that she knew a dozen or more of the men in the room—or at least knew who they were. She had seen them in Professor Karn's physics class. They were friends or sidekicks of Professor Karn's special protégé, Miles Oliver. And that made it twice as bad. Oliver knew her well enough to call her by name. They had even exchanged a few words from time to time.

Stop it, she scolded herself. Concentrate on getting out of this.

Her prospects didn't look good. She was in an enormous storeroom somewhere above the dolphin lagoon, near the huge airlocks meant for the habitat's landing craft. The place was crammed with work benches and tool lockers. These renegade men had broken into the tool lockers, helping themselves to anything that could be used as a weapon. Looking around, she saw hammers, lengths of pipe, monkey wrenches, pry bars, and, scariest of all, things like electric drills, reciprocating saws, and nail guns. Things that could only be used to hurt people, even kill them. What kind of men would do that?

She counted them again. If she ever got free, she could at least report on their numbers. There were between fifty-five and sixty; it was hard to be sure, the way they kept moving around. She couldn't understand how they hoped to take over the ship with so few.

Miles Oliver came over to talk to her captors. He had armed himself with a nail gun. Nina shuddered. She was familiar with the tools used by the maintenance crews that Martin worked with. The nail guns were small but powerful with a range of twenty feet or more if a workman's hand slipped and it fired into the air.

She let him see that she wasn't afraid. "Didn't you see this man hit me? Aren't you going to say something?"

He glanced at her indifferently. "That's what you get for being a bad little girl. You'll get worse if you misbehave again."

"It's you who's going to get worse. I'm going to tell Professor Karn what you've done."

He looked as if he were going to say something, then stopped. He turned to the man who was holding her. "Find some rope, will you, Pfyfe? We'd better tie her to a chair. You better gag her too."

He turned away to talk to someone else. She fought back tears of rage as Pfyfe tied her to the chair and stuffed an oily rag into her mouth. She wasn't going to let him think she was crying.

They were still traveling at thousands of miles an hour, but so was the lifeboat. Joorn kept his eyes on the viewscreen. They seemed to be closing the gap at a snail's pace. The lifeboat was only a few miles away now.

"Here we go," Joorn said.

He reached for the cord hanging overhead and yanked sharply. A klaxon blared deafeningly, a sound that was repeated throughout the ship. Joorn waited exactly ten seconds. "That should be time enough to prevent any broken bones," he murmured, and punched the Execute Program button. He settled back in his seat. Within another ten seconds, he was totally weightless.

Ryan's lieutenant, Grier, floated over. "That ought to flush them out, Captain. They won't know what's happening."

Alten was hovering about a foot above his seat, steadying himself with one hand to keep from rising farther. "Is there any word?" he asked.

"I'm afraid not," Grier said. "There are all sorts of nooks and byways in that sector but no living quarters, so it's usually pretty deserted. Of course I'm getting my information from runners, so it's anybody's guess what might have transpired in the last fifteen or twenty minutes." He grimaced. "It's awkward not being able to use my communicator. This must have been what it was like to fight a battle in the Middle Ages."

Alten came all the way up and braced his hand against his chair to aim himself at the door.

"I'm going down to see what's what."

"Ryan has about a hundred men in the search party, Professor," Grier said. "They're searching on a grid. You'll only get in the way."

"I don't care," Alten said. He sailed in a flat trajectory to the door, nodded to the half dozen guards Ryan had sent up, and let himself out.

"I don't like it," Grier said to Joorn. "If he blunders into them on his own, we could have two hostages instead of one."

"Man, I'd go too if I didn't have to stay with the controls," Joorn said.

"I'm sorry, sir," Grier said. "You're right, of course."

CHAPTER 22

Chu watched through the lifeboat's main viewport as *Time's Beginning* flashed by and came to a dead stop less than a mile away. Of course they both were traveling at tens of thousands of miles an hour, but they were almost motionless in respect to each other.

"Nice," he said. "Your grandfather lined us up with the boat lock adjacent to the dolphin lagoon."

All four of them, if you counted Jonah, were standing in front of the viewport. Actually, Jonah was floating in water. He'd moved his travel pod forward on its little powered wheels and was watching through its side port. He'd shut the big transparent lid to prevent spillage. There was just enough microgravity to allow the wheels sporadic contact, though there was a lot of unintended bouncing.

Torris—they knew his name now—was standing with his mouth agape, staring at the long, complicated shape that had taken so many minutes to pass by with its distal end still not in sight.

"It's the biggest thing he's ever seen," young Martin said. "I wonder what he thinks it is."

"It's a world to him," Chu said. "Bigger than his own comet and not made of ice. I don't think he can grasp that it's an artifact."

"And home to a quarter-million humans," came Jonah's computer-adjusted voice. "He'll adapt to it. We dolphins did."

A rectangle had yawned open in a bulge in the hull opposite, and Chu nudged the lifeboat sideways toward it with his attitude jets. "Your grandfather has us in his sights," Chu said. "There's not supposed to be any talk between us. Oliver's tapped into the ship's com."

"He'll feel the bump."

"There won't be a bump."

"There'll be *something*. You can always tell when a boat docks."

"It'll be too late for him to do anything about it."

The boat floated into its berth, and the airlock closed behind it. A groan of contracting metal came through the hull as the airlock filled with warm air.

"Okay everybody," Chu said. "Jack be nimble, Jack be quick!"

Torris couldn't have understood what he was saying, but he must have understood the urgent tone of voice and their body language as they turned toward the lock. He hastily pulled his helmet down and sealed his faceplate in place. He wasn't taking any chances. As far as he knew there was nothing in the boat's airlock except the vacuum of space.

"You don't have to—" Chu began, then gave up. "Oh, the hell with it!"

Martin was laughing. Torris was making frantic signs to the two of them to put their own helmets on. He must have thought they were stupid or crazy.

"It's all right," Martin told their beanpole passenger, and something in his own gestures must have gotten through, because Torris desisted. But he still kept his helmet on, just in case.

They headed for the airlock, with Jonah's rolling travel pod in the lead. On the way, Torris stopped to pick up his little bundle of table legs.

"He's not going to leave his souvenirs behind," Chu said.

There was no crew in the ship's lock to receive them as there ordinarily would have been. The empty chamber echoed with their shuffling passage and the rattle of Jonah's caster-like wheels on the metal floor. They waited until they were sure the pressure was equalized, then stepped through into an empty corridor.

Torris halted in his tracks, quite obviously amazed at the warmth and what to him must have been the thickness of the ship's air. He turned to Chu and Martin and made questioning noises in his own language.

"Yes, I know. It's a strange new world," Chu said. "And it's going to get even stranger to you."

They proceeded down the passageway in their low-gravity shuffle, with Torris continually getting ahead of them; he'd had a lifetime of practice in an environment where a misstep might mean death.

"There's a junction with the main corridor just ahead," Chu said to Martin. "According to your grandfather, this is the route Nina would have taken if she were taking a detour to see you."

Jonah's travel pod bumped the door open for them, and they followed it into the corridor just in time to see a door about a hundred feet ahead burst open and a noisy rabble of men pour through. They were armed with knives, sledgehammers, metal pipes, wrenches—anything you could think of.

"Oh Christ, is our timing good or isn't it?" Chu said. "Where the hell is Ryan?"

The men stopped as they saw Chu's party. They milled about uncertainly, not knowing what to make of the spindly twelve-foot figure in the primitive spacesuit. One of them pushed forward, shoving a small figure with her hands bound behind her in front of him. He was holding something with a pistol grip to her head. It looked like an automatic nail gun.

"It's Oliver! He's got Nina!" Martin cried, and started to run toward them. He forgot his absence of weight and bounced off the ceiling, flailing helplessly.

"Stay where you are, Martin boy, if you know what's good for your little sister!" Oliver said. "That goes for you too, Chu, and the fish tank. We're all going up to the control room."

"You're crazy, Oliver," Chu said. "You'll never get away with it. By now the captain will have the bridge guarded by half the security force."

"They won't do a thing, Mr. First Officer. Not when they see what we've got." Oliver prodded Nina in the head with the nail gun, and she gasped. Oliver laughed nastily. "And the captain will give the orders himself to keep hands off."

Torris was standing frozen, obviously bewildered, a frail towering figure holding a toy bow. Oliver glanced at him dismissively. "I don't know what you've got there, but we'll take it with us."

At that moment, Nina stomped on Oliver's instep, hard. He gave a cry of surprise and pain, and Nina dropped to the floor before he could regain his grip on her.

Without the slightest hesitation, Torris drew one of the pencil-thin table legs from the bundle tucked under his arm, fit it to his little bow, and let it fly. It caught Oliver in the throat, and the nail gun went flying. The force of the impact lifted Oliver off his feet and pinned him to the corridor wall.

Before anyone could react, Torris sent another table leg through the man who had been standing beside Oliver. The man stared stupidly at the thing sticking out of his chest. Dead or dying, he was flung back to crash into the knot of men behind him.

Now Torris seemed to consider whom to shoot next. He chose a man with a knife who had made the mistake of taking a step toward Nina. The slim metal rod caught him precisely in the center of the forehead as Nina rolled away from him.

There was no surge toward Chu's party. Oliver had been the only one of them who had a weapon that could kill at a distance. They broke into a panic and started to flee toward a corridor exit in the opposite direction. Torris sent the last of his metal shafts after them. It caught the rearmost runner between the shoulder blades.

Before the escaping mob could reach the exit door, it opened and a swarm of men wearing cloth brassards around their upper arms spilled into the corridor.

"Ryan!" Chu said. "Talk about timing!"

Martin was bending over Nina with the knife the dead man had dropped, sawing through Nina's bonds. Torris was looking down at them, not saying anything but eyeing the knife longingly. The ropes parted, and Martin raised his head and saw him standing there.

"All right, my skinny friend," he said, reaching up to hand Torris the knife. "I guess you've earned it."

Ryan's men were outnumbered two to one by Oliver's

demoralized band, but they were rounding them up without encountering any resistance. Ryan himself, wearing one of the security brassards, walked over to where Oliver's body was pinned to the wall and said, "Jesus!"

Martin helped Nina to her feet. She was shaky now that it was over but exhibiting admirable self-control.

"Where's Karn?" he said.

"I don't know," she said. "I didn't see him."

Ryan joined them. "We're still looking for him," he said. He glanced cautiously at Torris. "Is that what the human race looks like now?"

"I wouldn't try to take that bow away from him," Martin said.

"It was amazing," Nina said. "When I got away from that awful man for a minute, he had about two seconds to figure out what was happening. But he didn't hesitate at all. If he had, I'd be dead."

She glanced with a shudder over to where the corridor wall had been stitched with nails when Oliver had dropped the nail gun.

"He had to choose sides," Ryan said. "He decided Martin and Chu were the good guys."

"Don't forget about me," said a computer-generated voice from the dolphin tank.

Nina ran over to the tall figure and impulsively threw her arms around his hips. Her head just about came up to his waist.

"Oh, thank you, thank you, whatever your name is!" she said.

"It's Tor-ris," Jonah's enhanced voice supplied.

Torris, for all his strangeness, reacted the way any human male would. He looked unmistakably embarrassed and uncomfortable. He tentatively reached out to pat her head but thought better of it and jerked the hand back as if it were about to get burned.

Nina clung for a moment, then let go. "I'd better find Mother. She must be terribly worried. She was waiting on the observation deck with her graduate student, Laurel, for me to give them my account of the first sighting."

"Father will be worried too," Martin said.

"Tell him I'm all right."

She waltzed out, giving a wide berth to the swarms of security volunteers who were cuffing the prisoners and lining them against the wall. Ryan did not try to stop her.

"We'd better get him to the dolphin pool right away," Chu said. "I don't know when we're going to regain weight."

[CHAPTER 23]

"So he's safely ensconced with our finny friends?" Joorn said.

"Yes," Chu said. "Along with Irina and her graduate student, Laurel. And two extremely earnest young women and a rather excitable young man who've decided they've found their life's work. Irina says we're going to have to revamp our entire educational system to accommodate those who want to change their fields of study."

"They'll have their work cut out for them," Joorn agreed.

"She says we'll need anthropologists, linguists, archaeologists, paleontologists, ethnologists, and probably a host of disciplines for which names haven't been invented yet."

Alten, pausing as he rose to relinquish the first officer's seat to Chu, nodded. "Yes, and not just the descriptive sciences. Let's not forget a few other fields of inquiry that have suddenly become terribly important. Things like cosmological physics, planetary nebulae, and stellar evolution. Exactly how long before a red giant with the remaining mass of our Sol uses up the last of its remaining helium, and so forth."

"You'll have to argue it out with Irina. I wouldn't touch that 'descriptive sciences' crack with a ten-foot polemic."

"I got that one from Nina. She uses it a lot in her arguments with Irina about her future career."

"Well you better brace yourself. She's getting awfully interested in those so-called 'descriptive sciences.' You may lose your daughter to her mother's disciplines."

"All right with me." Alten got out of the way as Chu took his seat at the controls.

"By the way, Nina is still down there with them," Chu said. "She and Torris seem to be making progress understanding each other."

"Ear," Torris repeated. "Mouth," he said, tapping each in turn. He was floating on his back, half-submerged, in the medium he now knew was called *water* in the dwarfs' language. They seemed to have only one word for it, not the many words used in his own language to describe its various aspects.

The young girl he had saved with his makeshift arrow nodded vigorously. She urged him on with a smile of approval and sat back waiting.

He thought for a moment, then told her the equivalent words—first in the exaggerated lip movements of no-air talk, and then, when she didn't respond, out loud. He'd tried finger talk, but that was a total failure. Her people seemed to be used to always having air to speak in.

Her name was Nina. He'd practiced till he could pronounce it to her satisfaction. It was hard to judge her age. He hadn't decided how much of her small stature was because she belonged to a race of chunky dwarfs. But he could tell that she was still a child, several years younger than Secondmother, despite the fact that she seemed to be on an equal footing with the grown-ups who were examining him and jabbering away in their incomprehensible language.

One of them, a young woman, was talking now, pointing at him and sounding excited. These people talked more to one another than they attempted to talk with him. In some ways, it was easier to communicate with Jonah, whom he now knew was not a beast but a person despite his form.

His real name was not Jonah but a string of whistles, which Torris was able to imitate—albeit an octave or two lower—to Jonah's evident approval. Jonah was wearing the necklace with the talking medallion, and he only had to hear a word once to get it right from then on. About a dozen of Jonah's water-dwelling tribe were splashing about nearby, whistling back and forth, but Torris hadn't been able to identify any other names yet.

Now Nina was talking to the group of adults, showing them the marks she had made on something that looked like a square of flat resin, almost like a Face. They all had something to say about it, and they kept glancing over at Torris. Then Torris's stovebeast waddled over on its stubby limbs, looking for someone to attach itself to. They all shrank from it except for one woman who had the same hair and eyes as Nina. But Nina reached out to pat the furry little beast, forgetting how hot it was, and snatched her hand back before touching it again. The stovebeast pressed against her, recognizing her. Nina was the one who had taken charge of it when they'd first arrived in this enormous cave with its unthinkable expanse of water. She'd fed it fragments of something that must have been a form of meat because the stovebeast lapped it up eagerly. Torris was relieved; it hadn't been fed for some time and he didn't know when he'd need the little creature again. This Nina, he decided, had a good heart—*warm hands* in his tribe's idiom. Torris wondered how you'd say that in their language.

The huge cave had been filling up with people, many times more of them than there were in Torris's entire tribe. They kept their distance and just stared, chattering among themselves. Then something unimaginable happened. A huge disembodied voice spoke, seemingly from the roof of the cave. Torris didn't know what it was saying, but it had the even tones of unquestioned authority, like a priest delivering dogma.

All the chattering people began looking for something to hold on to. The waterbeasts, Jonah's friends, became suddenly alert. They'd been restrained in their play, trying—though not always successfully—to avoid breaking the surface tension of the water. Now they seemed expectant and a little careless. One of them leaped ten feet into the air, drawing a huge blob of water with it.

Then, like magic, Torris suddenly felt the return of the crippling weight he'd experienced in the little traveling cave with Chu and Martin.

He grabbed the basin rim he'd been leaning on and let the water support him, the way it had when he'd been in that weird rolling container with Jonah, a container he now realized was a sort of spacesuit for Jonah, with arms and grasping fingers that Jonah could operate from inside.

All across the expanse of the now-flat lagoon, the myriad little gouts of water that Jonah's friends had inadvertently stirred up and sometimes caused to detach and float in the air, collapsed and pelted down on the surface. The huge globule that had risen to the ceiling of the cave with the swimmer still in it dropped abruptly and deposited its accidental passenger with a splash. Torris could tell from the chirps and whistles that the others thought that was funny. They'd begun some kind of a game, splashing and leaping clear out of the water, now that it was safe to do so.

The enormous splash had soaked Torris's interrogators, who had leaped back in dismay, dabbing futilely at themselves, except for Nina and the woman who looked as if she might be Nina's mother. They thought it was funny too, and they both were laughing. Nina turned to Torris and said something, smiling mischievously. He didn't understand the words, but he smiled back out of politeness.

Then Nina got to her feet, wrung out the loose folds of her garment as best she could, and exchanged a few words with her mother. Her mother nodded. Nina turned to Torris and with words and gestures made him understand that she had to leave but would be back.

He watched her thread her way through the crowd of spectators, moving carelessly in the strange way these odd little people had of walking, clumping along as though their feet were glued to the ground at each step.

The other interrogators were crowding forward again with their unintelligible questions, but he ignored them for the moment and submerged himself up to his neck to relieve his unnatural weight. Jonah nudged him underwater, and he patted him absentmindedly on his snout and got another nudge back. It occurred to him that he had more in common with Jonah and his tribe than with these two-legged creatures who looked like people but could move about freely out of the water.

Except for little Nina. He had the beginnings of human language in common with her. He furrowed his brow, trying to remember one of the phrases she'd used several times in parting, to fix it in his new vocabulary.

Whatever it meant, he could tell that it signified a casual farewell, not the formal goodbye that in Torris's language meant a long separation.

Jonah seemed to know what he was thinking. Or perhaps he'd figured it out from the experimental sounds Torris was mumbling to himself. He lifted his head above water and squeaked in a recognizable if high-pitched imitation of human speech: "Bye now, Torris. See you later."

"Well what have you learned so far, young lady?" Joorn asked. He was lounging in the row of supernumeraries' seats, taking his ease now that Chu had taken the con and Alten had replaced him in the first officer's chair.

"He's really bright, Grandfather," Nina said enthusiastically. "It's only been a couple of hours, but he's already learned over a dozen words and tried to teach me the equivalents in his own language, complete with a lot of context I don't understand yet and a lot of gestures and body language that I do."

"How is it that you've taken the lead among all those professionals and budding graduate students your mother's brought into it?"

Nina blushed. "They're just getting started, Grandfather. I'm sort of the icebreaker. Torris is only comfortable talking to me so far. He thinks he has some sort of connection to me because he saved my life. I gather that among his people that implies some kind of mutual obligation."

"He must be a Confucian, then, mustn't he?" Chu said, looking up from the controls with a smile. "When you save someone's life, you're responsible for that person from then on."

"Jonah's been a big help," Nina said earnestly. "He's been recording everything and feeding it into a sort of three-way dolphin dictionary. His 'Rosetta' file, whatever that means. And Torris has been amazing. I think he knows more words in Delphinese than he does in English. You should hear him and Jonah chirping away to each other. I think he also feels some sort of connection to Jonah, maybe because he spent so much time in that tank with him."

"Martin can help too, when he gets off his shift after we're steady on course," Chu said. "We got a bit of a head start with Jonah in the lifeboat. Of course we're just engineering stiffs, not linguists."

"Laurel's already starting to make progress," Nina said, steadfastly defending the ad hoc forensic team. "She's specializing in ethnology, you know. Even with so little to go on, she says she sees similarities with the customs of some primitive tribes on old Earth. Torris climbing to the top of his comet's Tree, for instance. He told me very eloquently about it in pantomime and then mimicked going to sleep by resting his face on his hands and closing his eyes. Laurel says that the Australian Aborigines used to have a coming-of-age ritual called a 'walkabout,' where they wandered in the desert and didn't come back until they'd had some sort of mystic dream."

"Isn't that stretching it a bit, sweetheart?" Alten said from the second seat.

"Oh, Daddy, you're so . . . so *unimaginative* when it comes to Mother's field!" Nina said. Alten raised an eyebrow but had the good sense to say nothing.

Undeterred, Nina went on: "And then there was Andrew . . . "

"Andrew?" Joorn said, raising an eyebrow of his own.

Nina blushed again. "Andrew Nordraak. He's a little older than me . . . well, a lot older, but he's very nice. He's studying to be a paleoanthropologist, you know, the study of prehuman hominids, millions of years before man, like *Australopithecus afarensis* and *aethiopicus*."

"*Australopithecus*? *Aethiopicus*?"

Nina became defensive. "Well, it's very interesting, at least when Andrew explains it. He says that Torris's divergence from our kind couldn't possibly be the product of six billion years of evolution. It took only a few *million* years for the first hominids to evolve from an apelike ancestor. And only a few hundred *thousand* years for *Homo sapiens* and the Neanderthals to develop from *Homo erectus*. He said he'd be willing to bet that less than a half million years separates us from Torris's people."

"It'll take some DNA testing and molecular taxonomy studies to determine that, won't it?" Alten said mildly.

"Good for you, Daddy," Nina said. "You're getting there. That's exactly what we plan to do as soon as we can get Torris to trust us enough to submit to the blood tests and tissue samples."

"We?" Joorn said.

"You're making fun of me, Grandpa."

"Not at all," Chu interceded. "He's proud of you for making yourself part of the team. We're going to need all the good minds we can get to unravel this puzzle." He turned to Joorn. "This Andrew has a point, Captain. Where did Torris's people come from? They didn't spend six billion years evolving on their Bernal trees. They would have evolved themselves out of existence. After all, the Others came and went in six billion years, leaving the galaxy to us."

Alten lifted his head, his interest aroused. "The sun became a red giant less—far less—than a billion years ago. Perhaps whatever remained of the human race migrated to the Oort cloud and after who knows how many generations sank back into a preindustrial society."

Nina was shaking her head, and Chu answered for her. "Doesn't work, mate. It's still too many years before that happened. Whatever migrated to the comets would have been as far beyond us and Torris's people as *Homo habilis* was from the one-celled creatures that were swimming in the oceans at the dawn of life in the Precambrian."

Nina found the courage to contradict her father. "He's right, Daddy. Torris's people evolved from people like *us* less than half a billennium ago."

Joorn became thoughtful. "Half a billennium is enough time for the Trees and their human population to have spread through the entire Oort cloud, both ours and Alpha Centauri's. Torris has shown the ability of his people to survive in naked space with Stone Age technology, supported by the ecology of these Bernal trees that we see everywhere. Hell, there may be a human population of billions or trillions just surrounding this one star system. To say nothing about the Oort clouds of the other stars in the neighborhood."

"We have become the Others," Alten murmured. "In a way we never could have expected—in the form of a new branch of the human species."

"Daddy, we mustn't turn on the Higgs drive again," Nina said urgently. "Not till we're sure."

"Never fear, little lady," Chu said. "We can chug along at interplanetary speeds for the time being. That will get us out of the cometary halo and into the inner system. Maybe as far as what used to be the orbit of Jupiter. And we can see what happened to the planet we used to call home."

"But not till we find out more about Torris," Nina said. "Maybe he'd like to go home too."

CHAPTER 24

"Our numberers say that the Trees will be at their closest approach to each other in just a few days," Irina said, using Torris's words for the concept and pronouncing them carefully.

"Bad," Torris said.

"Why is it bad, Torris?" Irina asked.

They were looking at a floor-to-ceiling screen in one of the lecture halls, away from the gawking crowds. The ship's spin was at about half a gravity, so Torris was watching from Jonah's travel pod, his elbows resting on the rim. Irina's study group had grown to about a dozen people, arranged in a rough semi-circle at a respectful distance.

"Because now the war starts. People will be killed. Our women will be taken." He paused to consider it. "Theirs too."

He'd been using the word *war* at Laurel's hesitant suggestion to stand for the single harsh syllable that meant *bride raid* in his own language. Laurel had gone on at inordinate length to explain to the others about bride raids in primitive cultures.

"There's nothing we can do about it, Torris," Irina said gently.

"I should be there with them to fight," Torris said, showing them the little bow he took everywhere with him now.

"No, Torris! Don't say that!" Nina cried out.

Torris looked at her sadly. "Yes, but they would kill me, little Nina," he said placatingly. He brightened. "But maybe not. No one has ever returned from the great dark before. So perhaps it would be taken as a Sign."

Laurel looked helplessly at Irina. It was obvious that she wanted to say something, but it always took her a while to get her tongue around one of her convoluted sentences.

Torris turned to the viewscreen. "Can they see us?"

"Not really," Irina said. "Not as an object. We're too far away. Maybe we'd be barely visible as a faint mote of reflected light, rising and setting with the fixed stars."

One of the newly minted paleontology undergraduates spoke up before Irina could keep him from pursuing the matter. "It would take at least eight days ship's time to get close. We'd be accelerating at a fraction of a gravity on the auxiliary drive."

Torris understood at least the first sentence. He became pensive, and Irina could see him fingering his bow.

"Let's get on with it," Irina said hastily. "We still have a lot to do. Who's here from taxonomy?" She nodded as a hand shot up. "Nina, Jonah, heads up. You're going to have to help me explain to Torris about tissue samples."

"Here we go," Chu said, watching the figures unreeling in front of him. The numbers were slowing down, almost at a full stop now, except for those still flickering at the ends of their long strings.

"We're less than a half million miles from Torris's Tree," he said, "in a pretty stable co-orbit around the system's mutual center of gravity, somewhere between Sol and the Alpha Centauri twins, but closer to Sol. Proxima isn't a factor. It's orbiting the whole system, far out. We couldn't go into orbit around the Tree itself, of course, because we weigh more than it does, and we'd be the tail that wags the dog. We don't want to do anything to disturb it as a habitat till we know more."

Irina nodded. "We don't want them to be aware of us either," she said.

"No danger of that," he said. "We're just another Tree in the sky. A speck with an odd shape."

"I don't see any activity yet," she said, looking at the magnified image. "Those batlike creatures seem to be concentrating their efforts in the space around the top of the Tree."

"They pretty much stay away from the base of the Tree, where the people live. They've learned to be wary of arrows."

"Perhaps they're intelligent enough to remember what happened to the one that tried to gobble up Torris," Alten offered.

"He's still reticent about that," Irina said. "We might never know why his tribe sentenced him to death."

"Or he might not have the words yet," Joorn offered. "Keep working on it, Irina."

"The linguists have an interesting theory," she said. "They've been going through the ship's library, poring through all the languages of Earth up until *Time's Beginning*'s departure. It seems that contrary to what most people assume, languages don't evolve from simplicity to complexity. It's the other way around. Primitive languages can be quite complex, with all sorts of arbitrary rules. But as time goes on, they tend to lose some of their linguistic baggage. Sexing verbs to match the gender of the nouns, for example. Getting rid of the affixes that are attached to a stem or root. Dropping or trimming tenses or cases and other syntactic relationships. Modern English, so-called, is much simpler than Middle English."

"Chinese is a good example," Chu said. "Our grammar and syntax is as simple as you can get. It's positional. You just string words together and let them fight it out."

"I'll have to bring Laurel up here to explain it," Irina said. "She's discovered something called semiotics, and now we've got four graduate students specializing in it."

Alten shook his head in mock wonder. "Semiotics," he said. "And what is it that Laurel's discovered?"

"Laurel's team," Irina said.

"Laurel's team. What is it that this semiotics . . . *theory* tells us about Torris?"

"It *is* a theory, you know, not a hypothesis, Alten. What does quantum theory tell us about zero-point motion?"

Joorn held up a hand. "Let's not fight, children. Irina, what's this about?"

She was still locking eyes fiercely with her husband. "Is this about Nina?" she said.

"Irina," Joorn repeated with practiced patience.

She transferred her gaze to him. "Torris's language diverged from an Earth language presumed to be English not more than two hundred and fifty thousand years ago."

Joorn drew in his breath. "But Earth disappeared not less than a billion years ago."

"Precisely."

"Then that means . . . " Alten had that faraway look that meant he was doing calculations in his head.

"Are you forming a theory, Alten?" Irina said sweetly.

"More of a hypothesis," he said. "I'll need more information before it's a theory."

Before she could reply, the door to the control room opened, and Nina came scurrying in. She gave her father and grandfather a cursory glance and went running to Irina.

"Mother," she said breathlessly, "Andrew's group just finished sequencing Torris's mitochondrial DNA and comparing it with samples from the ship! They had separate teams working on protein sequencing and amino acid sequencing and measuring the antigenic distances and—"

"Slow down, Nina," Irina said. "Take a breath."

" . . . and they're almost identical. There's hardly any difference at all!"

"Do they have a number?"

"Yes, and they're sure of it. They went through over sixty PCR amplification cycles and made a phylogenetic analysis of the result."

"And?"

"And it agrees pretty much with the language divergence study by Laurel's people. They're too close to be a coincidence!"

"Nina," Joorn said gently. "What exactly does that mean?"

She turned to him, her face shining. "It means that it pretty well confirms that Torris's people began to diverge from us less than two hundred and fifty thousand years after you and Grandma left Earth!"

"But that's impossible!"

"No it isn't," Alten said. He paused sheepishly. "I have a theory."

Torris frowned, struggling with ideas that were turning his world upside down. "And you say that man created the God-Trees, not the other way around?"

Alten was impressed. Torris was showing admirable courage in facing concepts that must have seemed heretical to him. For a supposed primitive, he seemed to have a surprising grasp of notions for which there weren't even words in his own language. If Torris was typical of the comet-dwellers, Alten thought, they must be a very superior folk indeed. But then, they would have to be. Living in the dangerous environment of the Oort cloud without technology would kill off the fools very quickly.

"Yes," he said. "It was a long, long time ago, when your people and ours were one."

"You mean we were dwarfs too?" Torris said, and everybody laughed. After a moment, Torris, despite his embarrassment, laughed too, out of courtesy.

They'd brought him to the bridge so that Alten and Chu could use the ship's displays to make things clearer when necessary. It made things easier that Chu was there. He was a familiar face, and so was Martin. Jonah had come along in his travel pod, to help with the dolphin chirps that were as much a part of Torris's new vocabulary as English. And Irina had allowed Laurel to bring along two of her linguists, though everyone agreed that direct conversation would be filtered through Nina to avoid overwhelming Torris.

The ship's spin, in its distant co-orbit with the Tree, had been lowered to one-quarter gravity to allow Torris to get out of the dolphin pool. Nobody minded; daily life in the ship went on as usual, and the low gravity was a lark. Torris himself was tottering along like an old man, even at a quarter G, but he was managing quite well.

"And we returned from a long journey, like you?" Torris said.

"Yes, and probably even farther than we went. But your ship was faster, so although you left later, you returned sooner."

That was too much for Torris. He turned to Nina, and she confirmed it, elaborating with the help of Jonah and his dolphin dictionary.

"So we could do magic, like you?" Torris said with a hint of pride in his voice.

"Probably even greater magic," Alten said. "But to no avail. By that time the sun had grown into the red giant you call the 'Stepsister' and swallowed the world we both had left from, as well as the other inner planets."

To illustrate his point, Alten brought up Sol in the display. One of the linguists whispered to Nina, providing a word that meant, approximately, *a very large person* in Torris's language.

"But that is not big enough to swallow a world," Torris objected. "The Stepsister swallows the Sisters from time to time, but they are only stars too. It couldn't swallow a world any more than a hopper could swallow a meatbeast. It's only a dot."

"It only looks that way because it's so far away. Let's bring it closer."

Alten fiddled with the display and got a zoom going. The red dot grew rapidly until it was an inferno that filled the display from floor to ceiling. Laurel and the two assistants gasped. The others, who had seen it before, still drew back at the intimidating sight.

Only Torris remained unimpressed. "It's a fire," he said. "Like any other. It's bigger than a man, to be sure, but hardly able to swallow a world."

It dawned on Alten that Torris must have seen other globular fires in the air-filled caverns where people lived, fires that had separated from their anchoring by the pressure of rising air. There must be fires aplenty in a world mostly made of wood. But there was never any danger of them consuming the Tree; they would be snuffed out when they encountered a vacuum.

Then it struck him that Torris could not imagine a "world" larger than a comet. He looked to his daughter for help.

"Daddy, show him some landscapes with people in them," she said. "Punch in the 'Scenes from old Earth' footage from the re-creation archive. Here, I'll do it."

She reached across and tapped on an auxiliary keyboard that connected with the ship's com. An African veldt replaced the sun, wide-angle enough to show the distant curvature of the horizon.

There were wheeled vehicles with canvas tops and people in bright holiday clothes to provide scale. A welcoming committee of giraffes had approached the people, lowering themselves stiffly on splayed legs and bending their long necks to mooch food.

Torris gasped at the sight. The wheeled vehicles couldn't have meant anything to him; they wouldn't have worked on a comet, where there wasn't enough gravity to hold them to the ground. But the giraffes would have made eminent sense to a man who had been elongated by evolution in a microgravity enviroment.

It was the horizon that was the true marvel to him. He grasped its immensity immediately. "Far, so far," he whispered in his own language. Jonah provided a translation in a synthetic voice for Alten, adding that the Delphinese equivalent meant, literally, *a long swim.*

"Then this is the world we came from, your people and

mine?" Torris asked. "Bigger than the Tree, bigger than the Ship. Where people walk about in the open without airsuits, and everyone is heavy."

"Yes," Nina said before Alten could answer.

"But it is gone now, eaten by the fire you showed me."

"Yes."

"And the fire was once that yellow thing that I saw in the sky? And the sky was blue, not black."

"He's getting it," Laurel said to her assistants. She still had not lost the habit of talking about Torris as if he were not there.

"You see, the red star and the orange and white stars that you call the Sisters are . . . " Alten began weightily but stopped when Nina motioned him to silence.

Torris said nothing for a long time. His brow furrowed as he worked it all out in his head. He glanced at the canned astronomy lesson that Alten had brought up, showing the merger of a younger solar system with Alpha Centauri's twins, even though diagrams and animations didn't work with Torris.

Finally Torris was ready to summarize what he had learned. He furrowed his brow and said, "Then we all came from the red star, before it grew. And then we went far away into the dark, and some of us came back. But when you travel so far, time melts—like ice near a fire. So that more time passed here than for the other travelers."

Alten couldn't help marveling. For a preliterate autochthon to have grasped and articulated one of the basic principles of relativity was nothing short of amazing. He turned to Nina, and she shot back an I-told-you-so look.

He cleared his throat. "Just so, Torris," he said.

Torris looked troubled. "Our priest did not tell us these things."

Alten turned to his daughter for help. She looked at her mother, who nodded her permission.

"Your priest didn't know, Torris," Nina said. "It all happened so long ago that it isn't even a memory or a tale to be passed down, even turned to legend."

The taxonomy people had finally settled on an estimate of two to three hundred thousand years for the evolution of *Homo cometes*, about the same distance separating the Cro-Magnons from the archaic *Homo sapiens*. The sun had long since devoured the inner planets when they returned from whatever galaxy they'd tried to colonize, but the Tree-based ecology of the cometary cloud would have been spreading for billions of years. They might have made a go of it at first, but without a sustainable technological base and the resources provided by a planetary surface, things had inevitably gone wrong. Their technology might have been more advanced than that of *Time's Beginning*, but when equipment wore out or broke down, it couldn't be replaced. Over who knew how many generations, they degenerated to a primitive society, sustained by the giant Trees and the plants and animals that the early Oortian lumberjacks had brought with them to their work camps. And the returnees began to evolve themselves.

Nina looked at Torris's overdeveloped chest, incongruous on his stretched-out frame, and wondered what his lung capacity was. She knew for a fact that he could hold his breath longer than Jonah.

She shuddered, wondering if her shipload of Homegoers

was destined for the same fate. But no, *Time's Beginning* had brought along everything needed to get an industrial society going, and her grandfather's followers were determined to find a planetary surface to terraform. Moreover, from an earlier generation than Torris's forebears, they were less dependent on their technology and thus more resourceful.

She smiled, thinking of her brother, Martin. He could fix anything, from the mechanical reels that played out the cargo netting to the conjugate mirrors that made the Higgs drive work.

Torris hadn't been able to tear his eyes away from the display, which had returned to its close-up of the Tree. It must have been very frustrating to him. He could have no conception of the distances involved. He only remembered the unfortunate slip of the garrulous paleontology undergraduate, who had said it would be an eight-day journey. He knew he could survive eight days in naked space with his primitive equipment. Ning had survived even longer, though she had taken extra air supplies, and he himself had survived more than half that long.

It was to Martin that he appealed. "Take me back to the airlock," he said.

He used the word he had learned for the double barrier that kept out the airless Outside. It seemed more appropriate than his own word for an air-trapping space, to describe the hugeness and solidity of the space that had accommodated the—he had learned that word too—boat.

Everybody looked at him aghast. "Torris . . . " Nina began.

"I have decided," he said. "I will need several of those . . . tanks . . . your people use instead of airbags, and Martin, I will need your help in contriving a valve that will attach to my intake."

Martin was the only person he had seen work with hand tools; everybody else seemed to use magic.

Martin stared numbly at him but didn't say anything.

Torris went on. He said diffidently, "I would like to take some of those magic tools with me, to show to our priest, Claz, so that he will believe what I tell him, and forgive my heresy. That thing that one holds that pushes you when you are drifting in space. The thing that makes heat without a fire, like a stovebeast. And a gift for Claz—one of those knives made of that shiny hard stuff that isn't bone or wood."

He was becoming more and more agitated. Martin and Chu exchanged distressed glances, then turned to Joorn.

"Can't we do something?" Irina whispered.

Joorn nodded. Chu said to him, "We're pointed in the right direction, Captain. I can take us in without losing our quarter-G spin."

Torris calmed down immediately. He'd understood every word.

[HAPTER 25

Torris visited the bridge every day now, usually getting there on his own, though with the ship spinning at less than a quarter G, he tended to shuffle along like an old man. There was still a weak up and down, enough to make shipboard life fairly normal, though the vector resulting from the ship's one-tenth-G acceleration made everybody experience a disorienting tilt. But people got used to it, and Torris, with his exquisite sense of gravity, fared better than most.

Today there was a special sense of excitement. He had been counting the days on his fingers, and this was the day deceleration time would exactly equal the interval leading up to turn-around time. Jonah and Nina had explained it to him. Jonah was trundling along beside him in his travel tank today. The dolphin lagoon had weathered the turnaround just fine, and the slight tilt of the water's surface was hardly noticeable. It would be a great event for the dolphins when the surface flattened out, but Jonah had chosen to accompany Torris instead of being there with his friends.

"Soon," Torris said. "Soon."

Jonah became uncharacteristically reticent for a dolphin. Usually he chattered away nonstop, especially in the water, where the chatter was laced with a liberal admixture of ultrasonics. "Patience, Torris, patience," he squeaked, then repeated it using a word in Torris's language that did not mean quite the same thing. It was not a word Torris wanted to hear. He had spent the last few days whittling arrows from leftover dowels he'd found in the lumber warehouse, and he had taken to carrying his quiver around with him, along with the bow.

"I understand," Torris said. But clearly he did not. He was not used to evasions or ambiguities.

When they reached the control room, Torris found a few more people than usual waiting for them. Laurel had brought along a couple of new assistants, people whom Torris remembered as being especially curious about the customs of his tribe. And Martin had drafted two people from his workshop: a brute of a man who helped with the heavy stuff and a young woman named Marisa who had done the delicate work of fabricating the interface air valve.

Faces turned in Torris's direction, careful faces with disturbingly taciturn expressions.

"Just in time," Chu said, a little too heartily. "We'll be parking in about an hour." One of Laurel's assistants explained unnecessarily that parking meant coming to a stop.

"We're rather large," Chu said. "But we'll be too far away for anybody to make out details or our scale without a telescope. Perhaps they'll take us for another Tree drifting by."

Torris knew about telescopes. He'd been given a small one, a compact black cylinder that became miraculously longer when you pulled on it. He'd intended it as one of the gifts for Claz, but now he was having second thoughts. He'd readily discovered the secret of what a lens could do, and he thought that if he ever became the tribe's Facemaker—a big *if*, because he had to get Claz's absolution first—he might be able to cast a lens from the clear resin used for Faces. How to arrive at a meniscus to provide the necessary curvature was the problem. He speculated that the Tree's microgravity at the comet's surface where it was strongest might be the answer, along with the liquid resin's natural tendency to be attracted to the sides of the mold. For now it was just a daydream, but a strong one.

Still, Chu's pessimistic view was disturbing. Torris scowled. "Why do we have to be so far away that they'd need a telescope to see us plainly?"

"It's complicated," Chu said, resorting to the irritating word that the dwarfs liked to use. "Let's take it one step at a time."

Torris was about to protest when Chu did something that made the engines stop. Torris could immediately feel the pull of artificial gravity straighten itself out. There was no longer the illusion of a tilted room.

"We'll coast from here," Chu said.

It took another two days, but Torris woke up one morning with the knowledge that the ship's engines had fired again during the night. The dolphin lagoon was tilted, though he had slept through the turnaround.

"We're parking again," he said to Jonah. "Why?"

"It's complicated," Jonah said in a sardonic imitation of Chu that managed to sound like him delivered in a dolphin squeak.

Nobody was up and around yet. The tiled shoreline was deserted, with no sign of his usual interrogators. Torris heaved himself out of the water and struggled into his airsuit, leaving the hood with its Face thrown back. The air sack lay flaccid against his spine, its new hoses dangling. He gathered up his pile of arrows and filled his quiver.

"What are you doing?" Jonah asked.

"I'm going to the bridge."

"I'll go with you."

"You'll have to hurry then," Torris said, tight-lipped. He strode off without looking back, tall and straight despite the quarter-gravity.

"Wait!" Jonah called behind him, breaking into a dolphin distress call.

Torris forged on, not looking back. By the time he reached the first turn in the corridor, he could hear Jonah's travel tank rolling along behind him, wheels squealing as it scurried to catch up.

Braking had stopped by the time he got to the bridge. The dolphin pool would be flat again at the quarter-G rotation. Torris knew enough about traveling worlds by now to surmise that the one they called a 'ship' was probably drifting motionless with respect to the Tree.

When he entered, he found everybody staring grim-faced at the big screen. Alten was taking his turn in the captain's chair. Chu was sprawled out in one of the spare chairs, awake now but obviously having spent the night there. Joorn was supposed to be off-shift, but he was in the first officer's seat next to Alten, making the small adjustments necessary to keep *Time's Beginning* in tandem with the Tree. Nina and Martin were sitting together, a scanty breakfast lying untouched on the low table between them. Their mother was with them, though she usually showed little interest in ship operations per se. Nobody from her ad hoc anthropology team was there; they were probably all still asleep at this hour.

"Sit down, Torris," Alten said, glancing over his shoulder.

"Me too?" Jonah squeaked, but nobody seemed to think it was funny.

Torris lowered his gangling frame onto a chair, perching rather than sitting. It was a relief after walking more than a mile in one-quarter gravity, plus the extra G's of deceleration. Aching legs were a new sensation to someone who'd spent his life in free fall.

His eyes went immediately to the overwhelming view on the screen. It was the Tree, heart-wrenchingly close—almost as close as he'd seen it the day Chu and Martin had plucked him out of the void. He could see it whole, from the table-land at the top, where he and Ning had hunted game, to the comet it clutched in its roots. No one else in his tribe had ever seen it like this, except perhaps a few oldsters who had been alive at the time of the last bride raid.

Almost as close was another Tree—Ning's Tree—looking much the same. While he'd been away, the two Trees had closed the gap between them. The ship's numberers, he'd been told, had calculated that there would be no actual collision. The two Trees would soon start to drift apart, passing each other. But for a few tens of days, they would be close enough for a bride raid. When that would occur would depend on how daring the young men of both tribes were. Undoubtedly there would be a few rash fools attempting the crossing early, either making the leap alone or with a foolhardy friend for mutual protection. But tradition dictated that the main body go together to provide a force that could overwhelm the defenders with less risk. Sadly, according to the tales that had spread through the cometary belt over the aeons, the result was more likely to be a mutual slaughter.

"I should be there," Torris fretted.

"Torris, we're not as close as it looks," Alten said without taking his eyes off the display. "You've seen what a telescope can do. Well, this is like a thousand telescopes. And it's a telescope that thinks—in a way—and fills in things that it can't actually see, like the human brain does. No matter how near it seems, we're actually a quarter-million miles away."

"Daddy, he doesn't know what a quarter-million means," Nina said. "He can count up to twenty with his shoes off."

"You must let me out with the airlock," Torris said. "With one of your magic tanks of air." He had been stringing his bow while Alten talked.

"Torris, don't you understand that . . . " Alten began.

"And one of those"—Torris thought hard for a moment and triumphantly came up with the word—"thrusters."

"And he doesn't understand *a thousand* either," Nina said. "The highest number he can even visualize is 'two hands of a ten of fingers.' That's not even a hundred. You can double it if you throw in the toes. I couldn't even attempt the word for that."

They spent the next few hours watching the two Trees, while Alten jiggled knobs and tapped keys to keep the ship's position adjusted. The others kept watching the screen, though there was nothing much to see. The images looked unchanging from here, but an occasional laconic update from Alten let them know that the comets were still closing the gap.

The Trees' motion toward each other couldn't be detected

by the naked eye, but to the inhabitants it was probably another story. The inborn sense of motion that all primates inherit— the instinct that lets a monkey throw a stone and hit a target or a man swing a bat and hit a ball—would be letting them anticipate precisely when the Trees would reach their ultimate proximity before beginning to drift apart. Alten was using the same instincts, controlling the immense ship with his array of keys and knobs but on an inconceivably larger scale.

To Torris, though, it seemed as if Alten and the others were doing nothing. He kept importuning Alten and getting grunts in return. Both of them were getting visibly impatient and annoyed.

Torris appealed to Chu and Martin. "Why are we sitting here? I have my airsuit, my new arrows, my knife with the shiny blade. I am ready now. I could find my way to the airlock I think, but I don't know how to open the doors. I could take my stovebeast, but I know it would not be enough. And I am not a child to think I could reach my Tree with a leap. I need one of your magical thrusters."

He moved as if to get up. Nina looked alarmed and grabbed at her mother's arm.

Chu struggled to suppress a yawn and sat up straight in his chair. "Alten, why don't you forget the wide angle and show him a real close-up of his own Tree. On a scale that might show him human figures moving around. That'd be the lower branches, or a place on the ground where there are exposed roots."

"At that focus, the image'll start to break up," Alten grumbled, but he began making the necessary adjustments. "I don't know if they'll even be recognizable as human figures."

Torris leaned forward as the zoom started. His mind must have been interpreting the rapid change of scale as breakneck speed, a speed that must have seemed impossible to him. The imaginary observer slowed to a stop and seemed to be hovering less than a mile above ground. The image was blurred and it jiggled, but the tiny mites it revealed were indeed moving and could be seen to have probable human shapes.

Torris exhaled slowly. "I can see the cave mouth," he breathed. "There are people coming out. And there is the hill where they threw me out into the dark. There are people gathering there."

The others strained to see. But to those without Torris's educated vision, the images didn't make the same sense. Nina was the first to notice what happened next.

"Look!" she cried. "It's like a flea jumping. Someone's sailing into space."

She pointed. It was the tiniest of specks against the deep black of night, but it must have caught the reflected light of the three bright stars that lit the sky. It twinkled as it tumbled on its flight, and as minute as it was, there was a suggestion of arms and legs.

"He couldn't wait," Torris said.

Even as he spoke, another mite flung itself into space, following the trajectory of the first.

Alten widened the focus and drew back to show the space between the two Trees. The specks were the merest motes of dust, but they were still visible once the eye had caught them.

Torris became agitated. "My place is with my kinfolk," he said. "Surely Claz would forgive me."

Irina got Alten's attention. "Claz is his priest," she said. "He didn't want to talk about it, but we got some of it out of him. He can't go back. They'd kill him on sight."

For the next few hours, the people assembled in the control room watched the big screen, not talking much, sipping coffee or dozing in their seats. Nothing was happening on the big viewscreen to catch their attention. The two dust motes were still visible if you cared to search for them, periodically catching the starlight.

A couple of Irina's language specialists had drifted in and taken seats, and they had helped calm Torris down. It no longer seemed necessary to restrain him. He had sunk into a deep funk and was unresponsive to further attempts to communicate with him. He perched awkwardly in his seat, all legs and elbows, and kept his eyes on the screen, his face impassive.

Nina was watching Torris's Tree, the one on the left, but now she turned her gaze on the other Tree. The two were not visibly closer, but the image was sharper and clearer. Alten, in one of his periodic announcements, had informed them that *Time's Beginning* had drifted a hundred thousand miles closer in its co-orbit since they'd begun watching, and that had made a difference in the focus.

She thought she saw something, and after a few minutes she was sure. "Look!" she cried.

Silhouetted against the night, just off the sharp-edged limb of the approaching comet, a silver mist was rising. After another few minutes, the skim of mist had visibly separated from the limb and continued to rise. More minutes passed, and the mist resolved itself into a cloud of sparkling dust motes. The cloud began to expand.

A cry of anguish from Torris pierced the silence. "They come! They make the leap!" he shouted. He unfolded his long body and disentangled himself from the chair.

Martin and Chu were out of their own chairs in a flash and grabbed Torris before he could reach the door. He did not resist and allowed them to lead him back to his seat.

Nina tried to imagine what he was seeing. She was seeing a cloud of wriggling specks. Torris was seeing a swarm of space-suited warriors like himself, armed to the teeth with their little bows and bone-tipped harpoons and knives of bone or fire-hardened wood. They would be violent young men, excited by the thought of blood and women.

She turned her attention to Torris's Tree. From the long interviews with Torris that she'd sat in on, she had gained a vivid picture of what life was like in the ice cave where he'd lived with his tribe—the greasy fires that kept them alive; the weird beasts they hunted for food; the young mothers, no older than herself, with the babies they had to carry in airtight sacks with a stovebeast when they ventured outside; and the little boys impatient to grow up and climb the Tree and become men. A sense of dread overtook her and would not go away.

She imagined that cloud of overexcited young men descending on them, the carnage on both sides, the babies torn from their mothers, the old men run through with spears, the fires wantonly extinguished to be restarted when the invaders had gone, the survivors creeping out of their hiding places. It was too much to bear. A line of poetry from her English classes came to her: "The Assyrians came down like a wolf on the fold." Her mother had told her that things like bride raids had survived on old Earth long after mankind had achieved a technological civilization and were still going on in one form or another up to the day her grandfather and grandmother had left to find a new home in another galaxy. That had been six billion years in the past. Mankind had gone and returned, though in a bifurcated form, and now it seemed the old cruelties had taken root again, even in a dying Universe.

She withdrew into herself like Torris, unable to take her eyes off the site of the coming calamity.

Another hour went by. The coffee in front of her grew cold. Someone came by to refill her cup, took one look at her face, and removed the cup without a word.

Then there was something like a puff of steam, and she leaned forward to see more clearly. The puff resolved itself into a swarm of wriggling mites hanging in space. A collective gasp came from around her, then a babble of voices. She turned her head, afraid of what Torris might do, but he remained in his seat, his posture more tense, his lips drawn back to bare clenched teeth in an expression of utter savagery she'd never seen before.

The cloud settled down to a stable shape as the individual motes that comprised it adjusted their vectors with whatever reaction mass they'd brought with them. Alten edited out the two extraneous Trees for a tighter focus, till the viewscreen showed only the two clouds drifting slowly toward each other.

"It's the bride raiders of Torris's tribe trying to get across first," Laurel informed them pedantically, as though an explanation were required.

Chu was halfway out of his chair, ready to take his place at the controls again. "There's no way they could change course now, even if they wanted to. And two collections of hotheads wouldn't want to. Are they headed for a collision?"

Alten was punching keys as fast as he could, a fine sheen of perspiration beading his forehead. "I've got enough data for a preliminary estimate. I give it a day and a half to two days."

"Arrows go faster," Chu said, "and in a straight line in space. Do I have to quote Newton's laws of motion?"

Martin looked over his shoulder at Alten. He was trying to hold a struggling Torris down. "Plenty of time to see them coming and dodge them. If you're within reach of a buddy, you can use each other for reaction mass. If not, you can sacrifice something small, like spare ordnance." He was doing rough calculations with his engineer's brain. "They'll have to be within thirty or forty yards from each other to start shooting arrows."

Nina was beside herself. "Isn't anybody going to *do* anything?" she shrilled. "Besides talk about Newton's law and reaction mass and how close you have to be to shoot an arrow! We can't let them *kill* one another!"

Alten appealed to her. "The ship can't get to them in two days. Unless we use the Higgs drive and kill everybody within a million miles."

Chu stood up. "A lifeboat or a landing craft can," he said. "And on chemical thrusters. They got our ancestors to the moon, if you recall."

Martin had said something to Torris, who stopped struggling and untangled himself to stand by his chair, fingering his bow. He looked expectant.

"I want to go with you," Nina said.

"You can't, sis," Martin said gently. "But you can help. Go

find your boyfriend, Andrew. The two of you can stow a cargo net. Andrew will know how to attach a sounding rocket."

"Boyfriend? Andrew? What's going on, Nina?" Alten said.

"I was going to tell you, Daddy," Nina said. She ran off before Alten could ask anything more.

"Good move, Martin," Chu said.

"I'm going too," Jonah piped up from his travel pod.

"What could a dolphin do?" Chu said. "It's outside work."

"I'm a safety engineer, remember?" Jonah said. He departed at high speed, the little metal casters squealing.

"This is madness," Alten said. "Look at him." He pointed a chin at Torris. "He's just itching to get in the fight and kill a few of his opposites."

"We're not going to kill anyone," Chu said. "We're going to stop it."

"I can't authorize the use of the boat," Alten said.

"I can," Joorn said, stirring in his chair. "Try to bring him back intact, Martin." He turned to Irina. "I'm sorry, my dear. I know you're loath to let your only specimen of *Homo cometes* out of your sight, but Nina is right. We can't let them slaughter one another."

"I agree, Joorn," Irina said. "I never thought of Torris as just a specimen. He's a very brave and intelligent young man who saved Nina's life."

Laurel looked from one person to another with a distraught expression on her face. "I don't understand," she said. "He's a new kind of hominid, and we're learning so much! Are they going to put him in the middle of some kind of primitive feud?"

Irina patted her on the shoulder. "Don't worry, Laurel. There are going to be plenty of specimens."

CHAPTER 26

They were almost too late. The boat came to a violent halt at four gravities, nicely parallel to the two swarms of combatants at the point where they were just beginning to intersect. They had covered the last thousand miles in less than a minute. To the drifting skirmishers, the boat must have seemed to have appeared from nowhere.

Martin helped Torris to his feet. With all their inertia gone, it took only the slightest effort.

"Are you all right?" he asked.

He studied Torris with concern. The four gravities had been hard enough on him and Chu. For Torris, it could only have been a terrifying hell of utter immobility. He could only hope that no bones had been broken.

Torris didn't bother to answer. He immediately floated over to a porthole to peer outside. He'd needed only a single casual push of his toes, but he bumped up against his target with unerring accuracy. Torris was in his element.

"How far?" he said.

Martin checked with Chu. "About a mile," he said. "With a good starting push, you could be there in a couple of minutes. We've got a net drift toward them, so we'd be right behind you. Your push wouldn't subtract much from our inertia."

Torris nodded. Irina's linguists had taught him the words

that went with the concepts, but he'd grown up knowing them in his bones.

"And your nets," Torris said. "You will be like an enormous web beast, bigger than any creature or object they have ever seen before."

Martin knew what Torris was thinking. "We'll try not to hurt anyone, Torris. Of course there might be some accidental casualties."

"But it'll stop the fight," Chu interjected. "They'll have been dazzled by a tremendous flash in the sky. When their vision clears, the ship will be there. Like an omen before a battle—a comet in the sky or an eclipse. It must give them pause."

"They won't stop the fight," Torris said.

Jonah's computer voice cleared its throat. "Torris is right," it said. "It might spur them on instead. You humans have peculiar mentalities. Both sides are liable to interpret omens as omens in their favor. Remember the Bayeux Tapestry. The Norman conquest of England was preceded by the appearance of Halley's Comet in the sky. For William the Conqueror's troops, the dread omen was a morale booster. It applied to the other fellow."

"You dolphins," Chu grumbled. "We should never have programmed the encyclopedia into your database."

"Human history is amusing," Jonah said complacently, "if incomprehensible."

Torris was paying no attention. Martin was helping him get ready, fastening the airsuit's new gaskets and checking out his equipment. He had two of the compact air tanks and one of the miraculous thrusters that somehow propelled you with a giant's shove when you pointed it in the opposite direction.

He had a quiverful of the arrows he'd whittled aboard ship and a lightweight metal harpoon with a line that was thinner and stronger than web silk.

He turned to Martin at the airlock door and said, with obvious reluctance, "If your magic fails, Mar-tin, I will fight with my people."

"I understand," Martin said.

He closed the inner door behind Torris, overrode the automatic sequence, and, not waiting for full vacuum, released the latch on the outside door. He got to a porthole and pressed his face against it in time to see Torris, crouched on the sill, give a kick with his powerful legs and sail off into space.

"You better get cracking." Chu's voice was urgent over the speaker. "I'll give you five minutes to get ready before I deploy the nets. Jonah, that goes for you too."

"I'm already in my spacesuit, so to speak," Jonah said. "Martin and I know the routine. We've worked together many times."

Ten minutes later, Martin and Jonah were at opposite ends of the leading edge of the cargo net, stretching it out between them and helping it to unfold. Martin could see Jonah's pod, about a quarter-mile away, clutching a clew line at the far corner of the net in its mechanical claws, like someone unfolding a gigantic bed sheet. When he and Jonah were about three miles apart and the pod had disappeared among the stars, he gave Chu the signal.

The sounding rockets flared together, all along the luff of the net, like a row of Christmas lights. Nina's friend Andrew had spaced them about an eighth of a mile apart, a staggering exercise in the geometry of drapery for someone who had to fold and unfold tons of mesh in a working space only a few hundred feet long, with only the brainless loading robots to help him. Martin's opinion of the young man shot up.

Pulled by the rockets, the net unreeled evenly, without snagging. Martin's admiration shot up another notch. He and Jonah used their maneuvering jets to stretch the net taut between them. When it was fully unrolled, he and Jonah found themselves a good mile from the landing boat. The boat itself would anchor the net at the other end, where it necessarily narrowed to fit the sixty-foot width of the slot before it fanned out. The nets were part of the equipment of every lifeboat, which might be called upon to snare accidental—and valuable—jetsam from an orbiting ship. The thought of the original designers of *Time's Beginning* had also been that when the ship had colonized a likely planet and stocked its oceans, the nets would be useful for trawling. Martin wondered if they'd done that on Rebirth three billion years ago.

He sighted along the edge of the net and found Jonah, a tiny dot almost lost among the distant stars.

Torris was closer. As Chu had said, they would be drifting along right behind him, with the slight difference in velocity that Torris's starting leap had given him.

He located Torris, only a few hundred yards from where the two groups of bride raiders were starting to intersect but about a mile from his own position at one end of the net. He cranked up the magnification provided by his helmet and brought Torris into focus at an apparent distance of only fifty feet or so. Torris was drifting into enemy territory. And according to what Nina had told him, the ornamental beadwork on his airsuit would mark him instantly as an enemy.

That seemed to be exactly what was happening. One of the

drifting warriors Martin could see beyond Torris twisted his head and saw an enemy coming from the wrong direction.

The man scrambled to fit an arrow to his bow, but fighting while hanging in space has its dilemmas. He was facing the wrong way, with no way to turn around. But he must have been a quick thinker. A couple of his friends were within arm's length, and he used one of them for leverage. He gave him a shove that sent him crashing into a third man, who in turn collided with someone else. In the meantime, the push had started a slow spin that had him briefly facing Torris.

He was ready, and he had good reflexes. He released the arrow he had nocked, and it streaked toward Torris. He had a good archer's instincts, automatically compensating for the sideways deviation of the arrow caused by his spin.

But Torris had good reflexes too. The instant that the arrow was released and its course could no longer be changed, he used the little thruster that Martin had given him and gave himself a spurt that moved him sideways, out of the way.

Without a pause he released his own arrow, compensating for his complicated vector sum without having to think about it. His opponent's arrow went sailing harmlessly by, on its way to infinity, but Torris's arrow, following its own vector product, sped unerringly toward its target.

The man never saw it coming. By that time his spin had turned him full circle, and he took Torris's arrow in the back.

The whole encounter had taken only a few seconds, but it had alerted the enemy swarm. The original chain reaction of collisions caused by the unfortunate archer was spreading, and to it was added a second chain reaction, started when his corpse was given a kick by the force of Torris's arrow.

Now it seemed that every enemy invader within a hundred yards of Torris was leveling a spear at him or struggling to align a bow shot. They had the same problem the dead man had had. Most of them had been facing the swarm of warriors from Torris's tribe, who were just starting to make contact where the two swarms were beginning to merge.

It was getting complicated. In the distance beyond Torris, Martin could see a few individual hand-to-hand battles starting to take place at the interface. And some of the more impatient fighters from both tribes were starting prematurely to hurl spears or shoot arrows. Most would never find their targets except accidentally; the distances were still too great, and by the time an arrow reached its intended victim he would have drifted, if only a few feet.

But for Torris it was very different. He was in the midst of his enemies. Already arrows and spears were starting to come his way from relatively nearby. With the help of Martin's thruster, he could still dodge them easily, but as their numbers increased, he would lose the ability to keep track of them. A further ironic threat was the shower of missiles coming from his own people. Almost all of them would penetrate the enemy swarm without hitting anything, but they were ultimately aimed in Torris's direction.

There was a more immediate threat from the spearmen. About a half dozen of them were coming his way, having borrowed reaction mass from their mates. They weren't bothering with their bows; in up-close combat, all you had to do was thrust.

When they were close enough, he aimed an arrow at the nearest target, a big man with a colorful pattern of embroidery across his broad torso. At this distance Torris could see his face plainly, his mouth contorted as he mouthed a string of insults. He wobbled in his flight as he shook his spear but not enough to spoil Torris's aim.

The arrow hit him dead center, right in the middle of the embroidery pattern. Before the impact could carry him out of reach, the man next to him shot out an arm to grab his harness and flung him backward to provide ample reaction mass.

That propelled him to within stabbing distance of Torris. But as he thrust with his spear, Torris fired a quick blast of his thruster, and the spear shaft went past him, with the man following. Torris still had an arrow in his hand that he hadn't had time to fit to his bowstring, and he raked the man's airsuit as he flew past. The arrowhead was a stubby nail made of that strange shiny stuff that was harder than bone, and it sliced the airsuit open from shoulder to waist. The man sailed into the distance, trailing frozen blood.

The others closed in, their movements cautious now. They had Torris bracketed—above, below, and on both sides. He clutched the thruster in one hand, the arrow poised for stabbing in the other. He'd have to somehow get past at least one of them.

The spears ringed him, almost within thrusting distance now. They were too close for him to use his bow.

He waited, alert for any tiny movement that would reveal their strategy. If they were going to rush him, two of them could grab two others and use them for reaction mass. And then there was the fifth man. He could serve as a fixed obstacle. In any case, there might be one slim escape route open if he could guess which one it would be. He had the thruster, but they'd seen him use it, so it wouldn't be a surprise.

He saw them confer in lip talk, their helmets turned so he couldn't see. Then he saw their bodies tense. He tensed himself, getting ready.

Then he saw a sudden flash in the sky and a huge black shape blotting out the stars. It would be Chu, giving a final blast of his maneuvering jets to get into position.

His assailants turned their heads and gaped, their spears forgotten. Torris stared too and saw an enormous web spread out across the entire sky, made barely visible by the tiny glints of starlight that sparkled here and there along its strands.

The skyful of men had lost all purposeful movement. They were transfixed, helpless to flee. Their total drift as a group was toward Torris's comet, but within that volume of space they were essentially motionless, with only limited movement. The same was true of the swarm from Torris's comet, except that their drift was in the opposite direction. The two swarms were merging now, but they would eventually have passed through each other and separated again.

Except for what was happening now!

The net loomed nearer, engulfing the two groups of fighters over a distance of miles. Then it began inexorably to draw itself tight, shrinking to a volume of only a couple of hundred feet across.

Torris found himself crammed into a crowded pocket with the five men who had just tried to kill him. They'd all lost their spears, except for one who had managed to hang on to his. Jammed between bodies as it was, however, there was no space to use it. With his helmet pressed against the mesh, Torris could see into other pockets containing dozens, perhaps scores, of spacesuited men. Presumably everybody had enough air to last out the remaining time until they could be transferred to *Time's Beginning.*

Peering around the packed bodies, he thought he could recognize some members of his own tribe from their beaded suits, in forced proximity to their enemies of less than an hour ago. The total silence of airless space was eerie under the circumstances, but he was sure that there was a lot of wailing and crying going on. It would have been deafening in a closed space with air to carry sound. They were all expecting to die or worse.

He waited a couple of hours, his limbs getting intolerably cramped. One of the men who had tried to kill him pressed his faceplate against his and attempted helmet talk.

"It was the Great World Eater that was foretold," he said. "I saw it. But the priest did not say that it would be a web beast."

Before Torris could reply, there was a blinding flash in the sky, so brilliant that its glare penetrated the packed net full of men and turned every cranny between their bodies into a searing outline of white light.

It lasted only a few seconds, but its sudden shock triggered a reciprocal spasm through the entire mass of men. Torris's involuntary neighbor jerked as if he'd had an electric shock, and he lost helmet contact. When Torris's vision began to return, it was dotted with dancing specks of light.

He managed to turn his head and get an outside view. Some miles away, *Time's Beginning* was an enormous blot against the sky. He understood enough about the little men's control of celestial mechanics by now to know that the doomsday flash had been the final braking maneuver needed to put the giant starship at rest with respect to Chu's lifeboat.

His neighbor had managed to restore tentative helmet contact. His voice was like a buzzing insect. "It's the end of every-thing, as the priests have always predicted," he said.

Torris didn't answer right away. He could feel the slight tug of the force that resembled gravity and a shift of bodies within the net caused by inertia. Chu had fired his engines to close the gap. He craned his neck to see between the packed bodies. They were headed toward the wide slot in the side of *Time's Beginning* that marked the huge airlock, where lifeboats and cargo landers could dock. Those with an outside view could see it too, gaping like some gigantic mouth waiting to gulp them. The mass of trapped men was writhing with their hysterical attempts to struggle.

"It's the end of everything," his neighbor repeated.

"No," Torris said. "It's the beginning."

CHAPTER 22

"They still have their weapons," Joorn said. "It's too dangerous for Torris to go in alone. Initial contact is a job for Irina's specialists." He'd hurried down from the bridge to join them, so he was still a little out of breath.

"All the fight's gone out of them," Chu demurred. "Both sides are terrified. They've separated themselves into two groups, huddled on opposite sides of the auditorium."

"Besides," Martin added, "they're more or less pinned to the floor by the quarter-gravity. They're not used to it the way Torris is. They're not inclined to move much, and besides, they don't know how to use their bows when they're not in free fall."

"One of them, brave fellow, tried to shoot at my travel pod when I rolled out of the lifeboat," Jonah piped up. "But he couldn't even get his arrow nocked. It kept falling to the floor. When I lifted the lid and showed myself, he threw away his bow and prostrated himself to me. And here I thought I had a nice smile."

"Torris will know how to talk to them better than any specialists," Chu said. "Sorry, Irina."

"I agree," Irina said.

They were gathered outside the barred doors of the main auditorium on Level Two, only a stone's throw from the boat lock, waiting for Ryan to give them the all-clear signal. It had been a daunting job herding the demoralized mob even that short distance after they'd been released from the net, but Ryan's security force had been up to it. Some of the Tree people couldn't walk at all, even in the light gravity, but after Ryan's hefty cops had physically carried the worst cases out, the rest had bowed to the inevitable and dragged themselves along under escort. Torris, with a nod from Ryan, had slipped out in the confusion.

Ryan had wisely not tried to disarm them. The fight had gone out of them, and they were more docile hanging on to their weapons. Besides, they were thoroughly cowed by their fantastic surroundings: a cave not constructed of ice, where the air pressure made breathing easy and where there was warmth with no visible fires.

"Ryan was right," Martin said. "Give them a chance to get used to each other. At last report, he said some of them on the fringes of their groups were actually exchanging a few cautious words."

Jonah gave a chirp of dolphin mirth. "And why not? They're all in the same boat."

The others responded with pained looks.

Martin said earnestly, "They have nothing to fight about anymore. They're just a bunch of young jocks starting to bond after the game."

"Let's help the bonding along," Joorn said. "When I was a young jock six billion years ago, we played a game called football and had hamburgers and beer afterward. Irina, what would be the equivalent?"

"Torris eats hamburgers," Nina put in eagerly. "With ketchup."

She gave Torris a sideward glance. She and her mother had come to assure themselves that he was all right, but other than the initial greeting, there hadn't been any attempt at conversation. He had been silent through all the talk, his face unreadable, his thoughts elsewhere.

"They have alcohol," Irina said. "And they eat a sort of minced meat, usually raw, with a kind of fermented sauce on it for when they can't cook."

"Perfect," Joorn said. "The off-duty cafeteria on this level ought to be able to handle it." He turned away and spoke for some minutes into his portacom, then turned back to the others and said, "It's all fixed. Two hundred hamburgers and four hundred beers, and whatever crunchies the manager can think of. We'll have a covey of waitpersons to lay out a buffet when we go in with our team. You don't get into a fight when you're scarfing food down." He turned to his daughter-in-law. "Irina, you better brief your people."

Some of Irina's specialists in aboriginal customs had already drifted in. She took them aside and began to speak to them.

What Torris was thinking was impossible to guess. Perhaps he was irritated by the sight of the people who had been annoying him for so long with childish questions.

But he shook himself out of his reverie and turned to someone who was easier to talk to, his little friend Nina. "Nina, you must tell them. I must go inside now and speak to my people."

She didn't know what to say to him. "I know, Torris. You will go, but we will go with you, to see that you are safe."

"I must go *now*," he said with unshakable obstinacy.

She turned uncertainly to her brother. "Tell him, Martin," she appealed.

Martin tried to reason with him, to no avail. "Torris, you are under sentence of death from your own people!"

"They will not harm me," Torris said obdurately. "They will see that I have not been swallowed by the big dark." Then, with unexpected humor: "But that I have returned with peculiar little friends who can perform miracles. They will say that surely it must be the will of the Tree."

"But to the others, the bride raiders from the other Tree, you're their enemy."

"They are like frightened children now. They will listen to what I say."

In an amplified voice meant to reach Joorn and the others, Jonah added: "Particularly when they see that you command the very beasts."

Chu laughed and said, "Shouldn't it be 'beasts of the deep'? But then, they don't have any concept of the deep, do they?" He turned to Joorn. "Torris has a point, Skipper. Strike while the iron is hot."

Joorn made up his mind. "We'll go in as a group. Torris will be the point man. We'll back him up. Ryan's security men will be there in case there's any trouble, but they'll stay out of the way. Irina's people will be there to help if there are any difficulties, but they'll be in the background. Communication will be chain of command. In other words, everything goes through Nina." He smiled at his granddaughter. "You up to it, sweetheart?"

She smiled bravely back. "Torris is used to talking through me, Grandfather, but it'll work the other way too."

"I'll be there with my dictionary," Jonah said. "Don't worry, Nina."

"It's settled then," Joorn said. He called Irina over and conferred briefly with her, then called Ryan on his portacom and worked out the arrangements.

Chu stepped over to Torris and looked up into his spare, narrow features. "Did you understand all that, Torris?" he asked.

"Too much talk," Torris said, and strode past Chu and Martin to the auditorium doors. Joorn and the two of them looked at one another, shrugged, and followed, with Jonah's travel pod rolling behind and Irina's contingent bringing up the rear.

The fighters were segregated into two cohesive groups, about a hundred feet apart on opposite sides of the stripped auditorium, with a dozen of Ryan's security guards loosely arranged between them as a buffer. The buffer looked to be unnecessary, as no one was showing any tendency to leave the comfort of his comrades. Another twenty or so security men were watching from their raised position on the stage. They'd been able to separate their despondent wards without the need to question them or communicate verbally. One group wore suits painstakingly decorated with embroidery, like Torris's, while the other group used beads, denoting some kind of cultural difference.

The packed groups stirred when Torris's entourage entered, particularly when they saw the dolphin tank, apparently moving of its own volition. But nobody got up. They were all sitting, or slouching on the bare floor with their legs sprawled out in a tangle, obviously made miserable by the mild pseudogravity.

Ryan met them halfway across the floor. "He'll want to address his own people first," he said, looking askance at Torris, who was walking right by him. "We thought of using the stage for that, but these people have never seen anything like a stage or lectern. Close up is better. My boys are watching, but believe me, nobody's going to move if they can help it."

Torris had stopped between the two groups. Something had caught his eye among his former enemies.

A tall warrior rose from the mass of fighters, standing erect and unbent despite the drag of the artificial gravity.

"Ning!" Torris blurted out. No one had ever heard him raise his voice before.

He lurched toward the apparition, but before he could take two steps, a couple of security men reached him and grabbed his arms.

They looked ridiculous trying to hold him, but their muscular strength was overwhelming compared to his, despite the advantage of his height. It didn't look as if he were fighting them, but rather that he was held immobile by some natural force.

More security men rushed up and formed a protective ring around Torris. Others turned their attention to the tall figure making its way through the jam of sprawled people.

It paused short of the perimeter of the group. The security men relaxed but stood ready.

"Tor-ris," a voice said.

It was unmistakably a woman's voice, a rich and resonant contralto.

Joorn and the others stopped short. Nina tugged at her mother's sleeve. "It's her!" she said. "The one Torris keeps trying not to talk about."

The spacesuited woman stayed put. Her posture was not threatening. You could almost say it was relaxed, despite the obvious effort to stand straight in the unfamiliar gravity.

The security men relented and allowed Torris to drag them to within six feet of the group's perimeter, a distance that even the long arms of the Tree dwellers could not bridge. Like the others, she still clung to her bow, but with her casual stance, the security men, though wary, didn't seem to consider her a threat to Torris.

With her hood and faceplate thrown back, it could easily be seen that it was indeed a woman, and a striking one at that. There was manifest strength in her chiseled face, with its prominent cheekbones and the huge eyes of the Tree people. Her pitch-black hair, chopped carelessly short, only enhanced the exotic effect.

"She's beautiful!" Nina whispered to her mother.

Joorn's party tried to press forward, but they were stopped by the security guards. Ryan shot Joorn a cautionary glance that clearly said that he wanted to see how this would play out.

Torris and the woman were jabbering fervently across the gap between them, the words pouring out in a torrent. It was too fast and too distant for the aboriginal language specialists with Irina to keep up with it.

"I wonder what they're saying," Nina said.

"What were you doing with the bride raiders?" Torris managed, almost choking with the effort.

Ning's lips parted in the familiar half-smile. "Perhaps I was coming to capture you and carry you away, Tor-ris," she said.

"Are you mocking me?" he said angrily.

"I would not do that, Tor-ris."

"Because of you, I was branded a heretic and thrown into the dark to die."

"So you could not keep your lips sealed after all. I'm not surprised."

"Instead of being sentenced to death, I might have joined our own bride raiders and perhaps captured *you*."

"Or died in the attempt," she returned.

He ignored that. "But because of you, I did not get the chance to join our raiding party," he said bitterly.

"And yet here you are." She looked around, first at the huddled group of warriors from Torris's Tree, then at the cluster of strange little people gathered between the two groups. "Who are your new friends, Tor-ris?"

He could not stay angry, no matter how he tried. "They come from a star very far away," he said. He struggled with the fantastic concept that Alten and Chu had tried to introduce him to. "So far away that it is beyond the sky itself."

Ning had a quick mind, and she'd had time to think. "Are we in a sort of Tree, then? And do these little people live inside their Tree instead of in its branches or in the World it carries in its roots?"

"We're not in a Tree," he said. "It's a made thing."

"So big?" she said. "But how can that be? Where would they stand to make it?"

He didn't understand that himself. He tried to make sense out of what Alten had told him. "On something called a planet. I don't know exactly what it is, but it's bigger than a Tree, and everything is heavy on it."

"As we are now?"

"Yes." He became aware of the strain in her expression, the lines etched by the pain of standing upright. He was feeling it himself, but he, at least, had had time to strengthen the muscles in his spindly legs. Yet Ning, as always, was determined not to show weakness, not in front of him or her failed cohorts. Those nearest to her had started to try to follow the conversation, probably with little success.

"It must be a powerful charm then," she said.

"It's only the same force that we use when we whirl something around in a sling when we want to throw it a distance."

She looked alarmed. "Is that going to happen to us?"

He tried to reassure her. "No, they mean no one any harm. That's why they stopped the fight."

"It was not a giant web beast, then, as some of these ignorant fools are suggesting. It was only a net, like one we might make ourselves but inconceivably bigger."

She was interrupted by gasps and cries of fear coming from both sides of the auditorium. Jonah had emerged halfway from his tank of water and was regarding them with a toothy dolphin smile.

Ning was doing her best not to show any fear. "So even the animals do their bidding," she said. "What do they intend for us?"

"They will return us to our Trees. They talk of bringing peace between us. How they will do that, I do not know."

"They cannot force peace on us, no matter how we may fear them. We can only bring peace ourselves. Their priests, if they have them, must convince our priests that they are doing the will of the Trees—all Trees. And they must allow the priests to pretend they knew it all along and let it appear that the God-Trees have sent their little star people to back their authority."

Jonah had tried to approach but was blocked by Ryan's

watchdogs. He emitted a string of dolphin chirps in the mixed-language patois that he and Torris had devised between them.

"What does your animal say, Tor-ris?" Ning said.

"He says that you have a fine Machiavellian guile and that I should listen to you. The word that I did not know how to translate is the name of one of the star dwarfs, a sort of adviser to priests who knows how to manipulate people. And yet he is admired for his duplicity. I have not met him yet."

"Well then, Tor-ris, I will tell you that you must work with this Claz of yours. If he is like all priests, he knows where power lies, and that is with you. You are the chosen go-between of the little star people. You speak to their animals and command the great web beast that ensnared the warring bride raiders. No one will ever believe otherwise. When you and I are long gone, you will be remembered as the bringer of the message. You must use their awe of you before it dissipates."

"I'll speak to your people," he said.

He made a move toward her but was checked by the security guards.

Ning shook her head. "I will speak to them. They have seen us together, and they have seen the beast talk to us. You had better talk to your own people first."

From where Ryan's guards had him boxed in, Jonah said in intelligible English, "Good idea, Torris. Play prophet for all it's worth. We'll help you along with a miracle or two."

CHAPTER 20

The priest's name was Shamash, and he came with two ceremonial guards armed with spears. The spears were serious weapons, tipped with the precious shiny hard stuff that the little men had brought, a sacred material that was reserved for the use of the priestly class.

But Claz had been gracious and had not objected to the guards' presence, though he had not allowed them to be admitted to his inner sanctum. They were waiting outside in the communal chamber, being treated to a feast of roasted meat and fermented sap and enjoying the chance to boast to strange women.

Torris studied Shamash, taking his measure. Ning's priest was a big, overbearing man with a peremptory manner, and he showed the strain and fatigue of his crossing, though it wasn't as daunting a leap as it once had been. Even an older man could make the crossing in half a day now, thanks to the man-slinging catapults that the artisans of the other Tree were turning out under Ning's direction.

It also helped that the Trees had stopped their slow drift apart and were now locked in a gravitational embrace. Chu had explained it to Torris. It had something to do with the presence of *Time's Beginning*, which now rose and set every day, a distant speck in the sky that the people of both Trees made sacrifices to. The traffic between the two Trees had become almost routine.

"It's settled then," Shamash was saying ponderously. "You may not hunt in the upper branches of our Tree, and we may not hunt in yours, not even Ning the Huntress. In times of need, as now, you will send us gifts of meat in return for things we can supply, like the catapults that Ning has shown us how to make. In your own times of need, we will do the same for you. Our elders will decide together what goods are acceptable. Private goods may be traded freely. There will be no bride raids, but young men of both Trees may visit peaceably to choose brides. They may not be carried off by force but must give their consent."

"Agreed," Claz said.

"And all this is the will of the Trees?" Shamash asked.

"Yes," Torris said.

The elders, Cleb the Chronicler and Igg the Spearmaker, had remained silent. Claz had ordered them not to interfere, and Igg especially didn't look too happy. Torris knew that Claz planned to ease Igg out. Torris, despite his youth, would replace him as elder. There would be more prestige in it. Cleb would be no problem. He was reconciled to the death of Brank. A realist, he had at once accepted Torris's position as the mouthpiece of the star people. And as Chronicler, he needed access, no matter what his scruples.

Shamash had made the same calculation on his own Tree. He had overcome the objections of his elders to a woman and confirmed Ning's status as an intimate of Torris and of the race of little people whom the Trees had brought forth as their instruments. He silenced dissenters by warning them that they risked bringing doom on the tribe if they flouted the manifest will of the Trees. He and Claz were two of a kind.

"Now then, Torris," Shamash said with the show of deference that he always exhibited in the presence of other people, "you will come to our Tree at the next conjunction of the Sisters and join Ning in addressing our slingmakers."

"Yes," Torris said soberly, "and I will bring a gift of the starsilk thread that has been granted by Joorn, the chief of their tribe."

"The silk of their giant web beast," Shamash said. He always put on a good show of believing the giant web beast story. It was easier than contradicting the beliefs of his followers.

"Yes," Torris said. "And Ning will come to our Tree with one of her artisans and instruct Igg, our Spearmaker, in the art of constructing the giant catapults."

Shamash didn't like that, but he and Torris had already wrestled over that point several times. "Agreed," he said reluctantly.

"One more thing," Torris said. "The star people wish to visit your Tree again and study the ways of your people more closely. They have already spent much time with us. They will require no food or air from you but will bring their own. They will live in their own little caves, which they will bring with them."

That finally penetrated Shamash's show of imperturbability. His eyes widened. "They will bring caves? How can that be?"

"They are magical caves," Torris said authoritatively. "They resemble nothing so much as a flat air sack, which a person may carry with him. But when he touches a certain spot and utters some magic words, it suddenly springs up like a mushroom. Inside there is air and heat and whatever they require."

"It's true," Claz said. "I have seen them."

"But their safety must be assured," Torris went on. "And they will wish to talk to many more people this time, especially women. They want to know that people will not be afraid to talk to them."

"I will see to it myself," Shamash said. "I will tell the women that they may talk freely. As for safety, who would dare harm an emissary of the Trees? But I will have my own guards follow them discreetly and see that nothing untoward occurs."

"Fine," Torris said. He rose to his feet. "If that is all, I will go now."

Claz looked relieved. "Torris, you might look in on your father," he said. "He asked about you the other day."

Torris did not reply. There was something in Claz's tone that made his remark more than a suggestion, as if he were trying to reassert his priestly authority, and he didn't want to acknowledge that. He gave a slight nod to Igg and Cleb to observe the basic necessities of courtesy and went out through the heavy curtain.

As usual he drew the stares of the people in the communal chamber, but he was used to that now. Over by the fire, Shamash's spearmen had finished gorging themselves on meat and set aside the remnants of their feast. They were a little tipsy from the drink and were getting bolder with the women. That didn't go over well with the young bloods from Torris's tribe, some of whom were loitering nearby. It hadn't been that long since the bride raiders had faced each other with murderous intent. They'd been returned to their Trees without fulfilling their thirst for combat, and they'd chafed under the enforced truce.

Torris recognized one of his former tormenters among the loitering malcontents; it was young Uz, one of those who'd escorted him at spearpoint to the hillock from which he'd been cast into space. Uz was having a dispute with one of the spearmen, and the voices were getting louder. Torris saw his hand hovering tentatively in the vicinity of the knife dangling from his waist.

He hurried over to stop it before it could go further. "Uz, these men have been made welcome here by Claz."

Uz turned, a resentful look on his face. "They are making free with our women."

"They have not touched a woman. Nor will they, without the woman's consent." He turned a hard stare on the spearman in question. "Is that not so?"

The fellow caught himself in the act of reaching for the woman who was serving him. She backed guiltily away, her eyes averted.

"Forgive me, Speaker to the Starfolk," the fellow said, his words a little slurred. "I did not mean to . . . "

Uz said sullenly, "It's not right for them to come here and make their choices."

Torris spoke carefully, aware of the weight his words carried. "You may do the same, Uz. It is the will of the Trees, through their instruments the Starfolk, that we may select brides from each other's tribes as long as the women freely consent. If you wish to see which women may be courted, you and your friends may come with me at the next conjunction of the Sisters. I will see that you will be made welcome."

He immediately regretted making the promise. He would have to fix it up with Ning, but she would work with Shamash

247

to smooth the way, as he and Claz had smoothed the way for her Tree's candidates. It would be a touchy business, but the people of the two Trees were already getting used to each other. They could see that the new arrangement was better than fighting.

Uz nodded in resignation. Torris remembered how fearful he had been aboard *Time's Beginning* after he had been released from the net with the others. Uz had been almost incoherent when Torris appeared to calm the prisoners. He couldn't fathom that the man he had seen cast out to die had returned with this tribe of beings who it was said came from beyond the stars. And he had been in mortal terror when Jonah appeared beside Torris to speak in an amplified voice that surely was the voice of the Trees. He had adjusted to the fact that Torris was not a supernatural being, but like the rest of the returned bride raid veterans, he had accepted Torris's new authority without conscious thought.

"As you say, Chosen One," Uz said. "We will follow the will of the Trees."

He motioned to his friends, and they hurried off with him, with a lot of backward glances.

Torris waited until they were out of sight, down the passage that led to the outside lock, then set off for the cubbyhole where Parn the Facemaker plied his trade.

He found his father sitting cross-legged over a Face mold, carefully pouring a ladleful of heated resin into it, leaning close to make sure there were no bubbles. His father did not look up until he was sure that the cast was complete. "Yes?" he said impatiently, then he saw Torris.

"It's all right, Father," Torris said. "I'm no longer Shunned."

His father sat looking at him. Finally he said, "Don't stand so close in case you jar the mold before it solidifies and cause ripples, boy. Didn't I teach you that?"

"Yes, Father."

"So you have been among the star people? Nobody talks of anything else these days. They were among us for many turns of the world when they returned the bride raiders, poking among us, asking questions, walking among us without weapons as if they had nothing to fear. One of them came to talk to me, a little woman, no larger than a child. She wanted to know how Faces are made and if any sacred rituals are employed in their making. What nonsense! And what position I had in the tribe and was I equal to the elders or below them. As if I was expected to kneel to Igg, who is only a spearmaker. And she could not talk properly but kept glancing at a thing in her hand that looked something like a Face but had marks on it that kept changing. If she did not understand a word, she kept asking me to repeat it while she held up the Face-object. I could tell she was not a supernatural being but a woman. But try to tell that to ignorant people who look no farther than the ends of their noses!"

Torris waited it out. When Parn seemed to have run down, he said, "Will you allow me to see Firstmother and Second-mother?"

Parn's face looked haggard and suddenly old. "Your mothers have been very distraught. But I could not allow them to talk to you when you were"—he could not make himself use the word *Shunned*—"not part of us. Nor speak of you when you were gone. You understand?"

"Yes, Father."

"It's almost time for nightfeast. Firstmother will prepare a portion for you."

Torris tried not to show his surprise. When Parn had taken Secondmother, it had become her task to prepare food, though under Firstmother's watchful eye. Secondmother had learned fast, and it hadn't taken long before Firstmother no longer needed to instruct her.

"You have a new brother. Secondmother needs time to take care of him until he is weaned."

Torris said nothing. Parn's manner precluded any comment.

Parn became brisk. He blew on the faceplate to check its progress. "It's done," he said and put it aside. He got to his feet, the joints of his knees cracking. He pushed aside the meatbeast pelt that served as a curtain and entered the living alcove, with Torris following.

The two women were nowhere near the curtain, but it was obvious that they had been listening. There was a fire going in the far corner with two large chunks of meat roasting on a spit. They turned around as if in surprise but didn't say anything.

Torris scrutinized his new brother. He couldn't see the infant's face, which was buried in Secondmother's breast, but the tiny body was well-formed, with strong limbs and a shaggy covering of rough black hair on his scalp.

With a glance at Parn for permission to speak, Firstmother said, "So you have come back, my Torris, not only a man but an oracle."

Secondmother smiled shyly at him. In an impulsive movement, she held the baby out for his inspection. Once he would have been at a loss to know what to do, but his stay with the little people, who were always tender of each other's feelings, had taught him much.

"He is a fine baby," he said.

His father scowled. Perhaps it made him uncomfortable to see Torris cosseting the women when he himself had always preserved perfect comportment. "Tell me," Parn said. "Is it true that there are to be no more bride raids?"

"Yes, Father," Torris said. "The Starfolk do not believe in killing."

He knew that wasn't strictly true. The man who had stolen Nina—and wasn't that a sort of bride raid—had been prepared to kill her when Chu and Martin didn't surrender. And when Torris himself, acting on an instinctive understanding of the situation, had impaled the man with his improvised arrow before he could hurt the girl, the others had been grateful. It had created a bond between him and the star people. But it was all too difficult to explain.

"It will just cause trouble," his father said. "You can't change the order of things."

"The Starfolk," Torris said carefully, "believe that our people will prosper more working together than fighting. They propose to show us new ways to grow food so that we do not have to rely on hunting. They talk of herding meatbeasts and growing things."

"Blasphemy," Parn said. "I suppose they propose to show us new ways of casting Faces too."

Torris knew better than to attempt to answer that one. He relied on the phrase that Claz had popularized. "It is the will of the Trees," he said.

Parn sighed. "Everybody is saying that these days. I suppose that we humans are mere twigs in the grip of the Trees, and they can snap us in two or make us grow."

"We have much to learn," Torris said.

The two women had been whispering together. Firstmother made her way toward them and waited diffidently for a pause in the conversation. "Come over by the fire," she said. "The meat is sufficiently cooked now."

Irina had taken over one of the larger auditoriums for the info-meet report. She had expected maybe a few hundred people to show up. Most people, she thought, would watch it on their personal screens or catch up with it later on the Shipnet posting. But over a thousand people had filled the hall to overflowing, with an equal number clamoring outside to be let in. Joorn, to the dismay of the participants, had been given no choice but to announce that there would be a second live conference where questions could be asked.

Irina's specialists were sitting stiffly on straight-backed chairs on the platform, some half dozen of them, representing the departments that had burgeoned under them. One was Nina's friend Andrew, who had made himself the go-to expert on physical anthropology despite his youth. Another was Irina's original assistant, Laurel, who had just published a paper tracing similarities between the dialects of Torris's and Ning's tribes that suggested a common point of origin about a thousand years in the past.

"And so the field workers' report concludes that we've gone

about as far as we can go in acculturation without causing mischief," Irina was saying. "We can leave the Oort cloud and continue our exploration of the Sol-Centauri system with a clear conscience. Left to their own devices, they'll do just fine till we can check on them again. Torris and Ning, along with their priesthoods, will be the prime focal points of change, but they're bright people—they'd have to be to survive without technology in a space environment—and they're well on the road to developing beyond an aboriginal hunting society. I think Andrew has something more to say about that."

Andrew replaced her at the lectern. He looked very young but thoroughly in command of himself and his audience. Nina, sitting in the front row between Joorn and Alten, looked at him with eyes aglow.

"Conclusions first, then the facts," Andrew said mischievously. "Just the opposite of the way we do it in our little work groups when we're hammering out theories. We think we can now state with reasonable confidence where Torris's people came from, how long they've been here, and how they managed their miraculous survival with only an Eolithic culture." He paused. "I say Eolithic rather than Paleolithic because they didn't even have stones to fashion into their first tools, as the australopithecines did."

A hush fell over the audience. They were paying attention now.

"Their resources were only those of the ecology of vacuum-dwelling trees—wood; ice; the bone, sinews, and hides of the animal life that the tree supported; and the sugars and other products of the tree's metabolism. And oh yes, fire. They had fire when they started out. The australopithecines didn't. And I can assure you that fire-hardened wood has a cutting edge." He held up a bandaged finger. "Our experiments proved that."

Nina whispered to her grandfather, "Isn't Andrew marvelous? He actually made wooden knives and spearpoints just to be sure." She added proudly, "I helped him when Laurel and the others belittled the idea. I was the one who had to bandage his finger."

Joorn smiled benignly, but Alten maintained a stone-faced demeanor.

Now Andrew was using a cursor to trace a lot of confusing lines and arrows on an electronic easel he had illuminated, but nobody was bothering to follow the animation.

"We followed up the study of Torris's DNA with samples from those members of his tribe we could persuade to cooperate. Some thought the DNA swabs were part of a religious ritual, sanctioned by the priest, Claz. Other DNA, I'm sorry to say, we acquired surreptitiously. Some say unethically. We can debate that, but no harm was done, and given the sociometric circumstances, we can say that, objectively speaking, there was no invasion of privacy. What we found jibed with our study of Torris and Ning. The antigenic distance between us and them is no more than four hundred thousand years, give or take a hundred thousand years."

A hand shot up. "How can that be? We come from six billion years in their past."

Andrew smiled. "Good question. They were derived from the same genetic stock that we were, only about four hundred thousand years ago on our time scale."

More hands were waving. "Time dilation," someone offered.

"Exactly. Torris's ancestors got here the same way we did, only four hundred thousand years before our arrival."

"Have you any theories to explain that?" somebody asked belligerently.

"We have. The relativistic math works out in any number of ways, depending on what assumptions we make about velocity and distance. What it boils down to is that Torris's distant ancestors either were returning from a galaxy closer than the galaxy that we were returning from or that they had a faster ship capable of crowding the speed of light another decimal point or two. They found Earth and the inner planets gone—engulfed by the sun. The sun was earlier in its red-giant phase, somewhat bigger than it is at present, its hydrogen gone, but still feasting on its helium reserves. The same stellar evolution had happened in the Alpha Centauri system, now within easy reach, but the primary star there was even earlier in its red-giant stage and correspondingly bigger. Perhaps their ship was in some kind of trouble—it wouldn't have been capable of another star hop, or perhaps it had run down its supplies. So with Earth gone, they did the only thing they could. They headed out to the Oort cloud, now augmented by Centauri's Oort cloud, containing plenty of real estate—trillions of comets with all the ingredients needed for life. And the Trees that grew on them."

Another hand went up. "You mean the Trees were already there when they arrived?"

"We're getting ahead of ourselves, but yes. They'd had six billion years to evolve. Don't forget, Torris's forebears had only a four-hundred-thousand-year headstart on us—a mere drop in the bucket of time."

He gave them time to digest that, then said, "I don't know how many generations it took for them to forget the star-hopping civilization they came from—it could have been fifty or a hundred thousand years—but eventually they hit bottom. They were the equivalent of the naked apes that we once were when early *Homo sapiens* and *Homo neanderthalensis* went their separate ways with the aid of the simple tools that were available to both of them in their common environment—chipped stone, wooden clubs, and so forth. The Neanderthals didn't make it, but *Homo sapiens* did. They became modern *Homo sapiens*—or *Homo sapiens sapiens*, as we paleoanthropologists like to say. Wise, wise apes. And at some point—about thirty thousand years before agriculture became a way of life and the first cities arose in Egypt and Mesopotamia—something quite wonderful happened."

Nina grinned at her grandfather. "Guess what he's going to say next."

Before Joorn could respond, someone in the front row impatiently yelled, "What?"

"Grandfathers," Andrew said with a broad smile. "Grandfathers happened." He regained his professorial tone. "That's the only way I can put it."

He moved the cursor on the easel, and a procession of fossil skulls appeared, each with its own bar graph. A header helpfully proclaimed O-Y RATIO.

"Teeth are the reason we know this," Andrew said. "In the early twenty-first century, a pair of paleoanthropologists had the bright idea of doing a statistical analysis of large numbers of fossil teeth. There were plenty of teeth—enamel is harder than bone. It was possible to tell from the wear of the teeth displayed how old the individual was at death."

He paused for emphasis. "In other words, given an existence that was short, nasty, and brutish, had any of these individuals lived long enough to become a grandparent? And applying statistical methods that hadn't been used up until that time, it was possible to discover the O-Y ratio for any given population."

There was an uneasy stirring in the audience, and Andrew anticipated the next question. "O-Y simply refers to the relative numbers of old and young individuals of breeding age— *old* being someone of thirty or more. And they discovered the remarkable fact that the O-Y ratio multiplied abruptly and dramatically about thirty thousand years before the onset of civilization. That was the turning point. We begin to see the sudden appearance of conceptual thought. Cave paintings. Ornamental necklaces, some of them quite elaborate. A new, more thoughtful method of chipping the flint weapons that had remained unchanged for hundreds of thousands of years, as far back as the pre-sapiens hominids. Tools changed from crude hand axes to quite sophisticated stone knives with long, thin blades. Man changed from a hunter-gatherer into a farmer. Of course there were cultural overlaps. In ancient Sumeria, well into the Bronze Age, there were peasants who were still using those Neolithic tools."

The impish look reappeared on his face, and he said, "So we can thank grandfathers for civilization." Catching the look that Nina gave him, he added, "And grandmothers. They'd lived long enough to pass on what they'd learned. How to weave a better basket. How to make a sharper knife or improve your range with a throwing stick. How to paint shells to make prettier necklaces. In a word, *traditions*. The sense that there is a past."

He became utterly serious. "We believe that Torris's people were at this point when we found them. Certainly our survey found plenty of grandfathers. And grandmothers too—excuse me, Nina. They've had traditions for an unknown number of generations. Torris fell afoul of at least one of them."

He lifted his head and locked eyes with his audience. "We also believe that Torris's people are at this turning point now and have been since their O-Y ratio began to change. And we think we can help speed things up."

The fellow in the first row, whom Joorn now recognized as a classmate of Andrew's, raised his hand. Joorn believed that Andrew was not above using him as a plant to keep things moving.

"This is all very interesting, Andrew, but what a lot of us would like to know is where did this full-blown ecology based on the Bernal trees come from?" he asked. "How is it that Torris's shipwrecked antecedents found a ready-made environment able to support them after they'd finished cannibalizing their ship and sunk into savagery?"

"I think I'd better let Jen answer that," Andrew said. "Jen is our expert on evolutionary theory."

He made way for a lanky young woman with straggling ash-blond hair. Nina nudged Joorn. "Jen's new to the team, but she knows more than some of them."

The young woman began briskly rearranging Andrew's visuals. The hominid skulls, the teeth, and the Stone Age tools flashed by and disappeared. When the blur of images slowed down and stopped, there was only a picture of a tree growing out of a comet left on the screen. The tree was ten or twenty times taller than the comet's diameter, like a small potato sprouting a stalk bigger than itself. It looked very much like Torris's Tree seen from a distance.

"This is an artist's conception of a Bernal tree," Jen began. "It was drawn in the early twentieth century, before there was space travel or genetic engineering—at a time when most scientists thought that space travel would forever be impossible and before the very concept of genetic engineering even existed.

"Bernal's tree was derided by most scientists at the time, but in the years that followed, it was championed by a few visionary thinkers, notably the evolutionary biologist J.B.S. Haldane and the physicist Freeman Dyson. Here's what Dyson had to say about Bernal's dream."

The tree was replaced by the close-up of a face, presumably that of the physicist. Jen read from the text of an old book that was also displayed on the screen.

"'How high can a tree on a comet grow? The answer is surprising. On any celestial body whose diameter is of the order of ten miles or less, the force of gravity is so weak that a tree can grow infinitely high. Ordinary wood is strong enough to lift its own weight to an arbitrary distance from the center of gravity. This means that from a comet of ten-mile diameter, trees can grow out for hundreds of miles, collecting the energy of sunlight from an area thousands of times as large as the area of the comet itself.'

"'Countless millions of comets are out there, amply supplied with water, carbon, and nitrogen—the basic constituents of living cells. They lack only two essential requirements for human settlement, namely warmth and air. And now biological engineering will come to our rescue. We shall learn how to grow trees on comets.'"

She paused to let that sink in. A low murmuring had begun in the audience. Jen let it grow, then said, "And evidently the human race did just that. The process had already begun when *Time's Beginning* left Earth in pursuit of a quasar. Captain Gant and his contemporaries can remember the early stages personally. We already had forests on the moon. Now the lumber industry proposed moving to the relatively nearby comets of the Kuiper Belt—the Oort cloud still seemed impractically far away then. The trees could be bigger—big enough to make wooden spaceships and habitats. We don't know what happened in the next six billion years after our departure. The Others came and, evidently, went. Humanity—whatever was left of it in our little corner of the galaxy—undoubtedly became extinct too. But the trees flourished and spread—to the Oort cloud and beyond."

Nina could no longer contain herself. She stood up, shaking off Joorn's restraining hand, and said, "Tell them about the animals, Jen."

Jen smiled. "Ah yes, Nina, those wonderful animals. And the saprophytic plants that the herbivores feed on while waiting to be fed on themselves by the larger carnivores, like man."

She wiped the easel clean, and the images were replaced by footage out of the old Earth archives. The scenes were familiar to Joorn, if to few others in the audience. One of them, under the title LUMBERJACKS IN SPACE, showed crews of spacesuited workers guiding gigantic self-propelled chain saws that were delimbing boughs that themselves were thicker than a California redwood, against the background of an immense trunk whose size could hardly be imagined. Another sequence, titled FARMERS IN THE SKY, showed shirtsleeved and overalled men in what seemed to be some sort of dimly-lit cavern driving a herd of perfectly ordinary-looking dairy cows toward a milking shed, while a narrator burbled: "Hungry men have to eat, and these fellows are there to feed them." That clip dissolved into a scene that obviously had been filmed some time in the future, showing the same cavern with a lot of new construction. The milking line had been replaced by a warren of livestock pens. The placid Jerseys of the previous scene had been superseded by animals that still looked like cattle but had short, stubby legs and grotesquely enlarged briskets. The header this time was GRAZING PRIVILEGES.

"Gengineering was working its marvels on life forms other than the poplar tree," Jen said. "There was still some distance to go. These must have been an early effort. An animal that could graze—live off the land, so to speak—instead of depending on a hay crop, either brought from Earth or grown locally. It could live in vacuum for an hour at a time, holding its breath like a whale or a dolphin. It had nictitating membranes to protect its eyes and nostrils. Its limbs were atrophied, adapted for micro-gravity so that it couldn't inadvertently kick itself into space. Some of them must have been left behind when mankind vanished, and the fittest survived."

Nina leaned over to confide in her grandfather. "Jen didn't want to say so here, but some of the genes they used when they gengineered the animals that evolved into meatbeasts came from cetaceans. Whales once had legs, you know, and they lost them when they went back to the sea. Jonah became very upset. That's why he didn't want to come to the briefing."

"Can't say I blame him," Joorn said. "How would you like *Australopithecus afarensis* stew for supper?"

She poked him. "You're awful."

The inquisitive fellow in the front row spoke out again. "What about some of the other wildlife, Jen? Where on Earth would something like a flutterbeast or a web spinner come from?"

Jen spoke directly to him. "You know very well, Jason. You helped collect some of the specimens that went to the molecular biology lab. They were hitchhikers. Or, I should say, they were derived from the species that were the original hitchhikers six billion years ago. They had a long time to evolve. Longer than life itself had existed on Earth by the time mammals and reptiles and even flowering plants arrived."

She turned to the audience at large. "What do I mean by hitchhikers? Unwelcome passengers have been around ever since human commerce was invented. Rats and mice in grain shipments. Insect stowaways in just about anything. Barnacles attached to the bottoms of ships. Snakes, spiders, even bats trapped in some cranny before they could return to their roosts at daylight."

She gave a nod to Nina before continuing. "We have Nina to thank for noticing a distant resemblance to bats when the first flutterbeast was observed on our arrival in the Oort cloud. It was an amazing feat of intuition for a little girl at a distance of two astronomical units, when there was nothing to go on but an indistinct image whose fluttering movement could only be inferred from a blurred speck."

"I wasn't a little girl then," Nina whispered indignantly to Joorn. "I was almost grown up. You were there, Granddaddy. You remember."

Joorn patted her knee. He was busy studying the display

easel, where a series of visualizations by the study group's artist traced the presumed evolution of a house bat to the fearsome creature that had pursued Torris.

"By the time man departed," Jen went on, "bats had established a foothold in the caverns that housed the original lumber camps. Man had thoughtfully provided air and warmth for them, and there were plenty of moths and mosquitoes for them to hunt. We've still got moths aboard *Time's Beginning*, though we got rid of the mosquitoes before we settled Rebirth. We can only conjecture about the first steps that led to flutterbeasts. Perhaps when man disappeared, the caverns took millennia to lose their air—after all, there are still air-filled caves on Torris's comet, thanks to a little help from the inhabitants. Perhaps it was a gradual process of adaptation that took millions of years. When the moths grew scarce, there were plenty of insects outside, though they couldn't fly in vacuum. But neither could the bats. They adapted to new ways of hunting. Their wings became appendages modified to help them move through the branches. The claws became useful for clutching small animals. Sonar was no longer useful in vacuum, so the ears, with their large surfaces, became infrared detectors for hunting by body heat—the tree snakes had an easier time adjusting. And as time went on, the flutterbeasts became bigger, as the dinosaurs did, to take advantage of the economics of hunting large animals like meatbeasts. After all, T. rex's predecessors began as something the size of a chicken. When man arrived some billennia later in the form of Torris's ancestors, he became an additional source of snacks."

Jason couldn't resist being a smart aleck. "From chicken thou came, and to chicken thou shalt return," he said.

Jen made a face and forged doggedly ahead. "Spiders were another story. They had quite a headstart. In the first place, there were more of them. There are about thirty thousand different species, each with its own specialty. Most of them are too small to notice, but they're all around us—just ask anybody in the ship-cleaning department how many webs the cleaning bots sweep up in the course of a week. Some of them were—are—aquatic, like the fisher spider, which can stay underwater for an hour or more to hunt its prey, thanks to tiny hairs that trap air. Other species prefer to spin silken diving bells for themselves. They had a leisurely time of it over the millennia learning to live in vacuum. And, like flutterbeasts, they learned the advantages of growing bigger, including less surface area in proportion to total mass, which improved heat conservation. Some caught their prey in webs. Some, like the wolf spiders, hunted their prey or lassoed it by throwing a thread. We see the same two types among the web beasts. And yes, we got enough tissue samples thanks to the help of the Tree people to confirm the spider heritage of the web beasts.

"We have our work cut out for us to classify all the plant and animal species we've found here. We set out, six billennia ago, to seed another galaxy with terrestrial life. And while we were gone, our own galaxy was doing it for us here, in a way we never imagined. Perhaps it would be fitting for me to close with the prophetic words of Freeman Dyson himself."

She clicked the audiovisuals to sound only, and a sonorous voice filled the auditorium. Whether it was the voice of Dyson or some actor back in the vanished twentieth century reading his words was impossible to know.

"We shall bring to the comets not only trees but a great variety of flora and fauna to create for ourselves an environment as beautiful as ever existed on Earth. Perhaps we shall teach our plants to make seeds that will sail across the ocean of space to propagate life upon comets still unvisited by man. Perhaps we shall start a wave of life that will spread from comet to comet without end until we have achieved the greening of the galaxy. That may be an end or a beginning, as Bernal said. . . . "

Torris had never been to a cocktail party. He took a cautious sip of his martini and wrinkled his nose. "Is it a religious custom?" he asked. "You people gather together and drink dizzy juice to celebrate a leave-taking?"

Chu laughed. "It's called a going-away party. We gather together and have a drink to celebrate almost anything."

"I think it's a fine custom," Ning said. "Now that we are working with our priests to change things, it's a custom we should adopt. As soon as your friends from beyond the stars teach us to squeeze juice that tastes like this from Tree sap."

She held up her glass for another look at its contents. She was drinking Chablis with a splash of soda, a more judicious selection thanks to Irina's intervention. Irina had gotten to the bar too late to prevent Chu from ordering a martini for Torris.

"Why do you have to go at all?" Torris asked Chu.

"We'll be back for another look at you to see how you're doing," Chu said. "But we've done all we can for now. Now we have to proceed to the inner system to see what the red star has done to Earth, the planet we all came from when the Universe was young."

"I do not understand," Torris said. "Inner system. Planet.

Universe. Why inner? All I know is that the Stepsister is very far away."

"It is," Chu said, taking another sip of his own martini. "We have a long way to go before we even get to the outer planets, whatever's left of them."

"And you say that the Stepsister swallowed this planet Earth long ago and that it melted?"

"That's what we think." Chu knew that Torris was thinking of Earth as a ball of ice, somewhat larger than his own comet.

"And yet you say you want to walk on this Earth."

"That's right. A nice walk in the sun." Chu was enjoying himself.

"But if Earth is inside the Stepsister, how is such a thing even possible?"

"Your friend Nina ran the figures. And she's convinced her father and her grandfather that it might be possible."

"Nina? That little girl? Is she a numberer then?"

"Among other things."

Chu glanced over to where Nina was chatting with Andrew and some of his friends. She was holding something with a cherry in it. Chu knew that Alten thought she was still too young to drink. But he also knew that Andrew had probably sneaked her something like a Manhattan, an old drink named after the twentieth-century project that had originally split the atom. She saw Chu and waved. He waved back and lifted his glass.

Irina came over, trailed by her disciple Laurel. "What are you saying about Nina?"

"That your daughter's good at math," Chu said.

Irina laughed. "She had to be when she was growing up. To please Alten."

"Well, she picked up on something that was too simple for your genius husband to think about."

"That's what Joorn said." She shook her head. "Does it really mean what Nina says it does?"

"Think about it. What's the volume of a sphere with a diameter of ninety-three million miles?"

"There aren't enough places on my calculator."

"Exactly. Multiply pi by four. Then multiply that by the cube of the radius. Then divide that by the number of atoms in a cubic mile, say, of the outer layers of a helium star. Even a lowly starship skipper like Joorn or me can figure that one out."

"I can't."

"Then you'll just have to wait till we get there. If Nina's right, we'll show you."

[HAPTER 29](CHAPTER 29)

6,000,000,003 A.D.
A Walk in the Sun

The landscape was bleak and suffused with a ruddy light. The sky was a bloody red wherever they looked. The three of them cast no shadows whatsoever. The terrain was shot through with dangerous cracks but was otherwise utterly flat, without even a small hill to cast a shadow of its own.

"You shouldn't have come, Father," Alten said. "You're too old to take the risk. You could have stayed aboard the ship and watched from there."

"I've traveled two and a half billion light-years to come home," Joorn said. "I wasn't about to settle for a view from your helmet cam. Or a probe. I had to set foot on Mother Earth myself."

They were wearing the antiquated Venus coolsuits that had been packed away in storage for six billion years. Suits like these had been worn by men on Venus when *Time's Beginning* left Earth. They were bulky with insulation and equipped with Maxwell's Demons, the compact refrigeration units that worked by using sound waves to bat slow molecules in one direction and fast molecules in the other. The exhaust tubes rose high above their heads like medieval pikes, swaying precariously, the heat from them making the air ripple.

"Me too," Martin said. "I mean really and truly setting foot on Mother Earth."

Alten snorted. "More like Grandmother Earth to you. You're the youngest. You might have stayed behind and watched from the ship."

"Point of privilege," Martin said.

Joorn intervened good-naturedly. "The boy's right. It doesn't take a member of the Gant dynasty to run the ship. There's a perfectly competent third officer taking charge."

"Thanks for that, Skipper," Chu said. "Nice to know I'm not needed." He looked up at the burning sky. The sun reached both horizons. Technically it was sunrise, noon, and sunset at the same time. "We better move on before the soles of our boots melt. We've been standing in one place too long."

Joorn looked back over his shoulder as if to reassure himself that the lander was still there. It towered some eighty feet above them, but it didn't cast a shadow either. "Not too far," he said. "We have to give ourselves time to get back when the monitors beep us that the heat is starting to get the best of the ship's demon."

They shuffled forward about a hundred yards. It was easier than trying to push through the molasses that had been the atmosphere of Venus. Earth had no atmosphere to speak of anymore, and they really didn't need the suits to be powered. On the other hand, the heat was worse.

Joorn signaled for a stop. "Anybody see anything yet?" he said.

"You're kidding, right?" Chu said. "We could walk a thousand miles and the scenery wouldn't change."

Joorn nodded. "It would be nice to have some place to go to after traveling all those light-years," he said wistfully.

"Not much of a homecoming, is it, Grandfather?" Martin asked. "I can almost see why Professor Karn was against coming back."

They stared in mutual commiseration at the horizon. It was the same barren surface crust as far as the eye could see, a featureless plain with no shadows, even in the gaping cracks.

"We came a few million years too early, that's all," Alten said. "Nina's prediction was right on target. The sun's already begun to shrink. Earth will eventually emerge from the photosphere. The cooling process will speed up, and life will be possible again. And the white dwarf that the sun becomes will still shed enough heat to sustain some sort of life for another billion years."

Chu nodded. "And in its death throes the sun will continue to lose mass through flares and coronal mass ejections. So Earth's orbital radius will keep growing and speed up the cooling process."

That stopped Alten for about a half second. Then he said, "I see you've been brushing up on your astrophysics, Chu."

"I've been talking to Nina," Chu said dryly.

Martin said, "I ran through her arithmetic myself, Dad. It's counterintuitive, but it explains why we're walking around inside the outer chromosphere. The temperature's still horrendous—though it's technically down to only about six thousand kelvins here." He frowned with concentration. "But with a radius the size of Earth's orbit, the volume of the sun is so tremendous that its matter is tenuous enough to dilute it, especially in the outer layers of the photosphere. Like, putting your hand on a hot stove isn't the same as touching the point of a pin heated to the temperature of a hot stove."

Alten started to correct him but thought better of it. "Keep it up, son. We'll make a starship pilot of you yet."

"Not as good as Chu. And he'll need a good engineer."

Joorn said sharply, "We'll need a good astrophysicist too. If we're going to be zipping around the Sol-Centauri system, piloting the ship will be a full-time job."

Chu said, "That would be you, Skipper."

"I'm already about a hundred years past retirement age," Joorn demurred. "Are we arguing about who gets to refuse the job?"

Martin was getting restive. He kept glancing at the sky. "Where do we look next, Grandfather? Venus and Mercury are gone forever. Earth will be a hot potato for the next million years."

"We'll take a closer look at Mars next," Joorn said. "From the orbital observations, it looked like the surface baked to a hard finish but didn't melt. There was even a hint of green, though that will have to be confirmed—some of the algae we planted there six billion years ago may have survived and evolved. It may be a fit environment for the human race."

"And if it isn't," Alten said, "there's the four Galilean moons of Jupiter. When the sun boiled away Jupiter's hydrogen—including the metallic form that liquefied when the atmospheric pressure was released—it ended the dynamo effect that was causing Jupiter's killer radiation. It's become a nice neighborhood, and now there are four rocky bodies large enough to have gravity similar to Mars."

"Five, if you count Jupiter itself," Chu said. "It turned out to have a rocky core about the size of Earth. Even closer to the gravity we're used to, and just right for terraforming."

"And closer to our new friends in the Oort cloud," Martin added enthusiastically. "If Mother's team is right, there's a whole human civilization there—maybe a trillion people spread out all the way to Alpha Centauri. We can't ignore them. We have a lot to offer each other, and commerce of a sort has already begun."

"We'll see," Joorn said. "We're getting ahead of ourselves. Right now we have to keep moving. My feet are feeling warm."

They moved on till they came to the edge of a crack. They stopped and peered down into a chasm that was several hundred feet deep. There was a glint of lava at the bottom.

They were still staring downward when the dull red glow of the landscape all around them suddenly turned a blinding white. That was a lucky thing because their helmets' filters kicked in a fraction of a second too late.

Moments later, the lander's AI announced, "Coronal mass ejection. Return to lander immediately."

Joorn cursed. "How long before the heavy stuff gets here?" he said.

Alten was conferring with the AI. After a few more seconds, he raised his head and said, "If we can get off-planet in the next fifteen minutes, we should be able to keep ahead of it."

Martin started to run. Joorn stopped him with a sharp command. "Don't hurry. If anybody stumbles or falls and damages his demon, he'll be barbecue."

Even so, they made it back to the lander in record time. They skimped on recycling time in the airlock and let a lot of hot air into the cabin. Martin threw his helmet back but didn't stop to unlatch the clamshell halves of his suit. He got busy doing an engine check while Chu seated himself and started the ignition process.

"How's the engine temperature?" Joorn said.

"Fine," Martin said. "The lander's demon kept everything nice and cool."

The lander took off like a racehorse out of the gate. It had been calibrated for Earth gravity, but Earth had lost a tenth of its mass during its sojourn inside the sun. When its surface resolidified, it weighed about the same as Venus. Or the former Venus—the solar system's second planet had turned into plasma.

They were past the orbit of Mars and still accelerating when they looked back. A gob of glowing plasma, bigger than worlds, had enveloped Earth and was now chasing them.

"Don't worry, Martin," Chu said. "The CME can't catch us now. The plasma cloud's only traveling at about five million miles an hour, and we're outrunning the high-energy protons too."

"I'm not worried," Martin said stiffly. "I can do the math too."

"By the time the CME reaches the orbit of Mars, it'll have spread out to a width of about ten million miles anyway," Alten said. "Too diluted to even give us a summer tan."

"I *said* I'm not worried, Father."

Time's Beginning was waiting for them beyond the orbit of Neptune. From here, the sun was only a star, though as a red giant it was the brightest star in the sky. It still cast a measurable amount of heat though. At the limit of its expansion, it had melted the ice of Europa and stripped Jupiter of its hydrogen, after all. Neptune's orbit had been deemed a safe enough distance for the ship to park, though in view of the importance of the decision, Joorn had deemed it necessary to put it to a general vote.

Neptune was only four light-hours from Earth, but it took them some weeks to reach it because even at a one-G acceleration there wasn't enough time to attain near-lightspeed. By the time they arrived, they were tired, unshaven, and badly in need of a proper shower.

They paused at the airlock to drink in the magnificent sight of a full Neptune. It had managed to hold on to its hydrogen-helium atmosphere through the sun's red-giant era, and from close orbit it filled the sky, a luminous blue sphere that bathed *Time's Beginning* in its reflected light. The starship was parked in a co-orbit with Naiad, one of Neptune's smaller moons, to anchor it more conveniently. It was an unequal partnership, but it saved a lot of finicky orbital maneuvering.

Joorn led the way through the boat lock's access corridor. "You two can go on ahead and get yourselves cleaned up," he said. "I'm going to stop at the bridge and check in with Robertson. The time lag on the last transmission from him was over two hours."

Robertson, the third officer, had served as captain pro tem during their absence.

"We'll go with you, Skipper," Chu said.

Martin nodded. "I want to see what the ship's instruments made of that coronal mass ejection."

They traversed the corridors to the bridge, passing pedestrians from time to time. People called out greetings, curiosity plain in their voices, but no one was ill-mannered enough to try to engage them in conversation.

There were still guards at the entrance to the bridge, though it had been several years since the Karnites' second attempt at mutiny. Ryan was still ship's president, and he was taking no chances. Necessary or not, security guards at the bridge were an established custom now.

"Glad to see you back, Captain," said one of them, as he let the three in. "Some were saying they were afraid you wouldn't make it."

Joorn laughed. "Sorry to disappoint them, Paxton. But they aren't getting rid of me that easily."

Robertson had been alerted, and he rose to greet them. He nodded to Martin and Chu, and said, "How was it on Earth, Captain?"

"Hot," Joorn said. "How did things go aboard ship?"

"Fine." Robertson looked worried. "But . . . "

Joorn became instantly attentive. "What is it, Robertson?"

"It only happened a couple of hours ago. There didn't seem to be any point in exchanging messages with you because of the time lag. You'd be back here by the time . . . "

"What is it, man?" Joorn said impatiently.

Robertson continued doggedly. "It . . . actually happened at least two years ago anyway, since it's in the middle of the Oort cloud, and at that distance, the light from . . . "

"What?"

"It was the light from a Higgs drive. Hadronic photons and some of the characteristic decay products. And a little of the associated hard stuff—enough for us to detect but not enough to do any harm at this distance."

Joorn's jaw dropped. "A Higgs drive!"

Chu found his voice. "That means . . . "

"Yes," Joorn said.

"The Higgs drive turned off after penetrating the Oort cloud," Robertson went on, "and the source, whatever it was, continued decelerating using deuterium-helium-3 fusion or some other less lethal reaction like deuterium-deuterium."

"Like us," Martin said.

"They have some sort of ethics then," Chu said.

"That's not all," Robertson said. "We were able to continue to track them briefly. We lost them, but it looked like they were making a beeline to the part of the cloud where we left our beacons."

"Orbiting Torris's comet," Chu said.

"I'm afraid so."

"It'll take us at least two years to get back there," Martin said. "In the meantime . . . "

"In the meantime, anything could happen. Like the Higgs drive being turned back on."

At that point the door swung open and Nina burst in, brushing past the guards. She spared only a distracted glance for her father and Martin and flung herself sobbing into Joorn's arms.

"Grandfather, Grandfather, did Mr. Robertson tell you? Mother and I only found out about it a little while ago! What does it mean? What's going to happen to Torris and Ning and all those people? We've got to get back there right away!"

[HAPTER 30

6,000,000,005 A.D.
The Oort Cloud

The captain's name was Yung, and his ship was the *Tien Shih*—
the "Celestial Arrow." It had been launched some two hundred
years after *Time's Beginning* by the Chinese Commonwealth.

Yung was a tall, dignified man who looked about seventy,
though he must have been Joorn's age. He was wearing a naval
uniform that hadn't changed much through the ages: a white
high-necked tunic and plenty of gold braid. The captain's
saloon was elegantly furnished in a style that wouldn't have
been out of place on a sailing ship from the days of the China
Trade, with uncomfortable high-backed armchairs of carved
ebony, a straight-backed velvet couch, Chinese screens, and
lots of wicker. There was even a gilt cage with a live thrush in it.

He poured tea from an antique teapot, serving Irina and
Nina first and then the men. There was a painted tray with
elaborate little pastries that no one had touched.

"We planted our colonies in MR 2251-178," he was saying,
"a quasar as seen from Earth at the time. Like your 3C-273, it
had settled down into a proper galaxy by the time we got there.
If there ever had been First Ones, as in our own Milky Way,

they'd been gone for a good three and a half billion years. We seeded five of the galaxy's stars with our colonists, providing the nuclei for a galaxy-wide Commonwealth, thus discharging our obligations to our ancestors, extinct these six billion years."

He paused to sip his tea. He might have been laboring under strong emotion, but his voice remained under firm control as he continued.

"The remaining colonists—five thousand of them—voted to remain aboard *Celestial Arrow* and return to the Milky Way, just as your own Homegoing faction did. Though I must say, without the necessity of a mutiny like Professor Karn's. Everything was done lawfully. They were under no illusions about what we'd find here, but there was every confidence that we might, in some way, resurrect the Middle Kingdom in the galaxy where it was born. I'm sure that you and your people can understand that kind of ancestral yearning, Captain."

"Indeed we can," Joorn said. There was a murmur of agreement from the rest of his party.

"But we can discuss all that later," Captain Yung said. He broke into a smile. "It's an honor to meet you, Captain Gant. Your name is in all the history books, and you are a hero to all those who believed in man's destiny. Of course no one had the slightest inkling of what happened to your ship after it passed out of the Local Group, but you are an inspiration to boys like me. I became a spaceman because of you."

Joorn ignored the transparent attempt at flattery. "You said 'the first expedition,'" he prompted.

"Yes, there were five of them in the two centuries that separated *Time's Beginning* and *Celestial Arrow*. Nothing had been heard from them, of course. None of them would have reached its goal until long after the human race became extinct on Earth. By the time we ourselves launched, the First Ones had squeezed humans still further. They took over Alpha Centauri B and the two habitable worlds of Tau Ceti after our infant colonies there folded in despair and came home."

"You said you investigated the Centauri worlds before you proceeded to the Oort cloud in response to our signals."

"Yes, we left a team of archaeologists on Centauri B. They're still digging up the place, and they haven't found the slightest trace of a First Ones civilization there. It's their opinion that the First Ones became extinct some billion years after the last humans disappeared, or perhaps evolved into a nonsentient species. We were amazed to find a recognizable human subspecies, if that's what it is, here in the Oort cloud after we followed the beacons you left here. We've made our own studies in the last two years, of course. But our ethnologists will want to talk to your ethnologists."

Irina and Andrew, Nina's new husband, spoke at the same time. "Of course!"

Nina muttered under her breath, "Torris isn't a subspecies."

Joorn shot a warning look at her, but Yung just smiled politely and went on.

"Of course that's to be determined, *Fu Jen* Nina. But I digress. I was telling you about the five expeditions that followed yours. America and the European League jointly financed the first two before their populations balked at the expense. India managed one all on its own, and so did Brazil before it bankrupted itself. And the Islamic Federation agreed with itself long enough to send a Higgs starship off to 'proselytize the Universe,' as they put it, though one wonders who's out there to convert other than hypothetical varieties of First Ones at various stages in their evolution. We certainly didn't find any.

"At any rate, my own country's space advocates had been champing at that particular bit for some time. We were the wealthiest country on Earth, and we hadn't had a major trump in space since we'd been the first to land on Mars back in the twenty-first century. It had been over a century since the last of the Higgs ships had been sent quasar chasing, and our poor overpopulated, impoverished world was played out. So China set out to show we could do it again. I don't know if there were any expeditions after *Celestial Arrow*. Perhaps there were. But I rather doubt it. The world would have been getting increasingly dispirited in the years after we departed, for the same reasons *Time's Beginning* and *Celestial Arrow* were sent out in the first place."

"But we did it, didn't we?" Chu said vehemently. "Both of us. We planted our colonies, and we made it back home. The human race isn't finished yet."

Captain Yung looked taken aback at the outburst, but he quickly recovered. "And that brings up a delicate matter," he said. "How do we divide up man's birthright?"

"What's your proposal, Captain?" Joorn said.

Yung's eyes left Joorn and focused on an invisible wall between him and Joorn's delegation. He spoke in an impersonal voice to the wall as though it were the wall's responsibility to transmit his words.

"You can have the sun and its planets and everything up to the Kuiper Belt and its short-term comets. We'll take the Centauri worlds up to their Kuiper Belts. The intermixed Oort cloud will be the ocean we share, much as the Pacific was shared in the age of sailing ships. It shouldn't be a bone of contention between us. Now that we're part of the same multiple-star system, travel time between us will be a matter of weeks, not years."

"You get three stars and we get one—is that it?" Joorn said.

"Two stars," Yung said imperturbably. "Proxima's only a dying red dwarf, swinging out at a distance from the others."

"A dying red dwarf that will take hundreds of billions of years to die out. And with a habitable planet at a distance of only forty million kilometers, right in the middle of its Goldilocks zone. In fact, there was native life there when we left six billion years ago. Was it still there when you investigated the system?"

Yung spread his hands and offered a smile. To his credit, it was not a weak smile but a forthright one.

"You have me there, Captain," he said. "Of course we both know there was a human outpost there before the First Ones drove us out. But the planet that we're interested in is the Earthlike planet orbiting Alpha Centauri B. As a K-type sun, it escaped the fate of Sol and never will become a red giant, let alone a white dwarf. We can enjoy a comfortable existence there for the next billion years, if evolution is that kind to us. The gravity's about ten percent above Earth-normal, but that won't bother us. We Chinese are used to working hard. After all, the original settlers adapted well in only a generation or two. In the meantime, you get the Earth back."

Chu seemed to enjoy Yung's sales pitch. He said without rancor, "The Earth's within the sun's photosphere and will be for the next few hundred thousand years."

Yung smiled agreeably and said, "*T'ung i.*" He reverted to

English for the others and said, "I know you and the captain have a deep emotional attachment to the corpse of Earth, Mr. Chu.

"Otherwise you would not have done something as insane as attempt to visit it. It should be very gratifying to you to know that it will be part of your heritage as the sun continues to shrink. And until Earth becomes habitable again, you'll have Mars, the newly habitable Jovian moons, and Jupiter itself, now that it's divested of its crushing burden of hydrogen and has transformed into a habitable planet warmed by a red giant. And ultimately by a white dwarf that will continue to shed heat for as long as the human race is likely to exist."

Joorn gave him a grudging smile. "I give up, Captain Yung. You could sell a Maxwell's Demon to an Eskimo."

Yung looked blank, and Chu said, "That's a mythical race that used to inhabit Earth's polar regions."

"They weren't so mythical when I walked the earth," Joorn said, "even though they called themselves Aleutian Separatists then and had become an exceedingly prosperous sovereign nation, thanks to their control of the Northwest Passage." He fixed Yung with an innocent gaze. "You should read up on them, Captain Yung. They were an important factor in East-West trade in the days before the Chinese Commonwealth would have come to power."

Yung gave as good as he got. "Ah yes, the Chukchees. They became a part of the Commonwealth some hundred years after your time, when we took control of the Arctic sea route."

Nina broke in, her eyes flashing. "Why are we wasting time talking about irrelevant nonsense? What's going to happen to

Torris and his people? They're right in the middle of *our* supposed trade route!"

Yung recovered from his shock, and after an obvious struggle to refrain from harrumphing, said, mostly to Joorn, "We'll withdraw our study teams of course. There's no need to be territorial about it now that you've returned. There are inhabited Trees all through the Oort—possibly billions of them. We'll continue our studies elsewhere in the Oort and confine our efforts to the edges of the cloud closest to the Centauri planets, as I assume you will do in the part of the Oort neighborhood closest to your own planets. Is that satisfactory?"

"More than satisfactory," Joorn said.

"Neither of us could hope to exploit the trillions of comets in the Oort, anyway. Not for thousands or tens of thousands of years, if then. The people of the comets will fashion their own destiny as they grow and spread their culture. They're space travelers too, aren't they, aboard natural spaceships complete with superb life-support systems? And they're inevitably going to learn how to operate the Trees' natural light sails—those reflective leaves. They've already begun to do so, you know, without realizing it. We can teach them how to tweak the Trees' tropisms and turgor movements and hurry that along."

"Wait a minute. What are you saying?"

"The Trees are intelligent. Didn't you know that?"

CHAPTER 31

They all sat stunned, unable to speak. After several seconds of silence had elapsed, Joorn found his voice.

"Would you explain that, Captain Yung?"

Yung paused a moment to consider how to answer. "What do we mean when we say 'intelligence'?" he finally said. "Particularly plant intelligence. When we're talking about animal intelligence, we might begin by citing purposeful behavior in pursuit of an objective. A crow using a bent wire to snag a piece of meat. A chimpanzee choosing a correctly shaped twig to snare a termite. A cat using its paw to unlatch a cabinet so that it can get at the cat treats inside." He smiled. "My cat does that."

Andrew spoke up. "Getting closer to home, Captain, at what point can we say that some of the early hominids crossed the line between serendipitous behavior and purposeful behavior? What's the difference between *Ardipithecus ramidus* picking up a conveniently shaped branch and using it to club rabbits, and *Australopithecus garhi*, two million years later, whacking a rock with another rock to make it a better shape for cracking mussel shells?"

"Good point," Captain Yung said. "After all, even a paramecium hunts for food. But the earliest forms of emergent life were plants, not animals, and some of them were swimmers that actively sought out their food. As we go up the evolutionary ladder, we still find hunters, but now they're stationary, like Venus flytraps, and wait for their prey, like spiders, to come to them. And incidentally, their reflexes are faster than those of spiders, though of course we can't say they're thinking in any sense of the word. But there's another form of life-and-death combat going on in the plant world, only it's in slow motion. It's in the form of growth, and this growth has its own strategies. Now the question is: What kind of self-awareness, if any, is behind these strategies?"

Nina had been listening with increasing fascination. Now she delightedly exploded, "There are people who say that plants show signs of fear when they're in danger—an animal that wants to eat them, or a person that's plucked nearby members of its species. There was even one twentieth-century writer who said that flowers screamed when you picked them."

Yung nodded condescendingly. "It's long been noticed that when a crown rose is plucked, the roses around it seem to shrivel and close their petals to make themselves less attractive. Mimosas are a particularly good example. They react so quickly to being touched that some botanists speculated that they had actual nervous systems. Well, perhaps they do, in a way, but it's not like ours."

"You're saying that plants can be self-aware," Joorn prompted.

"Not only that, but that they can communicate with other members of their species and plan defense strategies together by sending chemical messages to one another through the air and groundwater."

Nina interrupted again. "Granddaddy, isn't that exactly what you told me when we first discovered the Trees and Daddy was getting upset because I was getting more interested in biology than physics?"

Joorn smiled benignly but continued to address his remarks to Yung. "And you maintain that these Bernal trees are doing the same thing in the vacuum of space?"

"More than that. Much more. Since Torris's people arrived some two hundred thousand years ago—" He broke off and turned to Andrew. "That was your estimate, wasn't it, young man? Two hundred thousand years?"

"Yes, sir," Andrew said.

Yung finished triumphantly. "Since then, the Trees have learned how to communicate with man."

Gasps came from several of his listeners, but Joorn only said, "You have proof?"

"We think so. Much work remains to be done, of course. By us and by you. We've interviewed more than twenty returned Dreamers here in the last two years, beginning with Torris, and—"

"You interviewed . . . " Laurel choked, then stopped.

Yung put on a good imitation of being apologetic. "I know your study group has formed personal ties with Torris and Ning, *nu-shih* Laurel. We don't want to interfere. But the work is too important to worry about niceties, and you gave us a good place to start. We'll share our data and move on, as we told Captain Gant. We'll begin our own project afresh more than half a parsec from here, in a swath of the Oort uncontaminated by previous influences. You've done an exemplary job here in beginning the transformation of this aboriginal society, but our goals might not be the same as yours."

"You were talking about proof," Joorn said impatiently.

"Yes," Yung said, totally composed and unhurried. "I was saying that we interviewed more than twenty returned Dreamers here. With the cooperation of the priest, Claz, of course. He made their participation mandatory—a matter of religion. One of our survey teams interviewed an equal number with the cooperation of a priest in a Tree a couple of astronomical units from here—a pair of locked Trees, actually, where the union of the two societies had already begun. Forty-odd interviews is a small sample, to be sure, but the correlations are too many to be coincidental."

"What sort of correlations?"

"To give one example, the Tree became aware of Torris as an individual because he was the agent of its cross-pollination by another Tree. The quantity of pollen given to him by Ning was of an order of magnitude greater than would be deposited by a pollinating insect, and several orders of magnitude greater than the thinly scattered grains of pollen that might drift across inter-Oortian space. The Tree was grateful for the gift—I guess I can use the word *grateful* to describe its vegetable emotions, if there is such a thing as vegetable emotion—and stored its tagging of Torris in its memory. Consequently, it was aware of it when its benefactor was cast into space. And when *Time's Beginning* arrived and its gravitational attraction began to affect its orbit and its engine luminosity and its infrared hull radiation became another source of photosynthesis, the Tree saw causality in the two events. As you can well appreciate, these influences would be a crucial form of sensory input for a sentient Tree. And when Torris returned and the Tree began to be overrun by your investigators, the Tree's impression of some sort of causality was only reinforced."

"Interesting, but where's the correlation?"

Yung leaned forward for emphasis. "Fully a year later, and half a parsec away, on a Tree that our survey party was reconnoitering, Dreamers started to have visions of a new kind of human, wearing spacesuits that weren't made of the familiar animal skins, darting about with thrusters emitting substances like hydrazine that they hadn't seen for two hundred thousand years."

"The Tree's memory of Torris's forebears, when they returned from quasar chasing," Andrew interjected.

"Yes," Yung said. "The Dreamers' impressions of *Time's Beginning* had to be filtered through what they were capable of imagining, so their perceptions relied on the perceptions of Torris's Tree. They tended to see the ship as a sort of large, undifferentiated mass, sometimes sprouting branches. But four out of ten—the more capable Dreamers—agreed on details, and with a specificity that couldn't possibly have been mere hallucination induced by the narcotic effect of their Tree's sepals."

"I see," Joorn said.

"What that implies is that the Trees have a racial memory going back at least two hundred thousand years. How far back into the billions of years without man, we'll never know. But they're beginning to spread the news of man's return. Their thoughts are exceedingly slow, and their communications even slower, depending as they do on the drift of pheromones through space. But the Tree people will speed that up. And eventually, as they achieve a higher level of communication, at the speed of light, we're talking a mere two years from one end of the Oort cloud to the other."

"And you propose to help them do it."

"My dear friend, it's inevitable. Eventually they'll turn their Trees into actual spaceships. And then it's off to the nearest stars. Perhaps, after millions of years, even other galaxies."

"They'd have to attach some sort of space drive to do that," Martin said, frowning.

"But of course. Isn't that what we're talking about? I'd expect that some thousands of years from now they'll have learned how to build their own Higgs engines. And of course, by then, they'll be mining the asteroids for their raw materials—landing on planets will never be a possibility for them."

"Neighbors who can't visit," Chu said. "The perfect partners for your intended empire."

Yung looked pained. "Please, Comrade Chu, *commonwealth*, not 'empire.'"

"It's all in the wording, isn't it?"

Yung showed his annoyance and said, "Cometary man will always be beyond the control of planetary man, through sheer numbers if nothing else. At any rate, they'll be your trading partners too."

Chu started to open his mouth, but Joorn gave him a reproving look. "A three-way trading partnership—us and the whole Oort cloud to share," Joorn agreed. "The immense travel time to the Oort ought to keep the two principal partners from overreaching."

Yung looked suspicious but refrained from any mention of the exploitation of the old imperial China in an era of communication by sailing ship. "We'll begin the process of withdrawal tomorrow," he said stiffly. "I'll arrange for our people to turn over our records immediately. The Tree people won't realize what's happening, so I strongly recommend that we arrange the change of guard in a way that makes sense to them."

Joorn stood up. "It's been a pleasure doing business with you, Captain Yung."

CHAPTER 32

ut what are they doing?" Ning said.

"They are packing up our Dreams and giving them to the priest Joorn and the numberers of *Time's Beginning*," Torris said.

They were perched on one of the semidomesticated boughs not too far above the cave mouth, looking down at the tiny figures bustling about below. The dwarfs from the gigantic world they called *Celestial Arrow* were folding the queer portable caves they had brought with them, and there was a steady traffic to and fro as they returned them to the chunky transfer vehicle they called a *tu chuan* that floated in space within easy leaping distance. Ning was big with child, wearing a cumbersome new airsuit she had sewn to accommodate her growing belly, and she was willing to settle for the easier game that grazed in the lower boughs.

"I don't understand," she said, her helmet pressed against his. "How can they take away someone's Dream?"

"With those tiny seed things they poke in your face when they ask their endless questions. The Dream is not taken away, but they may listen to it whenever they wish. And in some way, it is compared with the Dreams of others."

"Like the annals kept in the memory of a chronicler? When a new priest replaces a priest who has flown to the sky, the chronicler may recite all the Dreams of the past to him. Thus wisdom is preserved, or so they say."

"Exactly so."

She tossed her head, momentarily breaking voice contact. When he could hear her again, she was saying, "I don't know about the Dreams of unlicked cubs, but the questions they asked me were mere foolishness and went on and on to the point of drivel. Like why do women not hunt on your Tree but may form hunting associations on mine? And why is it that I hunt alone and not with a hunting sorority? And why are there no female numberers, though I for one was able to interpret the sacred slabs? There is no wisdom in questions like those—just the stupidities of human behavior."

"They are just trying to learn our ways," he said uncomfortably. "They plied me with all sorts of foolish questions when they first rescued me and then made scratches on those things they carry around with them. Perhaps they were only trying to learn to speak human language. The scratches give them a magical way of remembering words, as do the seed things they ask us to talk to. Once a thing is said, it may be remembered forever, even by the animal who speaks named Jonah. Joorn says that before they leave they will teach us to make scratches too, so that we may always remember our own words." He grinned, tired of explaining. "Cleb the Chronicler does not like that."

"All the same, I'll be glad when they're gone."

"You can't mean that."

"They are changing the way we live."

"Is that a bad thing? They are giving us gifts that make life easier, like my shiny knife and the threads that are stronger than ropes to improve your catapults."

"As usual, the benefits go to the priests and chroniclers, while ordinary folk must do things for themselves. I don't like being trotted out by Claz and Shamash as a justification for their holding on to their power."

"Like it or not, it's our duty to our tribes now. It silences the fearful or contentious who would keep the changes from happening. It keeps the priests in line. Think—our tribes are learning to live together now, learning to help each other through hard times. We've stopped the murderous custom of bride raids. Isn't that a good thing?"

She snuggled against him as best as the bulky new airsuit would let her. "Oh, Torris, I wish we could go about our lives without being followed around by gullible people who think they are worshipping the Tree of Trees." She patted the ungainly bulge in the suit. "I just want to see her grow up and teach her to be the best huntress who ever was."

"Teach *him*," he said, "to be the best hunter ever."

She laughed. "If the Tree has sent a boy, you can teach him to be a Dreamer."

He leaned over to look at the busy goings-on below, then touched his helmet to hers again.

"Look, there's Joorn with some of his people. I can recognize Chu's airsuit, and Martin, the son of Joorn's son, Alten. And there's that water-filled thing that Jonah rides around in. Isn't it clever the way he uses those grasping limbs to move about on the roots and branches, just as though they were real arms? They're going to meet with the other party of dwarfs from the sky. The one called Yung is grasping Joorn's hand in that weird custom they have—I suppose to show they're not carrying weapons. I don't recognize the man Joorn is pushing forward now, but he's old. I can tell by the way he's bent over. That's what happens to these star people when they age—I suppose because their bones carry more weight than ours. I wonder what they're talking about."

"It's good of you, Captain Gant, to allow our Professor Ma to meet Professor Karn," Captain Yung said.

Joorn made an effort to keep his voice cordial. "Professor Karn is not a prisoner," he said. "He's a highly respected teacher in our physics department."

Karn kept any hint of asperity out of his own voice as he put out his hand. "I've been rehabilitated," he said dryly. "But they do keep an eye on me. It's a pleasure to meet you, *Chiao-shou* Ma."

Ma, a withered old man who looked even more shriveled than Karn, said, "It's an honor to meet you, Professor Karn. It's more than a little surreal being introduced to an icon of the past like yourself. You might like to know that you were considered one of the great names in the history of physics in my day—two hundred years after you left Earth, along with Einstein, Hawking, and someone you never got to hear of, the great Multiverse theorist Harun al-Mudarris."

"Ah yes, Harun," Karn said in a sardonic voice. "He was one of my students. It's nice to hear that the boy made something of himself."

"Professor Ma is being modest," Yung said. "He was on the way to being an icon himself. The Commonwealth did not want to let him go. He was one of the jewels in their crown. In the end, they decided that there would be a greater luster in providing *Celestial Arrow* with one of the most eminent names in the physics community that our country possessed."

"Also," Ma said, matching Karn's wryness, "I was a thorn in their side. I was a partisan of the Karn plan for reaching the most distant quasar possible, and finding the beginning of time itself—or its end."

"So you became a thorn in Captain Yung's side instead," Karn said.

"Oh, he keeps an eye on me too," Ma said, with a hasty glance at a frozen-faced Yung to show that he didn't mean it seriously. "But there was no incentive for a mutiny. By then it was clear that the acceleration of the expansion of the Universe had increased so greatly that there was no possibility of ever catching up with the retreating boundary. Of course relativity itself was still intact, but effectively the edge of the Universe— if I can use such an imprecise term—was outpacing anything traveling at the speed of light because space itself was stretching. And still is, with an unknown consequence at the end."

Karn didn't like hearing that, any more than Newton would have liked hearing about relativity or Einstein would have regarded string theory. But he remained unruffled.

"Fascinating," he said. "But I imagine Captain Yung keeps a firm hand on your reins anyway."

Ma chose not to react to the insult. "We are continuing to study the implications of the changing cosmology," he said.

"We have some fine minds in our physics department. We would like to ask you to join us. Captain Yung and Captain Gant have both given their permission."

Karn looked at Joorn. "Can't wait to get rid of me, can you, my old friend?"

"Captain Yung's willing to take his chances with you, Delbert," Joorn said. "I think he can keep you in check. And it's a chance for you to do groundbreaking work in your own specialty instead of moldering away teaching freshman physics."

Karn turned to Professor Ma. "I accept," he said.

[HAPTER 33]

A new star suddenly appeared in the sky, brighter even than Sirius. According to the computer program that had been waiting for it, its magnitude was −1.48.

"There he goes," Joorn said.

"There he went, you mean," Alten said. "He was halfway to Alpha Centauri, more than a light-week from here, when he fired the Higgs drive."

"Very ethical of him," Chu said.

They were sitting in the captain's quarters having a drink while waiting for the expected event. Either Alten or Chu was technically the captain now, but after all the long years of tenancy since taking command, the captain's cabin was Joorn's permanent perch.

"Where's Martin?" Alten said.

"He's on the bridge with Robertson, wallowing in the ship's astrometry equipment," Chu said. "He's set his sights a bit higher since our trip to the sun."

Alten poured himself another splash of scotch. It was from the last bottle of Earth-distilled scotch in the Universe, the end of the ample supply that Joorn had taken with him six billion years ago. From now on, they'd be drinking imitation scotch from the ship's distillery.

"Naked-eye observation is good enough for me," he said.

"All I need to know is that Yung is on his way. And that he's taken Karn with him."

"You don't really think he'll try anything aboard *Celestial Arrow*, do you?" Chu said. "Yung is a tough cookie under that smooth exterior. Besides, the good professor doesn't have Oliver to do his dirty work anymore."

"I feel sorry for Delbert in a way," Joorn said, replenishing his own drink. "Seeing his lifelong obsession thwarted. Under house arrest here. And now under Professor Ma's thumb, lending his name to legitimizing an unwelcome view."

"Don't," Alten said sharply. "Don't feel sorry for him. Or guilty. We didn't make his dream impossible. The cosmos did that. When it became an incontrovertible fact that the Universe was not only expanding, but expanding faster and faster. Feel sorry for Professor Ma. Karn's going to take over his project. And who knows? Maybe together they'll discover another incontrovertible fact. Maybe time does have a stop after all."

Chu continued to stare at the bright new star. "We won't see Captain Yung for a while," he said. "He'll be busy terraforming the planets of Alpha Centauri B. And whatever's left orbiting the white dwarf that was once a star so much like Sol. And that Goldilocks planet of Proxima Centauri, no matter what he says. Maybe our descendants, a couple of generations from now, will be trading with his empire. No matter what he chooses to call it."

"He won't be able to colonize the Oort," Joorn said. "It's too big to digest."

Chu nodded in agreement. "He may be able to create a suzerainty or two, but that's just a drop in the bucket."

"We'll make our own friends," Joorn said, "starting with Torris."

Alten took a large swig of his father's scotch, heedless of the pained look he got. "I've been running some computer studies with Nina's help—maybe I should say Nina's instigation, and Andrew's. It's very long-range, but we could nudge Torris's Tree into an orbit in the Kuiper Belt. Along with Ning's Tree and whatever other Trees have joined them by then. A real archipelago of Trees forming the nucleus of a new cometary society. That would bring our friends closer to wherever we settle in the solar system and make a real partnership possible. Maybe even closer than the Kuiper Belt. Maybe as close as the orbits of Pluto or Neptune."

"But no closer," Chu said. "We don't want the comets to grow tails and melt away after a few circuits. Bernal's trees evolved to get their water from ice, not the easy way."

"The Trees wouldn't stand for it anyway," Alten said. "They'd spread their little light sails and head straight back to the Oort cloud. They're engineered to use any radiation they can get, but getting too close to a red giant would screw up their ecology."

"Where are our own people going to settle, Skipper?" Chu said. "Jupiter or Mars?"

"Jupiter's core is closer gravitationally to what we were used to on Earth," Joorn said. "But terraforming Jupiter, even the new slimmed-down Jupiter, is a big job. Maybe a job for future generations, when we start to have a population overflow. We'll put it to a vote, but I think our best bet will be Mars."

"Mars?"

"Yes. It's already habitable, though still a bit tropical. It'll be easier to terraform, with comet water from near-term comets and uninhabited comets from the Kuiper Belt. There'll be an ocean on Mars for the dolphins—Jonah will like that—and later for the whales whose fertilized eggs have been frozen in the ship's ovatorium for the last six billion years. The gravity will be friendlier to the comet people who visit us but not so weak as to cause us to evolve into a species somewhere between our present selves and *Homo cometes*. After all, there were people living on Mars in my youth, and the babies were doing just fine."

Chu lifted his glass. "Onto Mars, then." After a moment, Alten joined him.

[HAPTER 34

We call it a baby shower," Irina said. There was no word in Ning's language to suggest the impossible concept of quantities of water pouring down from overhead, so she settled for the closest equivalent she could find in Jonah's three-way dictionary—a word that meant carelessly letting a few precious drops escape when transferring a liquid to a storage bladder.

Ning looked puzzled. "It is another of your customs then, like a 'farewell party'?"

"Yes. It's another kind of party, this time to give useful gifts before the baby arrives."

"If it's a 'party,' why then can I not have the martini drink, as before?"

"Because it's not good for the baby."

Ning looked unconvinced. "A girl, you said?"

"Yes. Just as you wanted."

"How can you know that?"

"We are able to look into the womb. Do you remember when you allowed our doctor to examine you, she showed you an image of your baby?"

"Yes. She said it was the ghost of the baby," Ning said, resorting to a word in her own language. "But it looked nothing like a proper ghost."

Ning had peered dutifully at the jiggling monitor but had been unable to make sense of the ultrasound image.

Nina saved the day by arriving with a tall orange-juice spritzer in a glass with an inverted rim. Chu had slowed the ship's rotation to almost nothing for Ning's visit, but there was just enough pseudogravity to hold liquids in a glass if you were careful.

"Here, Ning. I think you'll like this," Nina said. "This is the kind of fruit we grow on our little trees."

The shower was going well. The room filled with chatter and the clink of glasses. It was mostly women from Irina's various study groups, but Andrew and a few other male researchers had shown up, some of them even bearing presents. Torris himself had stayed away; he had been told it was not the custom and was being entertained at the dolphin pool by some of the men and Jonah.

Laurel came over with a large wrapped package, which she presented awkwardly to Ning. "Thank you, Laurel," Ning said with her newly acquired shipboard manners. "What is it for?"

"No, no, that's just the wrapping," Irina said, and helped her tear off the paper. Ning was baffled by the tiny pink garments, but she was genuinely pleased by the little blanket. "To help hold in warmth," she said, "like the fuzzy skin of a stovebeast." Earlier someone had presented her with a supply of reusable hydrophilic diapers with phase control settings activated by running a finger along the hem, and Irina had had to explain how they worked.

The gathering grew noisier and livelier, and there was an intermittent parade of well-wishers bearing gifts. There was a baby stroller—useless in a microgravity environment where there would not be enough weight to hold wheels to a sur-face—and a plethora of rattles and teething rings, but some of the gifts were genuinely useful, like a baby-carrying harness that left the hands free and a wearable night-light with a per-manent battery. Ning received them all with a quiet dignity, seemingly at ease among all these strange child-size women, as if her attenuated form with the startling bulge of her pregnancy were the norm, not their gravity-molded bodies.

There was a brief flurry of commotion at the door, and Joorn entered with Chu and Alten. They'd all obviously had a few, and they were very jolly.

"Can a bunch of mere males come in and join the party?" Joorn asked. He caught sight of Andrew and the other men and nodded amiably but unapologetically, then crossed the room to pay his respects to Ning, followed by the other two.

Ning half-rose to greet them, the effort floating her a cou-ple of inches above the divan, where she'd been installed. "So, Joorn, and elders Chu and Alten," she said, an equal speaking to equals, "you don't respect the division of women and men either. A good omen for the new way of doing things that you are bringing to us. What have you done with Torris?"

"He'll be along later. He's with Jonah and the waterbeasts."

"The male waterbeasts?" she said with friendly mockery.

He laughed. "No, they've been reformed too."

"So, the other star people from Chu's kinfolk have left us after trying to 'reform' us. Will we be seeing them again?"

"I don't think so. They are looking for a new home in the part of the sky where the Sisters rise and set."

"And now you are leaving us too. Will we be seeing you again?"

"Yes. But not for some years. Not till your new daughter is halfway to becoming a woman. But we will leave you many gifts to help your Trees to grow and prosper. We hope other Trees will eventually join you."

"That is already starting to happen."

"What? What do you mean?"

"Torris's Tree has begun to speak to its Dreamers, to tell what some of the nearest Trees have decided. They are starting to alter their courses to bring them closer, though it will take many years before the first of them arrive. They know of *Time's Beginning* now. Torris and Claz, his priest, have learned this from their Tree's Dreamers, and our priest, Shamash, says the same of our Dreamers."

Joorn and Chu looked at each other. "Are we pulling the Trees' strings, or are they pulling ours?" Chu said.

Alten grew thoughtful. "We'll learn to talk to them more directly. Very very slowly. Through computer mediation. That's how we learned to speak Delphinese. And the dolphins to talk to us."

"Talking to vegetables," Chu said. "Maybe Nina had something."

Ning grew impatient with their gibberish. "So, Joorn, mover of worlds, *Time's Beginning* is not big enough for you. You are going to find a new home in the sky too. Where will it be?"

"Closer to the warmth of the Stepsister. But not too close. Perhaps your children will come visit us. If your Tree will let you."

"They are talking it over," she said quite seriously.

Joorn and Chu exchanged another look. "I'm sure they are," Alten said. "We can tell them of a place closer to the Stepsister called the Kuiper Belt. Closer, but not too close. Warmer, but not too warm."

It was too much for Ning. She frowned reprovingly at Alten and began to scold him. "If you are talking in riddles like a priest . . . " But just then, Martin came in. He spotted Ning and started toward them.

"Hello, Ning," he said with a boyish grin. "Congratulations on the baby. I brought you a little something I made for her."

He shyly held out his offering. It was a miniature hunting bow, painstakingly carved out of some limber wood like ash from the ship's forest. It was strung with monofilament, ready to go, and obviously a working bow. There was a bundle of tiny arrows to go with it.

Ning took the bow from him and tried its tension. She gave a nod of approval.

"At last, a present that is useful," she said.

[HAPTER 35

6,000,000,007 A.D.
Mars Orbit

ll through the great starship, people were clustered around the
outside ports to get their first naked-eye view of Mars. The
main observation lounge was crowded to overflowing, as were
any of the lounges that had an unshuttered window. Those who
couldn't get an outside view relied on the screens in their quarters or watched with friends. The ship was noisy with hundreds
of celebratory parties, some of them beginning to get unruly.

Joorn and his family were gathered on the captain's veranda,
along with Chu, Ryan, and a few friends. Jonah was there, with
another dolphin in her own travel pod. Her human name,
Jonah said, was Calypso, after the sea nymph.

Mars loomed hugely, filling the observation wall. They were
in close orbit, just outside the orbit of Deimos. The other Martian moon, Phobos, no longer existed. It had crashed into Mars
eons ago, leaving an enormous crater, the largest feature on the
Martian surface. It was now filled with water from the Kuiper
Belt comet that had preceded them more than two years ago,
the first of the rain of comets that *Time's Beginning* had nudged
into the inner system. Mars had seas again.

Joorn spoke to the dolphins. "There it is, Calypso and Jonah. Your new home. In two more years, when the atmosphere is up to around a hundred millibars or so, it'll be safe to move into it. You can't tell from here, but spectroscopic analysis shows that the blue-green algae that we sent ahead of us is already starting to gain a foothold, and we should have a decent food chain going in about ten years."

"The fish, Captain, the fish!" Calypso's computer-generated voice squeaked anxiously, together with all the pops and whistles she hadn't yet learned to edit out.

Joorn shook his head regretfully. "It'll take a little longer for us to get the Martian oceans stocked with fish. Till then, you'll have to come inshore for dinner. We'll keep the biohatcheries going full throttle for you."

"Your whale cousins will have to wait even longer," Chu added. "And then you dolphins will have to babysit the first generation."

Alten, stuffy as usual, said, "We're going to have to stay in orbit anyway, until the barrage of comets stops."

"Like Moses, looking down on the Promised Land," Jonah said, his beak curved in its permanent dolphin smile.

"Still studying human history, Jonah?" Joorn said.

"Studying it?" the dolphin replied. "I'm living it!"

"It isn't over yet, is it, Grandfather?" Nina said. "Human history, I mean."

"Not by a long shot, young lady," Joorn said. "We'll pick up where we left off. There once was a thriving human population on Mars, and there will be again. Old Mother Sol will continue to keep the climate salubrious for some millions of years, even in her dotage. And by the time she shrinks and Mars cools off, if we're still around, we—those of us who want to, that is—will move back to Earth and terraform it all over again."

"Don't forget *Homo cometes* in their trillions. And our neighbors on the Centauri planets," Alten said soberly. "By then we'll all have merged back into one human mainstream again."

Andrew, sitting on the loveseat next to Nina and opening another bottle of champagne, looked up and said, "We've had grand mergers before, haven't we? We all carry a few Neanderthal genes. To say nothing of the mixing of populations after the termination of the Dark Ages let us go about our business."

"The procreation business," Chu said, holding out his glass for a refill.

"What about us?" Jonah piped up with mock plaintiveness.

"You're in the human mainstream, like it or not," Chu said with a laugh. "Except for the procreation part."

"We'll take care of that ourselves," Jonah said. He added some chirps in Delphinese. Calypso replied with a long string of tweets and whistles that somehow managed to sound suggestive to human ears.

There was a sudden flash of light on the dull, red face of Mars, bright enough to make the window wall darken. A collective gasp came from Ryan's family, gathered together in a seating group across the room. The light flickered fitfully and died. In moments, a huge cloud of dust had boiled up and started to spread across the bulge of the planet's surface. Then the Marscape began to twinkle around the site of the flash as incandescent fragments from the cloud continued to strike the surface.

"What was it, Joorn, a comet?" Ryan's wife called from the couch where she sat with her children.

"Yes, one of the smaller ones, Kitty. It hit smack in the middle of the Valles Marineris. By the time we're finished, we'll have another ocean there, a long skinny one, two thousand four hundred miles from end to end."

"Mommy, can you make Uncle Joorn do that again?" one of the children said.

Kitty laughed and gave him one of the petit fours that Irina had made.

The festivities in the ship continued for some hours until night fell, when their orbit carried them past the horizon to the nocturnal hemisphere of the planet and people began to return to their quarters.

Irina served a light supper that she had prepared earlier, and people ate from folding trays. An eerie red halo surrounded Mars, casting a somber glow onto the veranda, but nobody felt like turning on the lights. The mood was subdued. The children had been coaxed to eat, had grown cranky, and eventually had fallen asleep on the couches. Joorn brought out the brandy, and people sat around drinking and not saying much, looking thoughtfully from time to time at the silhouette of Mars blotting out the night sky. The dolphins, logy from their vodka and clam-juice cocktails, had retreated to the bottoms of their tanks, coming up about twice an hour to breathe before sinking back down.

The little boy was the first to notice the new star in the sky. He'd been sleeping fitfully, then dropped back into a sodden doze. Now he sat up and tugged at his mother's arm.

"Mommy, Mommy, look! Orion's Belt has four stars in it! It wasn't there a minute ago."

Joorn jerked his head around. The others did the same. The

constellation had gained another star, brighter than Rigel or Betelgeuse.

His finger stabbed at his shipcom, but on the bridge, Robertson was faster. "Do you see it, Skipper? It was coming in fast, from above the ecliptic, but at only about point ninety-five c's. That means it's been braking intermittently. It would have just turned on its Higgs drive again. We must be looking at a course correction."

"What's your preliminary reading?"

"It'll enter the Oort cloud in about three years. It looks like it's making a beeline for Sol. That'll mean another two years before it gets here."

Alten was already punching numbers into the AI link he carried everywhere with him. "One of the five ships that left Earth after we did."

"Who will it be?" Nina said. "One of the two Euro-American ships? Or the Brazilians or Indians? Or the Islamic Federation zealots?"

"Or a ship that Yung didn't know about," Chu said. "One that was launched after he left."

Ryan had been alerted by the AI's security link. He walked over to join them. "Whoever it is, they seem to have decided on Sol, not the Alpha Centauri planets. It'll be up to us to deal with them, not Yung."

"We'll give them the Jovian moons," Joorn said. "Keep Jupiter for ourselves."

"If we can," Ryan said.

"Whoever they are," Martin said, "they'll be people. And there will be people here to greet them."

"There'll be others," Nina said.

Ryan nodded. The politician in him was beginning to emerge, and the others prepared themselves for a burst of his patented eloquence.

He didn't disappoint them. "Earth will always be a way station for the children it once sent out to the far reaches of the Universe. And there must always be people in Sol's system to greet them, even when Sol finishes disgorging Earth and the cradle of the human race is habitable again."

Joorn topped him. They'd played this game before. "So there'll always be humans in the Universe. Even billions of years from now, when the sky is empty of stars beyond our own cluster of galaxies, and the other clusters have become island Universes of their own, forever out of reach, there will be returnees—even disappointed fanatics like Karn—who've ridden the expansion of the Universe and come back to their home to refresh it. They'll find whatever dead matter remains—a burnt-out star or an evaporating black hole—and bring it back to life again."

Chu had grown pensive. "Yes," he said. "We human beings were meant to be the Jokers of creation. We were dealt to the Universe as a device for reversing entropy. And maybe Karn was right, in a way. Maybe the Universe is something like a gigantic protozoan. If it keeps expanding, it'll have to split. And maybe by that time, man will have learned how to cross over."

That was too much for Joorn. "Let's leave Eternity to our successors," he said briskly. "For now, in this billennium, there's enough to do. The Oortians must be raised to civilization. The Earth and the outer planets—Saturn, Uranus, Neptune, with their moons and their burdens of hydrogen that haven't completely evaporated—will have to be revivified. It's ironic that

Terra itself will have to be terraformed. And when we're up and running again"—he nodded to Nina and Martin—"that's for your children and grandchildren to do. We'll send out a new generation of restless souls to ride out the billennia in their time dilation cocoons and reseed the cosmos again. Each galaxy they colonize will become a new focal point for sending its children home."

There was a sound of clapping hands and a hearty "Bravo, Joorn!" It was Jonah's computer-modulated voice, and the clapping hands were a recording he'd squirreled away somewhere in his database. He leaned over the rim of his tank, dripping water on the carpet.

"But we dolphins have our own plans," Jonah said. "And so will the comet people. They can't ride your starships at one-G acceleration. They'll have to do it the slow way, on their intelligent Trees."

Everybody laughed. The gathering started to become lively again. Joorn poured more brandy.

"Drink up, people," he said. "We've got some work to do come morning."

Chu turned to the window wall and lifted a glass to the bright new star in Orion. One by one, the others followed his example.

"Here's to our new friends," he said. "Whoever they are."

CHAPTER 36

6,000,000,020 A.D.
The Kuiper Belt

[aptain Goncalves had a rather imperious manner, and he was not used to looking up at the people he was talking to. But he swallowed his pride and said, "And at this distance it is not too hot, *o Senhor* Torris, so your comet will not melt. But there will be more visible light, so the Tree will not object. It is a place where . . . "

His English failed him, even after twenty years of practice. He finished lamely with " . . . *onde nao entra o Sol*" and looked to Nina for help.

"Literally 'where the sun does not enter,'" Jonah piped up before Nina could answer. Nina's Portuguese was pretty good after twenty years, but Jonah's was better. He enjoyed tweaking Captain Goncalves, who had been painfully taught by Nina to speak to women as equals but who still, after all that time, could not bring himself to address a dolphin directly.

Torris nodded judiciously. As the acknowledged patriarch of his own people since Claz's death, he was willing to treat Goncalves with a measure of noblesse oblige.

"Yes, I understand," he said. "The Stepsister will not swallow the Tree or drink its ice, as it did with with your 'Earth' living place long ago. The Tree knows this and has persuaded its companions, which is why they have agreed to come with us for this journey."

"Just so," Goncalves said stiffly. He was willing to concede that the Bernal trees acted in a form of vegetable self-interest, like any plant, but he attributed this to clever tropisms, not the capacity to reason or communicate in any meaningful way.

Irina, in an ill-advised attempt to smooth things over, said brightly, "It's true, Dom Joao. Ning told me yesterday that the Trees are spreading the message through the entire Oort cloud and that some have already begun to set their sails to join our little colony in the Kuiper Belt."

Goncalves smiled with forced gallantry and replied, "We shall see, *dona*, we shall see. After all, Trees are attracted by other Trees, aren't they? Isn't that how forests grow?"

They were assembled in the captain's private lounge aboard the *Henrique*, the Brazilian starship named, inevitably, after Portugal's great explorer Prince Henry the Navigator. There was an observation wall, but instead of showing an outside view, it displayed a breathtaking vista of a Brazilian rain forest. At the moment, a jaguar was running across a sunlit clearing with a small animal in its mouth.

Tatiana, Nina's daughter, gasped. There had been cats aboard *Time's Beginning* in her childhood, but she'd never seen one this size before.

"That's the way Earth looked once upon a time, Tati," Nina told her. "And maybe the way Mars will look a couple of generations from now."

"And perhaps Callisto and Ganymede as well," Goncalves sniffed. "Though you Eurofolk got the tropics, and we got the temperate zone." His tone was polite but aggrieved.

Joorn and his family, with Chu and Jonah, had been Captain Goncalves's guests for more than three years now, and his hospitality was starting to wear thin—though, thankfully, the spacious apartment they'd been given provided plenty of privacy.

The *Henrique* was even bigger than *Time's Beginning* and consequently had greater mass, which had made it a better choice for coaxing Torris's gravitationally bound cluster of intelligent Trees to the Kuiper Belt. It also had a more advanced auxiliary ion drive for in-system work and a larger fleet of robot wardens for herding the Trees.

Joorn had left *Time's Beginning* parked in Jupiter's orbit when they'd boarded the *Henrique*. Alten had stayed behind to captain it, with Robertson's help. It was empty of colonists now and was being used for ferry work between Mars and the Jovian moons. The *Henrique* made a fine tugboat for hauling Trees, but Joorn did not trust Goncalves to have the tact to work with Torris and Ning—the human part of the equation. Irina and the others, who had bonded with Torris from the beginning, had jumped at the chance to work with him again, despite the length of the round trip to the Oort cloud.

Nina had brought her daughter with her so she could show her to Ning. Tatiana and Ning's formidable daughter, Ona, a huntress like her mother, had hit it off immediately. The two young women somehow managed to chat it up despite the language difficulties. Communication seemed to involve a lot of gesturing and giggling.

Tatiana watched as the jaguar disappeared into the underbrush with a last twitch of its tail. "Mother, do you mind if I leave now? Ona has something she wanted to show me."

"Don't let her take you hunting."

"She'd never do anything dangerous with me. She's much too sensible. She just wanted to show me the herd she's starting. She's into animal husbandry now. It's been taking hold on Ning's Tree the way Daddy hoped it would when you all left the Oort all those years ago."

Joorn broke off talking to Goncalves to say, "It's too bad Andrew couldn't come with us. He always says that animal husbandry is the first step in transforming a primitive society. That and grandfathers." He smiled. "His so-called O-Y ratio."

Nina annoyed Goncalves further by continuing to divert the conversation. "Andrew will have his chance to work with them again. A trip to the Trees will only be a matter of weeks now."

Tatiana said, "Wait till I tell Daddy what I've learned! I could go with him on his trips to the Kuiper Belt and help him. Do you think he'd let me?"

She skipped off without waiting for an answer. Nina called after her, "Be careful, Tati! Find someone to make the jump with you."

Tatiana called back over her shoulder, "Oh Mother! It's an easy jump. And I'll have a thruster with me anyway."

Goncalves was relieved to see her go. Having to deal with a young woman at what was supposed to be a serious meeting was an affront to his dignity. Ning had been bad enough, and when she had stopped coming to the meetings, leaving it to Torris, he'd been secretly glad, though she was supposed to be Torris's consort and the undisputed matriarch of her own Tree.

He'd always had a sneaking suspicion that the woman, only an aborigine, was finding fault with *him*!

They wound up the meeting with the bare bones of a preliminary trade agreement, a small one. Hunters or herdsmen on the conjoined Trees would supply quantities of butchered meat in return for simple, easily manufactured radios that would allow them to talk to one another in a vacuum over short distances without having to resort to sign language, or what they called "helmet talk."

Captain Goncalves excused himself and went off to attend to whatever minor adjustments were needed to keep the delicate gravitational dance of ship and comets in balance. The ship would be returned to full spin after Torris's departure, but Goncalves had been persuaded early in the game to reduce the pseudogravity by two-thirds—to Martian gravity—whenever Torris was aboard. At first, he'd considered it an unnecessary concession to a difficult aborigine, even more so when Ning visited.

They followed Torris down the tiled passageways to the airlock that had been assigned to them, trailed by Jonah sloshing along behind in his travel pod. Jonah had ignored Captain Goncalves's repeated requests to keep the travel pod sealed while traversing the immaculate corridors, and Joorn knew there would be more complaints about puddles of water by the *Henrique*'s housekeeping staff.

They crammed themselves into the airlock and helped one another get into their suits, then cycled through, ready to make the jump together. The Tree filled the black sky, less than a hundred miles away, blotting out the stars except for those that twinkled through the branches around the edges.

Torris did not wait for them. He took a mighty leap, propelled by his powerful legs, and sailed off into space.

"He's been talking to Ning on their private circuit, telling her we're on our way," Irina said. "He's too proud to use a thruster in front of us, but we'll catch up to him, and he'll be glad to hitch a ride."

They joined hands in a circle, except for Nina, who accepted an offer of a lift from Jonah, then stepped off the platform together and drifted a short distance from the ship. A moment later, Joorn fired a burst from his thruster, and the linked quartet jetted off in pursuit of Torris. Nina mounted the dolphin pod and, once firmly seated, gave it a thump to signal Jonah.

"How much longer will we be stuck with *o Senhor Poderoso*?" Jonah said in her ear. The Portuguese sobriquet he'd given the captain meant something like Mr. Self-Importance. "We're about done for now, and Chu and Martin could have us home in a week."

"Be a little patient," she said. "Give him more time to get used to dealing with the Tree people."

"He's had two years. He'll never be comfortable with them. He thinks they're some species of ignorant *indios*."

"Torris is way ahead of him," Nina said with a laugh. "Like the deal he made on the radios."

"He'll wake up about twenty years from now. By then *Homo cometes* will be city slickers."

"That's what Andrew thinks."

"Do you miss him, Nina?"

"Yes, I do," she said soberly. "Four years is a long time. From now on, we'll make these trips together. They'll only be short jaunts now. At a one-G boost, Mars is about as close to the Kuiper Belt as Dom Joao's Jovian orbit. We've got the advantage. Torris *trusts* us."

"I miss Calypso. And the rest of my pod as well. We're not used to being apart. From now on, I'm not going to go on these trade missions alone. I've already made a little side deal with Torris and Ning."

"You? What do you dolphins have to offer?"

"Fish!" Jonah said triumphantly. "That's the one commodity *Homo cometes* doesn't have. Once you humans have stocked the Martian seas for us, we'll start a fishing cooperative."

Nina laughed again. "Poor Dom Joao!"

"That's progress. Keep up with it, or get out of the way. What does Andrew think comes after city life?"

"A broader urban culture. An industrial civilization. It may take hundreds of generations to spread its way from a nucleus in the Kuiper Belt through the entire Oort cloud, but eventually, with their greater numbers, *Homo cometes* will be way beyond us planet dwellers. Then, watch out, Universe!"

They fell silent. They were beginning to catch up to the little chain of people ahead of them. By twisting her head, Nina could see enough of the sky to count easily a dozen comets scattered in the libration group around the center of gravity they shared with the *Henrique*. Some of them were close enough for her to make out the dumbbell shape of the Trees they nurtured. These were the Trees that Torris had tried to tell Goncalves about, the ones that had come on their own to join the Kuiper-bound caravan.

Jonah drew level with the linked group and fired a small braking burst to keep the travel pod in tandem with them. The little armada was closing the gap with Torris now. Nina could see him a couple of hundred yards ahead, spinning around to face them. Joorn held out an arm, and Torris reached for his hand and grasped it before the group could pass him. The contact started a slow spin of the entire group, and Joorn damped it with another squirt of his thruster.

They were halfway to Ning's Tree now, headed straight for the docking area. With helmet magnification, Nina could see the white bull's eye painted on the lower trunk where it merged with the exposed root ball, a rough circle about a mile in diameter. There were three tiny figures waiting outside the landing facility, a squarish structure carpentered entirely out of wood. That would be Ning, with Ona and Tatiana.

Another half hour took them within docking distance, and they separated, using their individual thrusters to slow themselves down. Torris hung on to Joorn and borrowed braking impetus from him. Any leap done with muscle power alone wouldn't have caused any landing problems, but the momentum Torris had gained by hitching a ride would have knocked the breath out of him—or worse—when he hit the Tree trunk. Nina stayed with Jonah, and he brought her in for a gentle landing.

Torris and Ning touched helmets for a mutual greeting. They'd had the little radios that Joorn had left with them for over twenty years now and were used to using them over distances, but old habits die hard. The language that Nina and the others heard over their own proximity circuits was entirely in the old helmet talk.

Ning motioned them inside. The wooden structure had a sturdy carpentered airlock made of wood edged with a gummy gasket, not one of the old barriers of greased animal hides. It was warm inside, not much below the freezing point. A central fire was going, and there was a caged area holding about a dozen stovebeasts for the use of travelers.

Ning and Ona threw their faceplates back, and the others removed their helmets. "Did the Proud One lord it over you again?" Ning said to Torris.

"He thinks he did," Torris said. "But little Nina kept him in check."

Everybody laughed.

Joorn said, "He'll be coming to trade every so often in the years ahead. Try not to take advantage of him too much. We have a saying: 'Don't kill the treehopper that lays the gold egg.'"

"What is gold?" Ona said. She was a stunning young woman with a glossy black mane, even taller than her mother. She towered over all of Joorn's people, but she did not slouch to bring herself closer to their eye level as would someone used to gravity.

"It's a metal, like the knife blades we provided your people, only softer."

"Then it cannot be valuable."

"It's not used for knives, Ona."

"Then what is it good for?"

"Trading, for one thing. Captain Goncalves would give you goods for it."

Chu exchanged a glance with Irina. "It's too early for money, Skipper," he said.

"Wait a minute," Martin said. He'd become Chu's chief engineer when Joorn retired, and since *Time's Beginning*'s colonists had put down roots on Mars, he'd been doing a lot of in-system work. "Now that the Trees are within striking distance of the asteroid belt, we can teach them asteroid mining, help them become self-sufficient in metals. They're naturals for airless, low-gravity work, aren't they?"

Torris was quick to pick up on what they were saying. "And this Goncalves star dwarf would pay for metals?"

Jonah must have been scrolling frantically through his human database. "That is gold, which is worth gold," he said. "An old Portuguese proverb."

"We'll do the prospecting, and they'll do the mining," Martin said excitedly. "You can't have an advanced technical civilization without metals, but they can't work under a planet's gravity. This is the only way they'll get their metals."

"We're getting ahead of ourselves," Nina said. She turned to Ona with a smile. "You're doing just fine, building up your meatbeast herd, Ona. This is work for your children. And your children's children."

Tatiana reached out and took Ona's hand. Despite the extreme difference in height and musculature, *Homo sapiens* and *Homo cometes* did not look at all incongruous next to one another.

"I've decided what I want to do, Mother," she said. "I don't have a scientific brain like you, but I know I can do useful fieldwork here, help Ona teach her people to begin an agricultural society."

"Fieldwork?" Nina said doubtfully. "That sounds daunting. It's not exactly like accompanying your father occasionally on one of his expeditions and living in a survival shelter with all the comforts. It's a way of life you're not adapted for."

Ona showed that she had inherited her mother's acerbity. "I will teach Tati," she said dryly. "There, I can help."

"I've already spent a night in the cave without my spacesuit," Tatiana said. "Shared meals. Helped the women with their communal tasks. Babysat for them."

Torris nodded in agreement. "If I could learn to live among you dwarfs, Tati can learn to live among our people."

Nina turned to Joorn. "Grandfather . . . "

"It's a start," Joorn said.

Just then, the inner door of the airlock opened, and a party of travelers came through, equipped with extra air sacks for a trip to one of the new Trees that had joined the convoy. They were burdened with unwieldy bundles that probably contained trade goods they would try to unload on the new arrivals.

They recoiled in alarm when they saw Jonah lolling halfway out of his travel tank, but they recovered right away. Everybody knew about the talking beast by now.

They made proper obeisance to the star travelers, then offered a further gesture of respect to Torris and Ning. They gave the dolphin tank a wide berth on their way to the stovebeast cages, where they exchanged their animals for fresh ones. They bowed again as they went out. They looked too burdened to rely on leg power for their jump, and would probably use the public catapult that Ning had installed.

"It starts," Chu said. "After six billion years, the human species has managed to get itself born again."

"We've made it this far." Joorn nodded. "And we're still only halfway to eternity. Karn was right. There's a long way to go."

"Goncalves won't be the last, you know," Chu said. "They'll be coming back for centuries. Maybe till the end of time."

Joorn shivered, perhaps from the cold the travelers had

brought in with them. Irina and her children drew a little closer to him.

Outside the crude little shelter, the stars continued to burn out and die one by one, the galaxies to flee out of reach, matter to disappear forever into black holes, the Universe itself to inflate beyond comprehension. But Omega was not yet.

ABOUT THE AUTHOR

Donald Moffitt was born in Boston. A former public relations executive, industrial filmmaker, and ghostwriter, he wrote fiction on and off for more than twenty years, often under one of many pen names. In 1977 he published his first full-length science fiction novel, *The Jupiter Theft*, under his own name.

Moffitt was a visionary novelist, praised for his scientific accuracy and his high-speed, high-tech stories. He lived in rural Maine with his wife, Ann, until his death in December 2014.

EBOOKS BY DONALD MOFFITT

FROM OPEN ROAD MEDIA

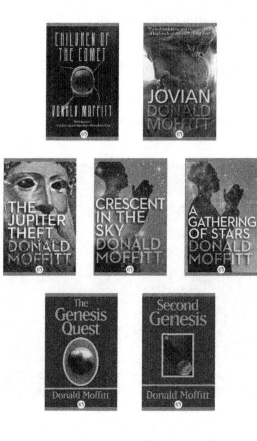

Available wherever ebooks are sold

OPEN ROAD

INTEGRATED MEDIA

Open Road Integrated Media is a digital publisher and multimedia content company. Open Road creates connections between authors and their audiences by marketing its ebooks through a new proprietary online platform, which uses premium video content and social media.

Videos, Archival Documents, and New Releases

Sign up for the Open Road Media newsletter and get news delivered straight to your inbox.

Sign up now at
www.openroadmedia.com/newsletters

31901056585609

CPSIA information can be obtained at www.ICGtesting.com
Printed in the USA
BVOW08s1158150915

418060BV00001B/1/P

9 781497 682948